A DEATH
at
Silversmith
BAY

BOOKS BY EMMA JAMESON

Jemima Jago Mystery Series

A Death at Seascape House

A Death at Candlewick Castle

A Death at Silversmith Bay

Magic of Cornwall

Marriage Can Be Murder

Divorce Can Be Deadly

Dr Bones and the Christmas Wish

Dr Bones and the Lost Love Letter

Lord and Lady Hetheridge Mystery Series

Ice Blue

Something Blue

Blue Murder

Black and Blue

Blue Blooded

Blue Christmas

Untrue Blue

A DEATH
at
Silversmith
BAY

EMMA JAMESON

bookouture

Published by Bookouture in 2022

An imprint of Storyfire Ltd.
Carmelite House
50 Victoria Embankment
London EC4Y 0DZ

www.bookouture.com

ISBN: 978-1-80314-116-9
eBook ISBN: 978-1-80314-115-2

For Donna, as always, and for Bobby, too

1

"OFF WITH HER HEAD!"

"This is good. This is right. The right choice," Jemima Jago muttered to herself as she fitted her key in the lock. All morning, she'd repeated the mantra. Throughout her two-and-a-half-hour voyage from St. Morwenna to Penzance; during the extra half-hour it took to get her little boat, *Bellatrix*, berthed on a Saturday morning; and throughout the long walk, lugging her suitcase with the broken wheel, all the way to her building, a modest four-story brick walkup with a courtyard and two exterior staircases instead of an elevator.

Her door was known to stick. Today it was up to its old tricks, requiring maximum effort. When the door finally popped free of the jamb, it did so with a *crack*, sending Jem tumbling into her old flat, unoccupied for nearly three months.

Sometimes the past strolls up and taps you on the shoulder. Sometimes it darts out of the dark and punches you in the throat. The smell that greeted Jem was definitely more of a throat punch.

"Oh!" She clapped a hand over her nose and mouth. It smelled like sautéed garbage. With top notes of... litter tray?

"What the actual..."

Jem would've said more, except it occurred to her that she might not be alone in her flat. Maybe somebody had broken in.

When she'd left Penzance for the Isles of Scilly, she'd cleared out her fridge and emptied all the bins. The chance that she'd left anything behind to rot, even a piece of fruit or a carton of milk, was precisely zero. As for her leaving behind a dirty litter tray—it wouldn't take a mathematician to figure the odds on that. She didn't own a cat.

Leaving her suitcase on the walkway and her front door open to facilitate a quick escape if need be, Jem felt around in her bag until her fingers closed on her mobile. As she feared, its screen displayed the red low-battery warning. That was bad. If she needed to ring 999, could her phone manage one last call before giving up the ghost?

Maybe I should start carrying a weapon...

Any American sleuth worth her salt would surely have an automatic handgun stashed in her bag. Perhaps a more genteel British sleuth would carry something creative—a walking stick, for example, or a hairpin with a wicked point. Currently Jem had half a granola bar, a tube of lip balm, a vintage gothic paperback, a maxed-out credit card, twelve pounds in coins, and her keys.

Keys it is. She gripped the ring so the longest key extended like a metal claw. *Scare me and I'll poke you to death.*

"I know you're here," she bellowed, devoutly hoping she knew nothing. "I've already called the police. You'd better clear out before they arrive."

Jem waited. No one answered. No sound came.

Shoulders dropping in relief, she started toward the kitchenette. Maybe the smell indicated a sewage problem. She'd heard of pipes backing up, sending unspeakably foul liquid into sinks or bathtubs...

A loud thump came from the bedroom. It sounded like a man stomping his foot.

Freezing, Jem took a deep breath. Then she called in a loud, belligerent voice, "Oi! You can't be in here! If you come out now and don't make trouble, maybe I'll let you run for it."

No answer.

She decided to ring the police for real, but her mobile's screen had gone dark. It stayed that way no matter how hard she tapped it. Until she could plug it in, it was a brick.

I don't have to stay here and see this through. I can run down the street, ring the building manager from somewhere safe, and let him handle it.

But the last time she'd rung the building manager for something she'd considered urgent—in that case, a backed-up loo—it had taken three hours just to get a callback. She couldn't loiter around Penzance while heaven-knows-who inhabited her outrageously stinky flat. Even if the smell wasn't a sewage problem or some form of radioactive waste, she needed to unpack and freshen up before meeting her friend Micki for a late lunch. Today they were going to Tatteredly's, a second-hand bookshop, to meet the owner and discuss her antiquarian stock.

From the bathroom's vicinity came a soft but distinct *mii-oooow*.

Well, that explains the litter tray odor, Jem thought, relieved.

Letting her breath out in a rush, she strode confidently into the poky hall that opened left on her bedroom, and right, on her bathroom. The right-hand door was closed. Jem knew for an absolute fact she hadn't left it that way.

Beside the closed door sat her feline intruder, mostly white with ginger spots and luminous green eyes. Like all cats, it seemed perfectly nonchalant about its surroundings: *What, this old heap? Inherited it. Nothing special but I call it home.*

Rather than flinch at the sight of Jem or show any propensity to flee, the cat tilted its head, regarding her with mild curiosity. Tucking its paws completely underneath itself, it assumed a loaf configuration. Jem saw it had no tail, only a tiny stub crowned with a furry ginger puff.

"How did you get in here?" Always a dog person, Jem had been exposed to few cats, apart from the feral sort that flee when approached, retreating to safer ground from which to issue burning stares. Was it okay to bend down and pat the creature's head? Or was that a terminal breach of feline etiquette?

She reached down to try it. In the blink of an eye the cat's legs reappeared and the creature skittered away from her touch. It didn't seem frightened, just offended. With another soft *miioooow*, it feinted toward the bedroom, then dashed back to the closed bathroom door. Standing on its back legs, the cat actually made for the doorknob with its forepaws, scraping ineffectually at the mechanism.

"You're a clever clogs. I suppose you're offended by this general reek, too. Fine. I'm going to regret this, but fine." Turning the knob, Jem opened the bathroom door.

The reek came from the tub. Jem's pretty shower curtain, jade green with an embroidered trim, had been pushed to one side. The tub was loaded with bags of rubbish. Some were tied at the top. Others had split or leaked during the stacking process, dribbling grot all over the white tile floor. The smell, which had been bad enough from behind a closed door, rolled out at her like an exhalation from the grave.

In disbelief, Jem tried to take it all in. There were burger wrappers, cantaloupe rinds, and coffee grounds—a mountain of it, wet and clumpy. There were empty tins crusted with food remnants. Plastic tubs that had once been filled with mayonnaise and salad dressing, now mostly scraped-out but still oozing. Some disgusting used kitty litter, crumpled damp tissues whose origin Jem couldn't bear to consider, and a disposable nappy—full, of course. Someone had rolled it into a crude ball, reusing the adhesive tabs to hold it together, but the repulsive thing was leaking. To be precise, it was leaking on Jem's bath mat, jade green to match the shower curtain but pretty no longer.

Flattened by the rank smell, Jem retreated into the hall as the cat strolled unto the breach, luminous green eyes sparkling. As far as it was concerned, this was the land of opportunity. Diving into a bag, it caught something with its teeth and pulled. Out came a yellow Styrofoam takeaway box. Prodding the lid like a movie animal performing a trick, the cat made it spring open. Inside was a congealed breakfast of eggs, blood sausage, beans, and toast. It looked as if it had been tossed away while new, at least twelve hours ago.

"Hey! Out of there!"

The cat didn't even glance her way. It was too busy munching scrambled eggs. As it settled down to get comfortable, more dark liquid oozed from the bag, sinking into the remains of Jem's bath mat.

"Oh, no, you're making it worse. I mean it. Stop that," Jem commanded, as she would've done to a naughty dog. "Come here!"

Startled, the cat looked back at her as if considering her a potential threat for the first time. Had Jem ever picked up a cat? If she had, it was so long ago, she'd forgotten. Did they bite like dogs? This one wasn't hissing or putting its ears back, but it had large paws and a muscular, ramped-up backside. She thought it could put up a good fight if it wanted.

"Kitty." Jem shifted to a cloying tone. "Leave off that mess and you'll get a treat."

The cat did not believe her. Turning back to its treasure, it started munching again, pulling the box aside to reveal something under it. The item wasn't food, but Jem thought it looked vaguely familiar.

"I'll bet I know how to get you away from there."

Moving fast, Jem snatched the Styrofoam box right out from under the cat's whiskers. She betted that once it was in her possession, the cat would follow it anywhere. She was right. With a high-pitched sound of distress, it darted toward her, and Jem saw all of that vaguely familiar thing, suddenly recognizing what it was.

Letting out an indignant *meow*, the cat leapt for the takeaway breakfast and very nearly made it, but Jem was too shocked by the revealed object to care. Absently, she carried the takeaway box into the hall, put it down for the cat's pleasure, and returned to examine the object on her bathroom floor.

It was in two pieces. The first was a long wooden shaft. The second, a thick wooden cylinder belted by circular grooves. One end of the cylinder was capped with a brass band. The other end was naked and clearly damaged, as if its matching band had been knocked off. On the broken side, the wood was stained dark. A clotted mess stuck to it. To Jem, it looked like strands of black human hair.

"Off with her head," she muttered, suddenly thinking of *Alice in Wonderland*. It had been ages since she'd seriously delved into classic children's literature. Hadn't the Red Queen threatened Alice—and anyone else who displeased her—with that fate during a croquet match? Whether or not she remembered that correctly, she was certainly looking at a decapitated croquet mallet, along with a second yellow takeaway tray, wads of damp paper, and still more coffee grounds.

Somebody binned a weapon. A weapon that definitely looks like it's been used. Doesn't matter how all this rubbish got in my flat. I have to ring the police.

Behind Jem, the door to her bedroom opened and a voice said, "Hey!"

2

THE SQUATTER

Jem whirled.

The person who'd emerged from the bedroom—*her* bedroom—was a right royal mess. A surge of adrenaline ordered Jem to run for it, but the dimensions of her poky hall, currently containing two adults and a cat eating its cold breakfast, wouldn't allow it, unless she literally kicked away the cat in the process. Luckily the intruder, in addition to being a right royal mess, was also a slender young woman. Had Jem been confronted with a burly man with wild eyes and an anaconda neck tattoo, she wasn't sure what she would've done. Sometimes in the heat of the moment she surprised herself.

"Oh my God!" the woman cried, squinting past Jem at the mountain of rubbish. "Did that really happen?"

There was something familiar about this young woman. Her black Sally Bowles bob was on sideways, her red lipstick had migrated to her chin and teeth, and one of her Liza Minnelli false eyelashes flapped when she blinked. Dressed as if for a night on the town, she wore a short, clingy sheath that showed off her lithe form and long legs. Every inch of skin was slathered in body glitter; her bare feet showed off purple toenails.

"Tori?" Jem asked in disbelief.

The intruder was clutching a pair of specs. Popping them on, she used her assisted eyes to take in the entire bathroom—rubbish, ruined bath mat, and Jem, trembling with fear and fury. For a moment she said nothing, just goggled, that loose eyelash scraping her lens like a windshield wiper. Then she whimpered, "Oh, Jemmie, I'm so sorry."

"Victoria Jago," Jem thundered, surprising them both. She was channeling Wendy Jago—Tori's mum and Jem's stepmother—who always broke out the full names when things seriously went awry. "What the hell is going on here?"

Tori crumpled. For a moment Jem thought her little sister—eight years her junior at age twenty-five—was overcome by remorse for her manifold sins: trespassing, squatting, taking in an unauthorized pet, and filling the bathroom with a mountain of rubbish that just happened to contain a bloodstained weapon. Then she noticed the distinct green tinge to Tori's face.

"Oh, no, you don't! Not here! Get to the kitchen sink!"

Tori blundered out of the bathroom, putting a foot in the cat's cold breakfast, staggering, righting herself, and then managing to trip over the infuriated creature with her other foot.

"Mii-oooow!"

"Tori!"

She wasn't fast enough to save the girl from going down in a glittery heap. It was fortunate there was no one around to witness this but Jem (a blood relation) and the cat (a cat) because Tori wound up with her nearly nonexistent knickers exposed, vomiting all over the rug. That outpouring mixed with the rubbish bouquet to create a smell that could have been weaponized for Britain's defense. Jem's stomach lurched and, before she knew it, she was running for the kitchen sink. She made it just in time.

"Tori," Jem called after the storm of nausea passed.

For several seconds there was no sound from the hall, where the retching had recently stopped. Then, weakly: "Yeah?"

"Are you okay?"

"Yeah."

"Good. I'm going to kill you."

"Fine."

"Tori?"

"What?" she screeched, sounding like she was crying.

"Why is there a bloodstained mallet in my bathroom?"

Silence. Jem turned away from the sink, fetched a glass from the cupboard, filled it with tap water and forced herself to take a sip. Her stomach flipped but she kept it down.

"Tori! Answer me!"

"Stop shouting. I don't know." Now she definitely was crying, raggedly, like a small child who knows she's done wrong and weeps in hope of lessening her punishment.

"At least tell me why you filled my bathtub with rubbish," Jem said, marching back into the hall. There she found Tori lying wretchedly on the floor, looking for all the world like Streetwalker Victim #3 in the sort of gritty crime drama that kills off a few anonymous female characters every episode.

"All right. Up you get." She caught Tori's hand, helping her rise. "Stop sniveling. And let's cover your bits while we're about it," she added, yanking her sister's hemline, such as it was, into position. "Want me to guess? Fine. I'll go way out on a limb and say you spent last night at a club and drank your dinner. Feel better, now the poison's out?"

Tori nodded. The false eyelash went *scrape-scrape* against the lens of her specs as she gave Jem an imploring look. "I think maybe I'm in trouble," she quavered. "I need your help."

"Did you hurt someone?"

"No, of course not."

"Did you see someone get hurt?"

"No, nothing like that."

"What's with the rubbish stuffed in my bathroom? Did you help someone cover up a crime after the fact?"

"I didn't mean to," Tori said, face screwing up as she fought back more tears. "But now I think maybe I did."

3

CLEAN-UP AND CATCH-UP

The story Tori proceeded to tell Jem was odd, full of infuriating blank spots, but overall it didn't sound alarming or criminal. Concluding that her sister was still too inebriated to explain herself to anyone, much less the police, Jem decided to put off ringing them a little longer. Her first responsibility was to get Tori in a fit shape to face them.

Without an accessible shower/bath, it wasn't easy to clean up Tori, but Jem gritted her teeth and set about it anyway. First, she steered Tori into the kitchenette and plucked the Sally Bowles wig off her head, revealing the brown curls pinned up beneath. Next, she carefully peeled off the false eyelashes, discarding them on the counter, where they lay like fat black caterpillars. Wetting a dishtowel, she added a bit of Fairy Liquid and scrubbed Tori's face, eliminating all of the smeared lipstick, most of the mascara, and at least a quarter of the body glitter. Wetting a second dishtowel—the first was all but ruined —she handed it to Tori and told the younger woman to de-glitterfy her arms and legs once she'd wriggled out of the sheath.

"And all this time," Jem said, examining the dress, which

resembled an oversized muffler after Tori was fully extracted from its clutches, "I thought you were in Liverpool with Dave."

David Jago was Tori's twin, born seven minutes before her. Ever since Tori had arrived in the world almost literally on his heels, she'd viewed the two of them as a package deal. If he zigged, she zigged, and if he jumped, her feet flew off the ground in perfect tandem.

"Now you're back in Penzance," Jem continued. "You might have said."

"Pull the other one," Tori snorted. "When you moved to London you practically went up in a puff of smoke. You know who told me you were back in Cornwall? Dean. You know who told me you two split up? *Dean*, a man I've never actually met, who seems to have a better relationship with me than you. And you've got the cheek to say I might have said?"

"Whew! Feel better?"

"A little. You know it's true."

"I know. You may be pleased to learn I've improved a bit since I came back to Cornwall. The Scillies have been good for me."

"You're very tanned," Tori said. "Blonde streaks in your hair, too."

"Yep. Sun and surf. I can't wait to take you out to St. Morwenna on my boat. You'll love it. But first we need to find you something decent to wear before you meet the cops."

Jem went to the bedroom in search of clean clothes. She had on island wear—T-shirt, jeans, and plimsolls—which was fine, but Tori was in desperate need. The police were just like everybody else, except more so—if Tori presented herself visually as Streetwalker #3, they might not give her the benefit of the doubt as they listened to her story about the bloodstained mallet and the rubbish.

Glancing around the bedroom, Jem saw that her sister

hadn't really made herself at home. Apart from the unmade bed, there were few signs of occupancy. Only Tori's dancing shoes, discarded in the middle of the floor, and a tote bag full of toiletries, which was apparently her sole piece of luggage. Poor kid must've run away from Liverpool in a hurry.

Though more or less estranged from her father, Kenneth, and her stepmother, Wendy, Jem felt much warmer toward Tori and Dave. They were fun-loving, interesting people who didn't deserve to be blamed for anyone else's behavior, especially Kenneth Jago's. However, as Jem grew up, moved to London, got married, excelled in her career as a Special Collections Librarian, got divorced, and finally returned to the Isles of Scilly, she'd allowed Tori and Dave to slowly become names on a Christmas card list and little more. She was glad Tori was back in Penzance. It would give her a chance to start mending fences, as she'd recently done on St. Morwenna.

She dumped the contents of Tori's tote bag onto the bed. It contained a toothbrush, toothpaste, a blow-dryer, a make-up kit, two thongs and a bra. Poking around her own bedroom like a stranger—it looked small and rather sad after staying with Pauley Gwyn at Lyonesse House on St. Morwenna for eight weeks—she found a small pile of Tori's dirty clothes. There was a pair of jeans that looked okay, but none of the crumpled T-shirts would cut it. Opening her own wardrobe, Jem selected a crisp white button-down Oxford and a blue wool sweater.

"Right," she announced, returning to the kitchenette with the clothes, toothbrush, and toothpaste. "Brush your teeth and put these on."

As Tori obeyed, Jem retrieved her own kit from her suitcase in the hall, and returned to the kitchen sink to embark on her own spot of dental hygiene. All the while, her mind turned over Tori's tale about the rubbish pile in the bathroom, trying to analyze it as a lawman might.

"Tori."

She turned to find her sister, already in jeans, trying the white Oxford for size. It was too big—Tori was four inches shorter than Jem and more finely boned—but acceptable.

"Do you really expect me to wear that sweater on top? I'll look like a great blue sheep."

"Yes. Put it on. Haven't you ever seen how women on trial dress?"

"Like librarians. Point taken." Tori pulled the bulky sweater over her head. As she poked her face through the neck hole, she looked like a child playing dress-up.

"Listen, Tors," Jem said. "I've dealt with the police a lot lately. There were a couple of murders in the Scillies, and I helped solve the cases."

"No way. Why didn't I see it on the news?"

"I don't know. It was in all the local papers."

"You're a detective now?"

"Sort of. Strictly amateur."

"Naw, this is bollocks. You're having me on."

"No, really. *Bright Star* even sent a reporter to talk to me."

"Oh my God, you're going to be in *Bright Star*?" Tori squealed, impressed at last.

"Maybe. I keep waiting to see if I'm featured, but it hasn't happened yet. Maybe bigger stories crowded me out." *Bright Star*, the nation's second-best-selling red-top paper, couldn't be expected to run a profile on Jem if Piers Morgan said something really outrageous or the Duchess of Cambridge wore another showstopper.

"Anyway," Jem continued, "my point being, I can't lie outright to the authorities, not even to smooth things over for you. If there's anything you haven't told me—anything that happened last night that puts you in real legal danger—we need to arrange counsel right away."

Tori made a sound between a scoff and a tongue-click. "I like that."

"What?"

"You don't trust me. You think I'm holding out on you."

At least she sounded sober enough to argue properly. "All right, let's go over it again from the top. What are you doing in my flat, uninvited, living out of a tote bag, when Kenneth and Wendy live ten minutes from here?"

Tori scowled. "You know I couldn't go back there. They've never stopped treating me like I was fifteen years old. Living there would be like house arrest. When I took the train from Liverpool, I didn't know what I'd do. Then I watched a YouTube video about squatting. Turns out the squatter has all the rights, at least in the short run. I knew your address because Dean gave it to me. When I said I'd drop by for a visit, he mentioned you were actually off doing a library job in the Scillies and might not be back yet. So I found a video on lock-picking..."

Jem groaned.

"You should thank me. By the way, security's important. You really ought to install a deadbolt."

"I'll take that under advisement. When did you break in?"

"Wednesday afternoon."

"And nobody noticed a strange woman coming in and out of my flat?"

"Please. Ms. Bolton across the way is so cheerful. No wonder her Year Three class loves her. And Mickey and Tommy downstairs are adorbs. I've offered to babysit whenever their dad likes. Everyone seems to think I'm you, and that you're finally getting around to meeting your neighbors. You've been isolating on Planet Jem again, haven't you?"

"Maybe. Spending a lot of time with my old friends in the islands, too. But even though I'm glad to see you, this behavior is completely out of bounds. You can't just pick an empty flat and take it."

"I can. I did," Tori replied, with the blunt cheekiness Jem well remembered and had mostly enjoyed. Cleaning up and putting on fresh clothes seemed to have restored her native defiance. While in her twin Dave's shadow, it was easy for people to think of him as the bossy, brassy, daring one, and Tori as his cheerleader. Without him, she could shine.

"Now let me give you a bit of legal advice," Tori continued blithely. "You've returned to your empty property to find a squatter in residence. What do you do? First, you type up a letter—just a paragraph or two, really—asserting the right to reside in this flat. Maybe you can get your landlord to do it, assuming you can find him. That letter is called a notice of possession. Seal the notice in an envelope and pop it through my letterbox." She pointed at the rectangle set into the front door. "And then you wait until I reply. If you feel unsafe sharing the flat with me, you'll probably need to bunk with a friend or go to a hotel."

Jem raised both eyebrows.

"Oh, and I realize it might require a tiny outlay of cash, but you'll also want to hire a solicitor. If I don't respond to your assertion of rights, you'll have to turn to the law. The wheels of justice grind slowly," Tori concluded with a grin, "but you'll get your day in court. You'll have me out of here in a fortnight. Two months at the most."

Crossing from the kitchenette to the living room, Jem seized her trusty cricket bat from its hiding place inside the umbrella stand. She smacked its spine against the palm of her hand. "I'd rather settle out of court."

"It's illegal to threaten violence against a squatter!" Tori yelped as Jem charged at her. It wasn't much of a chase—Tori was running on fumes—and when Jem caught her they erupted into peals of laughter. There was a slightly manic quality to the sound, given there was a bloodied weapon in the bathroom and the flat reeked like a wheelie bin, but it felt good to laugh.

"You cow. I've missed you. I've missed the hell out of you," Tori said, voice breaking.

Putting the cricket bat aside, Jem gave her sister a hug that was long enough and hard enough to satisfy even the touchiest-feeliest American. "I've missed you too, kiddo. Why'd you leave Liverpool? Don't tell me you and Dave quarreled?"

"All he cares about is his job. And *Brooke*." Tori pronounced the name like it was a foot disease. "They're having a baby. He doesn't have time for me. Brooke kept dropping hints that I needed to move to my own place. Do you know what the rents are around Goodison Park? When I told Dave I wanted us to move back to Penzance, he said if I'd rather be off, there was no time like the present. Tosser! He didn't think I'd do it. So I threw my stuff in a tote and hopped the first train before I could change my mind."

"Good for you," Jem said, and meant it. "High time you stepped out of Dave's shadow. Just because he's happy in Liverpool doesn't mean you have to be."

Tori's eyes shone. Apparently she'd been waiting a long time to hear someone say that, and now that it had been said, she needed a moment to let herself believe it.

"Thanks for giving me something to wear," she said at last. "Sorry I said that. About dressing like a librarian. Not that you are right this minute. But usually, with the granny skirts and the sensible shoes."

"Oh." Removing her specs—big and round, they could be called stylish or owlish, depending on who you asked—Jem polished a lens. "What you refer to," she said loftily, "is actually my protective coloration. I prefer for people to underestimate me. I like to see the look on their face when they realize how wrong they've got it. But, Tors, we've wasted enough time. We really must ring the coppers and get this over with.

Remember, just the facts. Try not to offer them anything extra."

"Can't you tell them?"

"The main part is yours to tell. But if they get mean or sniffy, clam up and let me handle it."

"You think they'll be mean?" Tori sounded worried.

"It's happened before," Jem admitted, and picked up her mobile.

4

WHO ARE YOU CALLING SILLY?

Because it wasn't an emergency, the police dispatcher advised Jem that they might wait anywhere from twenty minutes to two hours. That was fine with Jem; she'd set herself the awful task of cleaning up the hall rug. Even with rubber gloves and disinfectant wipes, it was a foul job. But anything that reduced the stink in the flat was worth some momentary discomfort. All the windows were open, and though she'd thoroughly spritzed the place with deodorizer, there was only so much you could rationally expect Febreze to do.

In the kitchenette, Tori put the kettle on and started rummaging in cupboards. "Is there any builder's?" she called, meaning her favorite brand of tea.

"You're the squatter in possession of my flat. You tell me."

"Then I reckon we're out. This isn't good. If I'm going to be interrogated, I really need a cuppa."

"You'll be questioned, not interrogated. Make coffee."

"I used up the last of it yesterday morning."

"Then consider it karma," Jem said heartlessly, "for helping yourself to the groceries I bought. Come give me a hand."

"I don't think I can. I know I'm the one who sicked it up,

but, Jem, seriously, I don't dare look at it. My tummy's so bad I might—"

"Calm down, the worst is done. It's nothing but a scrubbed damp place on the rug now," Jem interrupted. "We'd better locate your cat. What do you call him? Or is it a her?"

"I don't know," Tori said, venturing from the kitchenette into the hall.

"What do you mean, you don't know?"

"I respect its privacy."

"That's a strange way to treat a pet."

"First, I think he's male, based on the way he carries himself. Second, he isn't actually what you'd call my *pet*. Don't think he'd fancy being called a pet. He's more of a fellow traveler."

"Tori, what are you talking about?"

"When I picked your lock, I turned around and saw him on the walkway, watching the operation. When the door opened, he strolled in ahead of me like he was giving me the tour. I thought maybe he was yours. Or that he lived here with the previous tenant."

"Right. How long since you cleaned his litter tray?" Now that the sick was cleaned up and the bathroom door was shut, the smell of ammonia had begun to predominate over the other stinks.

Tori looked embarrassed. "I'm short on cash, so I set up a cardboard box with some newspaper in the bottom. I reckon it's soaked through by now. He probably needs a better place to wee."

"It's official. I'm never getting my security deposit back." Jem blew out a sigh. "What do you call him?"

"Wotsit. Like the snack. Because of the little ginger curls on his white fur."

"Wotsit!" Jem called in a firm, friendly voice that would've made any dog worth his salt bound headlong into the room. It came as no particular surprise when the cat didn't appear.

"Wotsit!" Tori called half-heartedly. "Sorry. We really don't have that kind of relationship where I call and he comes. He lives his life, I live mine."

"There aren't that many places to hide around here. He must be under our noses," Jem said. After a quick check under the sofa, she went to the bedroom for a look. From under the bed came a faint squeaking. She flipped up the duvet, leaned down, and looked.

Under the center of the mattress, at the precise spot where a human hand would have the hardest time grabbing him, sat Wotsit the cat with two prizes—both of those yellow Styrofoam boxes of takeaway breakfast. One had been scarfed down so thoroughly, only the beans remained. The other, on top of which he was protectively curled, was apparently meant to be his dinner.

"You little piglet. When did you go back to the rubbish heap and get the second one?"

He stared back at Jem inscrutably. Something in his expression suggested he'd accomplished many things while she and Tori were simultaneously being sick, all of them to his advantage.

"All right. No one's taking your food away," Jem told him. "But the police are coming, so don't freak out. Just stay put and don't be seen. I'm not sure I'm allowed to even have you."

Rising, she straightened up just as the long-expected knock at the front door finally came. It was followed by a woman's voice announcing, "Devon & Cornwall Police."

"Ready?" Jem asked Tori, who nodded.

"Wait. You're still barefoot, Purple Toes. Put some shoes on. I'll go break the ice."

When Jem opened the front door, she found herself facing a

blonde police officer with apple cheeks and a snub nose who said, "Ms. Jago? Pleased to meet you. I'm PC Kellow."

Looking like that in a stab vest and regulation bowler hat couldn't have been easy, but PC Kellow pulled it off. She was lovely. Behind her, unlovely, stood a mountain of a man. Stepping forward, he took in Jem with unblinking eyes, not bothering to introduce himself. Perhaps he thought he needed no introduction. To Jem, something in his expression suggested he knew her, or at least knew of her, and that he considered that knowledge an advantage. She didn't appreciate the unspoken *gotcha* in his gaze, and his intensity made her skin crawl.

Seeming a bit surprised that her colleague had stepped forward only to stare at Jem without speaking, PC Kellow said, "And this is DS Conrad. He works with the homicide unit but happened to be available when your call came in."

Jem nodded. Despite the fact it was mid-September and warm by anyone's standards, the man had on a brown overcoat over his suit, wearing it the way a credenza wears a dust cloth. Under low and bushy brows, his small eyes gleamed. His hair was sparse, and the mustache under his hooked nose seemed molded out of his flesh. Perhaps he'd started life as a ginger, and while his hair faded, his face grew redder, the whole process continuing until finally his hair, scalp, mustache and skin were more or less the same color.

"You're Ms. Jemima Jago," he announced as if it might be news to her, in a voice that sounded like gravel crunching. "The Scilly Sleuth."

"Excuse me?" She bit back, *Who are you calling silly?*

From beneath his overcoat, DS Conrad brought out a folded tabloid. It was an issue of *Bright Star*.

"You didn't make the cover, I'm afraid." He held it up so she could see who did: the usual mix of reality TV stars, misbehaving politicians, and royal lightning rods.

"They ran the piece?" She didn't want to give this odious

man the satisfaction of seeming interested, but she couldn't help herself.

"Indeed. Wait till you see the picture they published. Not flattering, I fear." Refolding the tabloid, he stuck it back inside his overcoat. "If you want a peek, you'll have to invite us in."

"Oh, of course. Sorry." As Jem stepped back to allow them in, Tori emerged from the bedroom. Properly shod with her curls brushed out and the blue sweater making her look young and innocent, she was a sight to inspire confidence. Jem shot her an approving smile. Maybe they could get through this without being taken down to the station to assist the police with their inquiries, to quote the undying cliché.

"Whew!" When the stink hit PC Kellow, she cringed. Her pug nose seemed to grow even smaller in self-preservation. DS Conrad didn't react. Jem had the feeling that if she asked him, he'd say he hadn't noticed. Hardboiled coppers weren't known for being delicate about their surroundings.

"We can sit here to talk," Jem said, leading them to kitchenette's table. "But I'm afraid there's only three chairs."

"No worries. I'll stand while I take it all down." PC Kellow withdrew an oversized smartphone with a heavy-duty case—her department-issued handheld, no doubt—and readied her stylus for note-taking.

Jem and Tori sat down and waited, trying not to be impatient as DS Conrad stalked about, peering into empty corners and scowling as he examined the sink.

Is this a put-on? Jem wondered.

He seemed deadly serious, his small eyes flicking around the kitchenette as if a corpse might tumble out of a cupboard. Back on St. Morwenna, Jem would've said something snarky, especially if she was the one about to be questioned, but this was Penzance and Tori was clearly nervous. For her sake, Jem maintained her most respectable, librarianly air.

"Did someone vomit?" DS Conrad asked at last.

"Yeah. Because of that reek from the bathroom. It was too much for me," Tori said.

Gently, Jem kicked her under the table.

"Sir," Tori added.

Sighing, DS Conrad pulled out a chair and lowered his bulk into it, looking for all the world like an elephant balancing itself on a tricycle. He wasn't really that large, but apparently he was so inflexible that even bending at the waist to sit required a major negotiation with himself.

They began with the basics: Jem's full name and occupation, Tori's full name and occupation (or in her case, lack thereof), and other details that left PC Kellow and her superior in no doubt of who they were dealing with. Then DS Conrad brought out *Bright Star* again, opening it on the table facing Jem and Tori.

"Let's get your fame out of the way first. I'll give you and your half-sister a moment to read it."

It was a two-page spread headlined, THE NEXT SHERLOCK OR JUST A 'SCILLY' SLEUTH? There were five photos: a beautiful shot of Tresco, the Isles of Scilly's most luxurious location; a picture of each murder victim in happier days; Jem at a café (photographed during the interview); and one of her school pictures—Year Five—in which Jem had sported a too-short haircut that made her resemble a sentient bottle-brush. She thought she'd mended fences quite well since her return, but clearly she still had detractors on St. Morwenna if someone had given a reporter *that* picture to run.

"Wow," Tori breathed. "I thought you were exaggerating, but if anything, you downplayed it. You're really something, Jemmie."

DS Conrad emitted another sound. It could have been faint displeasure.

Ignoring him, Jem read the piece rapidly, guarding her face. Whatever had made this copper take against her, he'd gone to the trouble of bringing along a tabloid article for the express purpose of ruining her day. As with most things *Bright Star*, the story was written in a style a few notches above Biff, Chip, and Kipper stories, full of unkind suppositions about why a divorced librarian had run off to the remote Scillies to play Agatha Raisin. Rather than focus on Jem's efforts to catch two killers, the author had zeroed in on Jem's wayward childhood. During the course of the interview, Jem had been promised the story's angle would be local-girl-makes-good, but the final result was more enigmatic-ex-delinquent-makes-waves.

Jem yawned. "I expected better. Next time I'll hold out for TV, where I can tell my story my way." She refolded the tabloid and pushed it back across the table.

"Your half-sister looks star-struck," DS Conrad said.

"No need to keep saying half," Tori said.

"Has that term become politically incorrect these days?"

"No, it's just unnecessary. We're not fractions. We're sisters." Tori, looking and sounding as if she were in desperate need of some paracetamol and a gallon of hot tea, added, "Why did you bring that here? I saw your name mentioned. Are you embarrassed that Jem solved a case for you?"

Under the table, Jem kicked her again, harder. Tori jumped, giving Jem the sisterly look of death that made it clear to their guests she'd received a reprimand. DS Conrad's answering smile was completely without warmth, amusement, or charity.

"I am never embarrassed when justice is served," he rumbled, crunching gravel deep inside. His head appeared directly attached to his chest. If he'd ever had a neck, it had crumbled into the general rock pile. "It was pure coincidence that I had the paper in my possession. I was bringing it to show PC Kellow. I thought she'd like to see The Saint's new sweetheart."

PC Kellow, who'd been standing nearby, ready to resume her note-taking and regarding the trio with polite attention, stiffened. When she looked at Jem, her cornflower-blue eyes were suddenly hostile.

Cornflower-blue eyes, apple cheeks, and a disposition like sour milk. That covers the whole ruddy farm.

Surprised at herself—it wasn't like her to take against a perfect stranger so fast—Jem mentally kicked herself under the table. This wasn't the time to get nasty, even if provoked. PC Kellow had gone from polite to visibly displeased. DS Conrad was leering as if he'd scored a point. Rather than meet them in kind, Jem told herself to stay cool and on guard. There was at least one hidden agenda here, and they hadn't even trotted out the story of Tori's night on the town.

"I don't know what you mean by that 'sweetheart' comment," Jem said, back in starchy librarian mode, "but it sounds as if you're joking, and we called the police because we consider this quite serious. Perhaps you'd like to see the blood-stained mallet, or ask us some questions?"

DS Conrad didn't answer right away. He seemed to be one of those interviewers who liked to insert long, possibly meaning-less silences into the exchange, doubtless to unsettle and unnerve. At last he turned to Tori and said, "Proceed. From the beginning."

5

IT HAPPENED ONE NIGHT

"Right. Well. Here's the thing. I grew up here in Penzance, but a few years back, my brother Dave and I went off to Liverpool because he got his dream job. USM Finch Farm." Tori, clearly still proud to utter the words, paused slightly to allow DS Conrad and PC Kellow time to be impressed. "He's always loved footy—we've always loved it, but him more than me. He played a bit in school and wanted to go pro. That didn't happen, obvs, but he applied as deputy kit administrator at Goodison Park and got the job. I went along and he found me a place in the Everton Premier League club office.

"We lived together and it was all right. Even after he moved in with his partner, Brooke, and they got pregnant, it was still all right. But then my boyfriend Marko threw me over for a numpty cow with big udders, and Dave started hinting that I was taking up space that was needed for the baby. That's when I realized I hated living with him and Brooke. I hated my whole life in Liverpool." Her voice cracked as if she might dissolve into tears.

Jem's foot was poised to deliver a third kick, but she held

herself back. DS Conrad's reaction was impossible to read—he exuded nothing but faintly amused contempt—but PC Kellow's nascent animosity had faded, giving way to calm professionalism. Maybe a little honest emotion wouldn't hurt.

"Anyway, Dave didn't care. I've spent my whole life bending over and under to make whatever he wanted work. But when I needed him to bend, or at least consider bending, or even pretend to care, he wouldn't do it. He just looked at me like I was mental. My parents still live in Penzance, but I didn't want to turn up on their doorstep. They've never cottoned on that I'm not fifteen anymore. It would've been no boys, no parties, and a ten o'clock curfew. But I had to find someplace to stay. I'd left Liverpool with just an overnight bag and not much cash. I was thinking of finding a hostel or something when I saw a YouTube video about squ—"

This time Jem administered a very soft kick so Tori wouldn't jerk in her chair again, but she also wouldn't casually admit to breaking and entering.

"When I saw a video," Tori corrected herself, "that reminded me of my sister Jem..."

"I'd issued a blanket invitation for Tori to come and stay with me anytime, and given her a spare key," Jem put in quickly.

"...so here I am," Tori continued more smoothly. "But it felt lonely with Jem still off on St. Morwenna. I'd lost touch with most of my school friends, and I was missing Marko. I felt pretty low, like no one in Liverpool cared that I'd gone and no one in Penzance cared that I was here. So yesterday I decided to make it a big Friday night on the town.

"I bought a dress and a wig and some make-up. I got all dolled up, incognito, and went to a club called Noughts & Crosses. It's on the far end of Silversmith Lane."

PC Kellow was taking notes again; DS Conrad nodded almost imperceptibly.

"I started drinking Jägermeister with nothing in my tummy but half a sandwich. Big mistake." Tori offered the detective sergeant a weak smile that wasn't returned. "A bloke started flirting with me, so I pulled him out onto the dance floor. Halfway through the song, his girl turns up, breathing fire and ready to do me harm. She called me a—never mind—and I had a few choice words for her, and she gave me a slap and I scratched her cheek. She started it, but since I drew blood, the big gorillas on security decided I should be bounced. And that's when Josh spoke up for me."

When Tori pronounced his name, her eyes lit up and she seemed momentarily reinvigorated. "He was wonderful. So handsome, like he fell from heaven. Not only did he stand up for me against the brutes, he insisted I be allowed to stay. He was my white knight."

"So they didn't bounce you?" PC Kellow asked.

"Oh, no, they flung me out. Tossed me into the alley behind the club. There I was at one in the morning, drunk and shivering, feeling like a ruddy fool. Right away I saw I wasn't alone—a guy was there, having a wee behind the bins. He would've been cute if he hadn't been doing *that* right in the open. I turned my head and started walking away, fast, and ran straight into Josh. He'd left the club in protest after they threw me out!"

She grinned at Jem, expecting support. Jem forced herself to smile appreciatively. It was hardly a romance for the ages, but maybe you had to be there.

"Anyway, I told him a lad in the alley was being disgusting, and he laughed and said it was only his friend T.J., who wasn't housebroken. By then T.J. was zipping up, thank goodness, and he wanted to know what we were laughing about. He really wasn't so bad, and the next thing I knew, the three of us were mates—Josh, T.J., and me. I spent the rest of the evening with them. They're the reason I ended up dragging home those bags of rubbish. Well. Them, and Jägermeister."

"Names?" PC Kellow interjected, her stylus poised.

"Josh and T.J.," Tori repeated slowly, as if the constable had been caught napping.

"I mean surnames."

She shrugged.

"You have no idea?"

"If they ever said, I don't remember."

"You say you spent the evening with them," DS Conrad rumbled. "I presume you mean sexually?"

"No." Tori's eyes went wide. "Why would you say that?"

He spread his hands, as if to say they both knew why. "I withdraw the question. Proceed."

Tori still looked insulted, so Jem patted her shoulder. "It's okay. These interviews always get personal. Even offensive."

"There's no law against a night on the town. There's no law against having a drink and making new friends," Tori declared hotly, staring down DS Conrad. He appeared as troubled by the intensity of her glare as the average boulder is troubled by the intensity of a gnat.

He said, "In a public place, it is an offense to be drunk, or to be drunk and disorderly. From your own statement, having been forcibly expelled by a club, you were both, Ms. Jago. The same goes for the friend you found urinating in the street."

"Are you going to arrest me after the fact?"

That earned her a good, hard kick, and Jem didn't care if she jumped or not. "Tors, darling, I realize you're hungover and embarrassed. You need some caffeine and some quiet time. But the sooner you finish your story, the sooner this will be over."

"Fine. For your information, outside of weeing in an alley, T.J. was no worse than any other bloke out for a fun Friday night. And Josh really was my white knight. So scrummy. There I was, ready to cry over being chucked out, and he starts telling me all the times the club's been shut down. Illegal hours, electrical faults, license problems—Josh had all the dirt on them. He's lived near Silversmith Bay all his life."

"Do you know his occupation?" PC Kellow asked.

"Gastropub."

"Which one?"

Tori looked blank.

"Does he own it, or manage it?"

"Lord, none of the above. He washes dishes and mops the floor."

To Jem's eye, PC Kellow's expression didn't change. Tori, however, must've detected a hint of disdain, because she added, "He was doing an apprenticeship with an electrician, but there was family trouble and he had to stop. He'll take it up again soon, and then he'll have a job that pays brilliantly. Maybe better than yours."

"No doubt. Sounds as if you and Josh did become good friends between one o'clock in the morning and daybreak," PC Kellow said. "I'm surprised you didn't pick up his surname while going over his career plans."

"I was drunk," Tori said, cheeks growing pinker. "Which bloody well better not be a crime, or this whole country's in trouble. Anyway, the three of us walked the streets, talking and having a laugh. Looking for an after-hours club, but we couldn't find one open. Then Josh said we could go back to his place on Weaver Road. Need me to spell it?" she asked PC Kellow.

"I know it well, thank you. Semi-posh neighborhood. Sky-high rents. Josh the dishwasher must be rolling in it."

"Of course he isn't. They're just ordinary blokes. T.J. lives with his gran, who can't be disturbed on account of her illnesses. And Josh lives in his parents' house as a lodger. In the basement, with a separate entrance. It was snug in there—telly, mini fridge, one of those beds that folds up against the wall. We opened a bottle and talked for hours. I haven't had so much fun in forever. But we were drinking Clarke's Court Spiced Rum, and I should've known better. On top of the Jägermeister, it knocked me down. I don't remember passing out, but I must've, because I woke up in Josh's bed around half-six."

Jem maintained her scrupulously blank expression. She had strong opinions about Tori going home with two blokes she met in an alley and passing out in their presence; it didn't take a body language expert to see PC Kellow had them, too. Still, Tori was grown up, fairly savvy, and fully responsible for herself. If Jem decided to give her a woman-to-woman, sister-to-sister dressing down about personal safety in the big bad world, she'd do it when they were alone, not in front of judgy strangers.

"I know it was stupid, all right?" Tori burst out, no more fooled by Jem's deliberate blankness than by PC Kellow's compressed lips. "It was meant to be a wild night, that was the whole point. For one night, I didn't want to be the rejected twin, or the rejected girlfriend, or the daughter forced to come home because she couldn't hack it in Liverpool. And when I woke up in Josh's bed, I was fine—unhurt, unbothered, absolutely fine. Sorry to disappoint you."

"Were your new friends asleep?" DS Conrad asked.

"No, they were gone." Tori sighed. "What woke me was the sound of Josh's dad knocking on the open door. He heard a noise and came downstairs to check it out. He expected to find Josh just in from the club alone. Wasn't best pleased to find me lying in bed." Eyeing DS Conrad, she added, "Can't blame him, he's an old man. Maybe as old as you."

"Poor sod," he said evenly. "How did the white knight's old dad react to finding you? Did he hand you the keys to the street?"

"No. Josh came back just then. He said T.J. had gone home, and it was getting light out, so he offered to walk me to Jem's place." Taking a breath, she stopped, squeezed her hands together.

Jem noted the gesture with a pang of alarm. Until this moment, except for flashes of temper, Tori had recited the story just as she'd told it to Jem, mostly in the same words. It wasn't that Jem distrusted Tori—as a kid she'd been honest to a fault—but something smelled bad, and it wasn't just the bathroom. In Jem's experience, people sped up when determined to finish telling a difficult story. It was before embarking on a lie, especially a big one, that they slowed down. And Tori had definitely slowed down.

"So, you know, we started saying goodbye to Josh's dad, and I noticed Josh seemed worried. Also he seemed to have sobered up a lot in a short time," Tori continued, gaze darting from face to face. "I asked why he left me alone instead of waking me up. He said he'd only expected to be gone a few minutes. His parents don't allow smoking anywhere in their house, even Josh's basement room, and T.J. *must* have his ciggies. So T.J. went outside for a smoke, and Josh went with him. They started walking down Weaver Road." She paused again, for no reason Jem could see.

"Go on," DS Conrad said.

"If you know the area, you know that Weaver runs sort of parallel to Silversmith Lane, with a long alley between them. Anyway, Josh and T.J. walked down Weaver and across the alley—"

"Why?" PC Kellow cut in.

Tori blinked at her. "Because they felt like it, I reckon. Maybe because Josh works nearby. So does T.J., sometimes, but not regular. He's the gig type. Always something short-term." She paused again, hands coming together, squeezing hard, and breaking apart. "Anyway, while they were walking, these gang-bangers in black leather turned up..."

"Gangbangers," DS Conrad said. "In black leather."

"Sorry, I've lost the thread." PC Kellow sounded irritated. "Ms. Jago, are you relating something you witnessed? That you therefore know happened? Or are you repeating a story that Josh told you? In other words, what he *said* happened. After the fact, I presume, while walking you home."

Tori blinked at the constable as if she had no idea. "Um... this is what he told me. By then we were outside, the sun was coming up, and I could see Josh was really upset. He was almost green and his hands were shaking. When I asked why, he said while I was asleep, he and T.J. walked to the alley between Weaver Road and Silversmith Lane and that's when some gangbangers in black leather ambushed them."

PC Kellow seemed about to interrupt again, but DS Conrad forestalled it with a raised hand. Jem was glad neither of them was looking at her face, since this was the first she'd heard of any daybreak leather-clad ruffians.

"I don't know how many there were. Probably three. Three or four," Tori said, nodding to herself as if four was a good number. "One of them had a knife—I mean, obviously they all had knives—and they wanted money. Josh didn't have his wallet —he'd left it back in his room—so he had nothing to give them, but T.J. was forced to hand his wallet over. There was only a fiver inside. After they took the money, T.J. asked if he could have his wallet back, and the lads laughed and said go fish for it. And they flung it inside one of the big bins behind Silversmith Lane." She paused, not looking at Jem.

"Proceed," DS Conrad said.

"Well, Josh helped T.J. hunt through the bins for a while, but then he went back to his place to check on me. So he was worried about T.J., you see. He was willing to walk me home, of course, but he also thought if T.J. was diving into wheelie bins to try to find his wallet, he needed help. The binmen were due to turn up around seven—"

"On Silversmith Lane?" PC Kellow cut in.

"Well... we thought... anyway, Josh really wanted to go help him, so I said I'd help, too. I really should've just walked back here alone—I was still legless—but we'd had such fun that night, I would've felt disloyal if I didn't pitch in."

Consulting what looked like her personal mobile, PC Kellow said, "In that zone, pickup occurs on Tuesday and Friday."

"Fine. I reckon Josh and T.J. got it wrong, then." Tori flashed a smile that seemed rather desperate. "I would think the police would be more concerned about gangbangers roaming the town after dark. That's down to you, isn't it? Keeping the streets safe?"

DS Conrad regarded her steadily. PC Kellow had put her personal phone away and was back to taking notes.

"Anyway, when we got to the alley, T.J. said he'd been through the other bins and couldn't find it, so it had to be in The Siren's wheelie bin. The Siren's a gastropub, and its bin is the biggest. It was—"

"The pub where Josh works?" DS Conrad cut in.

"Yes, I said that, didn't I?" Tori replied, falling into his trap so neatly she didn't even know she'd done it. Jem had no idea why Tori was trying to conceal details, or why she'd added that transparently fake bit about the knife-wielding wallet thieves, but all she could do now was listen.

"Where was I? Oh, the bin. It was stuffed from top to bottom. A lot of the rubbish inside wasn't even from the restaurant. People who live nearby throw stuff in too, when they can get away with it. Josh climbed inside, searched with the torch on his phone, and then started shifting bags over the side. That's when, well, we noticed people about, coming to work and whatnot. We thought we heard the binmen's truck on the move, too, so we decided to take away the unsearched bags and go through them someplace else."

"The three of you dragged those bags all the way here?" PC Kellow asked.

Tori nodded.

"Because there was too much activity around The Siren—
people and trucks and so on?"

She nodded again.

"So the three of you, laden with rubbish, made a ten-minute
walk to this building and concealed— Excuse me." DS Conrad
pretended to cover a slip of the tongue. "And *placed* the bags
here for sorting?"

"That's right," Tori said. Her eyes bounced back and forth,
but never met Jem's.

"I'm surprised you didn't go to Weaver Road. It's closer.
According to you, Josh and T.J. both live there. And strictly
speaking, it wasn't your problem, it was T.J.'s. Moreover, unless
his empty wallet was a family heirloom, I can't imagine it was
worth so much effort," PC Kellow said.

"But I told you, T.J.'s gran is ill and can't be disturbed," Tori
shot back. "And of course Josh's place wouldn't work. His dad
was already cross. My place was best—sorry, I mean Jem's place,
but I didn't know she was coming back today. And have I
mentioned we were still all metabolizing the booze and thinking
straight was next to impossible?"

"All right. Keep going," PC Kellow said.

"Well." Tori seemed nonplussed. "I've told it, haven't I?
What more do you need?"

"Did you find the wallet?" DS Conrad asked, a touch of
malice in his tone.

"No. The operation, um, fell apart after we got here," Tori said,
again pausing to wring her hands, longer this time. "Even though
the guys carried the rubbish, it stank to high heaven, and all that
running about was making me ill. I expected Josh and T.J. to sort the
bags outside, in the courtyard, but a police car was following us by
then—I guess we looked odd—and the guys wanted us out of sight.
Josh and T.J. started arguing—sort of turned on each other—and
before I knew it, T.J. said forget the damn wallet and shoved off."

"You're telling us that after all that, he just left?" asked PC Kellow. "And then you and Josh went ahead and *still* dragged the rubbish into your sister's flat, even though the person to whom the wallet belonged had given up?"

"Mustn't browbeat," DS Conrad said mildly. "Proceed."

"Josh pleaded with me," Tori said, turning away from her interrogators to look at Jem. "He pleaded for me to let him bring the rubbish inside. I was so tired—ready to pass out, really—but I said okay. And once we got it all in the bathroom, indoors, in such a small space..." She shook her head. "It was all too much. I told him to go home. I said I'd ring him after I'd had a nap and we'd finish looking for the wallet. Then he left, and I went to bed, and fell asleep."

"Passed out?" PC Kellow suggested.

"Both, I guess. Then Jem came home, and found me, and found the mallet."

Jem fought the urge to start her own interrogation. In the presence of the authorities, under the kitchenette's stark fluorescent light, the story's denouement sounded even more ridiculous the second time around. It wasn't only the added details—in the first version, T.J. had carelessly dropped his wallet while climbing into a bin, and the trio carrying the bags home had been presented as a sort of drunken lark gone wrong. This second time, Tori had refused to give Josh's surname but accidentally revealed his workplace, added a dramatic confrontation at knifepoint, and said Josh begged her to let him bring the bags inside. That last bit had the ring of truth, even if Jem didn't know why.

Unless he knew a bloodstained mallet was in one of those bags. And he wanted it out of the alley and away from the binmen and anyone else who might find it.

Since Josh was only a name to her, she had no trouble believing he might be involved in a murder, or trying to cover one up after the fact. What troubled her was Tori—had she known? Could she have been a willing participant?

6

THE SAINT

"I have listened to your story. Now I think," DS Conrad said, drawing out his pause until Tori was practically vibrating with anxiety, "you'd better ring your new friend Josh and ask him to come over. Not just so he can answer a few simple questions, but for his sake. He was so very committed to finding his friend's wallet, after all."

"I didn't get his number."

DS Conrad raised his eyebrows. Because those brows were exactly the same color as his forehead, it gave the impression of an edifice shifting; the puff of smoke that precedes the avalanche.

"I thought I did. But I didn't. We were—"

"Inebriated. Drunk. Legless. Pissed. You've said," he replied dryly. "What a shame about the number. Fortunately, you've been to his home—"

Tori looked so alarmed, Jem decided it was time to say something. "You know," she announced, "if anyone's interested, we have a mallet clotted with blood and what looks like human hair in my bathroom right this minute." She was careful not to sound angry; she'd dealt with enough liars to know that most tried to cover themselves by leaping straight to anger, and while that might fool ordinary people, it never worked with the police. They had tasers, truncheons, and the force of the law behind them. "Would you two mind looking at it while I put the kettle on? My sister's running on fumes. If I can get a little chamomile tea into her, and possibly a cup of soup, I reckon she'll have an easier time answering questions."

DS Conrad studied her for another overlong, excruciating minute. "There have been no deaths reported to the police, natural or suspicious, in the last thirteen days. However, a great deal of people live on the margins of our society. They live and die, for the most part, without ever involving the authorities if they can help it. Therefore it's certainly possible, Ms. Jago, that you've innocently discovered a weapon used to commit GBH or murder." Putting both hands on the table, he heaved himself to his feet.

"It's also possible," he continued, looking down at Tori, "that this young woman, along with her male companions, committed GBH or murder last night, and fell out with one another in the process of hiding the weapon. It's happened before, and will happen again. If that's the case," he said, holding Tori's gaze until she looked away, "I assure you, I will soon find out."

After a visual inspection of the bathroom and broken mallet, DS Conrad and PC Kellow were satisfied that a visit from Exeter Police HQ's Forensics Team was necessary. Jem was steeled for them to remain in her flat, possibly asking all the same questions again just to be cruel, but PC Kellow received a call on her shoulder radio and DS Conrad seemed to have other irons in the fire as well.

When PC Kellow reached the door, she turned back and issued one last warning: "Ms. Jago—both Ms. Jagos. Please don't leave the West Country without calling Exeter Police HQ and asking for me. Leave a message if I'm not in. I'll be in touch ASAP to say whether or not your travel request is approved."

"That's a bit much, don't you think?" Jem asked. "I planned on returning to the Isles of Scilly next weekend."

"Ah, well, that's the trouble with being helpful to the police, isn't it? Which you're so very good at, apparently, and which we naturally appreciate so much. It requires tiny sacrifices for the greater good." The flash of dislike in her cornflower-blue eyes seemed aimed at Jem personally. Why? Was it the *Bright Star* article? Maybe coppers hated amateur sleuths in real life as much as they did in novels.

As for DS Conrad, he held back his parting shot until he'd actually stepped over the threshold into Jem's walkway. Though solidly built, he wasn't especially tall—no more than five foot nine—and Jem found herself looking down on him as he rumbled, "Give Saint Ignatius my regards."

"I never pray to middlemen," she said, and shut the door in his face.

"What was that about?" Tori asked.

"I have no idea. I'm sure he was dying for me to ask, and I wasn't about to give him the satisfaction."

Soon after the police left, the forensics team arrived, swathed in jumpsuits, masks, and gloves. The bloodstained mallet head and broken shaft, as well as the contents of the rubbish bag it was discovered in, was carefully separated and slipped into individual sterile pouches. To Jem, that seemed like overkill, considering the items had been marinating in their own filth all night, but procedure was procedure. She didn't intend to forget about Wotsit's twin takeaway boxes under the bed, but she was so busy trying to persuade the team to haul *all* the rubbish away—why stint in the pursuit of justice?—that detail escaped her until the team was gone. As for her hopes about a total cleanup, the lead technician quite understandably pretended not to hear Jem's suggestion.

Tori, whose hangover seemed to worsen as the techs in white overalls worked, said nothing until they filed out, taking their evidence bags and scientific equipment with them. Then she moaned, "Thank God they're gone. I feel like death. Could we go out for an espresso? And maybe some croissants? There's a great place near the statue of Sir Humphry Davy."

Jem, who'd narrowly kept a lid on her emotions thus far, bit her lip to keep from saying something she'd regret. Instead, she counted to ten, took a deep breath, wished she hadn't on account of the lingering stink, and said, "Tors, we have to get this place sorted. The bathroom's still full of rubbish and smells like a midden heap."

"I know." Tori gave her the big wounded eyes and pitiful voice of little sisters everywhere. "If I can just have some caffeine and keep a bit of food down, then maybe I could—"

"Nope. No maybes. We're not leaving this flat until the bathroom is back to normal. Once that's out of the way, I'll be the first in the shower. I have to get the fug out of my hair and change into fresh clothes, because I'm going out this evening. Once I'm gone, you can do what you like. Go out for a nibble. Order in. Wait around to see if Josh, assuming he even exists, comes back to search for his potentially imaginary friend T.J.'s potentially imaginary wallet. Because you're such a liar," Jem added, losing the battle with herself, "I don't know what to believe anymore."

If the remark injured Tori's feelings, she was too queasy and wrung out to show it. "He's real. They're both real. I might have messed up some details."

"Gangbangers? *Black leather?*"

At least Tori had the decency to look a bit ashamed over that one. "Yeah, that came out sounding doolally even to me. Josh and T.J. were mucking about, climbing into bins and checking for goodies—clothes, food a little past its sell-by date, all that stuff—when T.J. lost his wallet, and by the time he realized it, he had no idea which bin it fell into. I couldn't very well say that to the police, now could I?"

Jem sighed. "I don't know. I think Conrad mostly works murder cases—I can't imagine he'd consider it the crime of the century."

"Please. He was dying to nail me on something. And you! You can't pretend he didn't have it in for you."

There was a certain amount of truth to that. The fact he'd turned up alongside PC Kellow was odd enough, since for all they knew, the broken mallet could've been ketchup-stained rather than bloodstained. Jem had the uncomfortable feeling he'd seized the excuse to come simply to see her, and she didn't know why.

Deciding to let Tori's concession about phony details stand for the moment, she shifted into Girl Guide Unit Leader mode.

"Come on. Up you get," she told the younger woman in a tone of merciless good cheer. "You had a nice long sit while the coppers and forensic people did their bit. Time for us to crack on."

Crack on they did, with Tori—white-faced and conspicuously pitiful—scrubbing the bathroom's tub and tiles while Jem hauled the leftover rubbish downstairs to her building's communal bins. The jade bath mat was binned along with it. That was £22.99 she'd never get back, unless she took it out of Tori's hide. As for the matching curtain, she saved it by using scissors to snip away the stained panel. The truncated result was a functional, if smaller, shower curtain that would just have to do, at least until her finances recovered from purchasing *Bellatrix*. Maybe in ten years. Or a hundred.

"I. Can't. Go. On," Tori announced defiantly after the Dettol had been poured, swabbed, and spritzed everywhere. To prove it, she stretched out on the living room floor and stayed there. Wotsit, determined to test her declaration, jumped on her chest, sat there, then turned around, pointing his tailless rump toward her face. Tori stayed flat on the floor, and when Jem emerged from the shower a quarter-hour later, Tori was still there. Wotsit had reassumed his loaf configuration nearby. As if sensing Jem's gaze upon him, his eyes opened to slits, saw nothing worth moving or meowing for, then shut completely. She was dismissed.

"I'm off to do a mini-shop," Jem told Tori's supine form. "I'll cover it and you can pay me for your half later. Any requests?"

Tori emitted a moan that sounded like, "Caffeine."

"Understood," Jem said, and went out to seek some. She was halfway to her destination, the Tesco Express on the corner, with her mobile pressed to her ear when Micki Latham finally picked up. The number of rings necessary to connect with her friend wasn't surprising; Micki worked odd hours and frequently forgot to keep her phone juiced up. In addition to those odd hours bartending on St. Mary's, the largest island in the Scillies, Micki was now guest-singing with a band called Tommy and the Knockers.

Although primarily a folk band, Tommy and the Knockers also played soft rock and cover tunes at a variety of West Country venues. Micki, who sang like an angel but suffered from stage fright, had overcome her phobia in order to perform with them once a week. As one of Micki's chief encouragers, Jem was fiercely proud of her friend. After years of letting the phobia get the best of her, she was finally running headlong toward her dream.

Micki usually picked up with a cheerful, "Hiya, lovely!" Today she began with a stiff, "I shall hear your apology."

Jem snorted. "Very funny."

"I'm quite serious. You ruined my afternoon."

"What? I sent you a text as soon as I knew I'd be late."

"So you did. A five-word text that said, 'Can't make it, talk soon.' That was almost three hours ago. *Three hours!* I don't have a flat in Penzance anymore. There's only so much window-shopping a gal can do. Just at present I'm cooling my heels in a café, enduring hurtful looks from a waitstaff that plainly want me to shove off, and wondering what the hell gives you the right to treat me this way."

Her tone was so aggrieved, Jem stopped dead in amazement. As she was passing through the supermarket's automatic doors at the time, she momentarily stopped the flow of traffic, causing the patron on her heels to plow into her.

"Sorry! Sorry!" she called as the man walked away, shaking his head in disgust.

"Are you?" Micki demanded.

"God, yes, excuse me for living," Jem shot back. She was so accustomed to Micki's typically friendly, go-along-to-get-along vibe, it was almost a shock to find herself on the defensive. "Something came up. I spent the afternoon with my sister Tori, two coppers, a forensic team, and a thousand kilos of stinky rubbish."

"You're kidding. Tell me you didn't find another corpse."

"I did not."

"I didn't even know you had a sister. Did I?"

"Maybe not. She had a wild night. I turned up to find her sleeping it off in my flat. Plus a cat roaming around like he owned the place and what seemed like a murder weapon in the bathroom."

"Get out."

"I am out. I'm in the supermarket, picking up a few things, since Tori cleaned out the cupboards," Jem said, making for the aisle with pantry staples.

"But what sort of weapon? Gun? Knife?"

"Croquet mallet. Broken and bloody," Jem said, transferring a bag of Lavazza ground coffee and a box of PG Tips into her trolley.

"Like in *The Shining*?"

"I think that was a roque mallet. This is more *Alice in Wonderland*."

"But Alice and the Red Queen didn't use mallets. They played the game with flamingos."

"Huh."

"Librarian, heal thyself. Read a book."

"I'll get you for that. Never mind, here's the rundown." Breezing through the details as quickly as she moved through the aisles, Jem snagged all the other requisites—bread, cheese, eggs, wine—as she filled Micki in on everything, including the *Bright Star* article that dubbed her the Scilly Sleuth. As she talked, her side of the conversation occasionally drew glances from her fellow shoppers, but she didn't sweat it. In Penzance, unlike the Isles of Scilly, there was a common class of individual known as the stranger. Being around strangers after a long time in the islands was wonderfully freeing. It didn't matter how interesting or startling strangers found her description of the day's events, because she would probably never see them again. Ah, the mainland, home of something the Scillies didn't have: voluntary anonymity.

"I don't know, Jem, that's a weird one. How old is your sister?"

"Twenty-five."

"Has she always been a muppet?"

Jem chuckled tolerantly. "Just going through a bit of a rough patch. I think it's positive overall—she left Liverpool because she's finally becoming her own person, not just an extension of Dave. I only hope she takes some time to figure out what she likes and how she wants to live before immediately transferring custody of herself to a boyfriend. You should've seen her whenever she mentioned this bloke Josh. Misty and tremulous every time."

"Her knight in a shining back alley. But I shouldn't talk. I've probably dated worse. Listen, if you want to cancel our plans, I'm sure Gina will understand."

"But your sister-in-law—"

"Ex-sister-in-law."

"—ex-sister-in-law went to so much trouble," Jem said. "She got out of bed early to do a special inventory of Tatteredly's oldest and most unusual books just for me. I can't just say thanks but no thanks, something came up."

"But if you're involved in yet a third murder investigation—"

"Just barely."

"—and spoiler alert, she promised to give me a bell if she unearthed any special finds, but I haven't heard a peep. Maybe all the big inventory revealed was more Jeffrey Archer novels and Dan Brown books."

"Yeah, but even if Gina came up empty-handed, I'll never forget how she came through for us with *A Child's Garden of Verses*," Jem said, referring to a stolen first edition that figured prominently in her very first case. "I'm overdue to thank her in person."

"All right. How much longer will the shopping take?"

"Already in the queue." She didn't add that it seemed like a long line for late afternoon. Everyone else had one or two items, while Jem had a full trolley with semi-skimmed milk on the bottom and a plastic litter tray on top. "I just need to pay for this stuff and drop it off at the flat, and then I'll be on my way. It's five twenty-seven. Tatteredly's doesn't close until seven, right?"

"Yeah. And Gina always stays after to tidy up." Micki's mood seemed to have worked itself out; she once again sounded like her usual friendly self. "That bookshop is her whole life, especially since she split with my brother Eddie. Even though she didn't send me a message, that doesn't mean the inventory was a wash. Maybe she's waiting to surprise you with a real showstopper."

"I wish. You said you were at a caff. Which one?"

"I already cleared out. Sick of the pitying glances. Guess where I'm heading? The Siren, since you mentioned it. I've eaten there before and it's not half bad. I'll grab a pint while I wait for you."

As Micki said the word pint, Jem saw the woman ahead of her pass a bottle of Saints Triumphant Bordeaux to the checker and suddenly remembered about DS Conrad. Describing him to Micki, she asked, "Isn't he the one who tried to fit up Rhys?" She meant Rhys Tremayne, her old flame, who still lived in the Isles of Scilly and had recently got into hot water with the Devon & Cornwall Police.

"Yeah. Rhys said he looked like a troll who got caught by the sunrise, turned to stone, kept calm and just carried on."

"I didn't care for him. It was almost like he came to my flat just to see me for himself. Kept trying to insinuate something about me and someone he called The Saint. The last thing he said was, 'Give my regards to Saint Ignatius.'"

Micki gasped. "Jem. That's it."

"That's what?"

The other woman let out her distinctive, wheezy *heh heh heh* laugh, like a squeaker toy on its last go-round. "Some detective. You must really be tangled up in Tori's drama if you didn't cotton on right away. It's Hack!"

Hack was the preferred nickname of Sergeant Hackman, the Isles of Scilly's new chief of police. Jem had met him during the course of her first case, and unofficially assisted him during her second. If Rhys was her old flame, then Hack was her new one. It was hard to decide which burned hotter, or which was more likely to set her world ablaze.

"What about Hack? Just tell me. I'm finally at the head of the queue," Jem barked, passing items to the checker.

Slowly, as if speaking to someone with ornamental shrubbery where her brains should be, Micki said, "Hack and DS

Conrad used to work together, and there's no love lost between them. The Saint is probably his nickname for Hack. That means 'Ignatius' is Hack's forbidden first name!"

Delighted, Jem let out a spontaneous whoop of triumph. The checker jumped, reflexively stepping back from her cash register, and trod unseeing into the path of a man carrying a carton of milk, half a dozen eggs, and a bottle of elderflower syrup. All three items hit the floor. Jem, recognizing the man she'd accidentally obstructed on the way in, met his eyes and mouthed, "Sorry." The look on his face convinced her to snatch up her bagged items and be on her way.

7

"I WISH TO GOD I'D NEVER MET YOU!"

"All right. You've had dinner, and you've had a second quick one. There's nothing left but foam. Shift it," Micki Latham demanded, sliding out of their cozy booth at the rear of The Siren.

In her late thirties, Micki had dark skin, dark eyes, and a cloud of long, curly black hair that looked good no matter how she wore it. Today she had on one of her favorite ensembles—heeled sandals, a backless dress, and a straw hat, all in the same shade of medium tan. Jem, who was fair-skinned with brown hair and toffee-colored eyes, would've looked drab as dirt in such a get-up. On Micki, it was practically haute couture.

"There's something off about you," Jem said, eyeing her friend speculatively. "You never badger me like this. And you sounded downright cross this afternoon when you first picked up."

"Only because I've wasted all day waiting around, feeling like a social outcast." Micki glanced restlessly around the room, eyes settling everywhere but on Jem's face. "We should have been to Tatteredly's hours ago. What's wrong with saying, can we get on?"

"Nothing." Jem collected her bag, still eyeing Micki suspiciously. It had been an awkward meal, though she wasn't sure why her friend had been so uncharacteristically silent. Over the course of three months and various adventures, including two murder cases, she thought she'd come to know the other woman pretty well, but apparently not. Something seemed to be eating Micki, something she refused to talk about. That in itself was surprising; as an extrovert, she shied away from few if any topics. While tending bar she listened, commiserated, and dispensed advice, all with genuine interest and a feather-light touch. But tonight she seemed to be holding back. Or maybe she was holding on—keeping a grip on herself so she didn't say or do something she might regret.

"Where's the check?" Jem asked.

Micki shrugged. "I reckon he forgot."

The man who'd waited on them, a beefy sort between forty or fifty with a red face and a wispy comb-over, had disappeared after setting down their plates and never returned. Apparently he'd become overwhelmed serving drinks to other customers and forgotten all about them. Now he was mopping up behind the bar. As Jem and Micki approached, he looked up and blinked at them in surprise. "You ladies all set?"

"We are," Jem said, feeling a bit sorry for him. He looked like he could use six months' holiday, or perhaps just six days'. "You're the jack-of-all-trades tonight, eh?"

"I'm the owner. God help me," he said. After leading them to the nearby cash register, quoting them the bill, and accepting both payment and tip without comment, he said, "Want some free advice?"

The man's jaw was tight, and he seemed about an inch away from tearing off his food-stained apron and walking away forever. Jem shrugged, unsure what she was letting herself in for.

"Never buy a restaurant. Never, ever buy a restaurant."

"Noted. Given how short-handed you are, can I assume Josh isn't working tonight?"

"Josh?" The owner, already back to wiping down around the taps, stopped and stared at her. Behind his plastic-framed specs, which had smudged oversized lenses, his gaze was intense to the point of rudeness. "Who wants him?" he asked suspiciously.

"Me. Jem Jago." She stuck out a hand, which he didn't take, forcing her to awkwardly reel it back in.

"I don't actually know him," she continued bravely, holding his gaze as if his hostility was perfectly normal. "But he's a friend of my sister's. That is, I thought she said he worked at The Siren. Maybe—"

"Josh works here. Should be beside me now, the skiving little git. But as you see, I'm all by my lonesome, left to sink or swim."

"Sorry about that," Micki told him. Equally briskly she told Jem, "It's a quarter to seven. If we're going to Tatteredly's, let's go."

At the name of the bookshop, the owner's gaze shifted from Jem to Micki and back again. His big hands wrung the bar rag convulsively.

"Sorry, I thought it was just around the corner," Jem said.

How long is this mood of hers going to last?

"We're close," Micki said. "It's just at the top of the street. But you said you were eager to meet Gina, so let's do it."

"Only..." the owner began. He looked down at the rag he was twisting and stopped, putting it aside. "If I were you, I wouldn't bother. Lot of grot in there. Wouldn't set foot in the place if you paid me." With that, he turned away to begin wiping down the ice machine with a vengeance. Jem exchanged a glance with Micki, and by common consent they headed out of The Siren's now oppressive atmosphere and into the fresh air.

The walk to Tatteredly's was lovely. A warm wind blew off the harbor and the pedestrian traffic was minimal, as most businesses had already closed for the night. In mid-September, Penzance entered the golden hour around seven o'clock—that time especially treasured by photographers, when the light turns rosy and the low sun seems to buff away the world's sharp edges. Along Silversmith Lane, lengthening shadows cloaked the old street's concessions to modernity—cashpoints, road signs, zebra crossings—allowing its more picturesque qualities to shine. Between iron streetlamps, baskets of flowers hung from hooks and flags rippled in the breeze. In Cornwall, there was always some sort of festival going on.

Curving as it climbed, the lane's pedestrian walkway carried them toward the Market House, one of Penzance's best-known landmarks. Once a corn exchange and guild house, with a few cells underground to imprison those who disturbed the king's peace, it had undergone nineteenth-century renovations. These days it was topped by a lantern-shaped lead dome, its unglazed windows allowing visitors to enjoy the air as well as the view. Jem and Micki approached the Market House on its west side, popular with tourists because of its Greek columns, red phone boxes, and the statue of Sir Humphry Davy, inventor of the miner's safety lamp. Just at the moment Sir Humphry's head was being used as a pit stop for a rather self-satisfied looking gull.

Micki halted at a crossing to wait for the light. "Uh-oh. The sale tables aren't out front."

Jem followed the other woman's gaze across the street to a shop with a green canvas awning that read TATTEREDLY'S USED AND RARE BOOKS. The door was closed, the shades appeared down, and the pavement outside the shop was deserted.

Micki said, "Usually there are tables loaded with cheap paperbacks outside. Pulling them inside is the last thing Gina does before locking up and going home. Maybe something came up and she had to be off."

"Oh. Well. It'll be too bad if she gave up on us, but I couldn't blame her. Besides, it *is* Saturday night. Maybe she had a date."

"Maybe. I know she took up with some bloke not long after she told Eddie to hit the bricks."

"Sore topic in the family?" Jem asked.

"Her new bloke? Nah. It was to be expected. Gina was the best thing that ever happened to Eddie. Poor sod muffed it up somehow. Now he has to live with the consequences."

The light changed and they crossed, Micki withdrawing her mobile from her bag and glancing at the screen as they reached Tatteredly's.

"Thing is, I don't have any messages. Gina wouldn't scoot without at least texting me."

Jem eyed the shop's front window. "Looks pretty dark inside." She glanced over her shoulder to see who else was still open. Silversmith Lane's dramatic curve made The Siren seem farther away than it really was. From Tatteredly's on one end to The Siren on the other, ten or twelve shops were sandwiched in between. The various businesses along the row had nothing in common but glassed fronts, local gray stone, and signs proclaiming their particular trade: patisserie, electronics repair, herbalist, vintage clothing, hair salon, and so on. "If I'm honest, they're all dark. Surely they all lock up at about the same time."

"You don't know Gina. She's never cared what other people do. See how there's no hours posted on the door? That's because they change from day to day, according to her whim. Besides, the interior lights *are* on, see? It just looks dim because the shade's halfway down."

Micki approached the door, painted green to match the awning with a sticker advertising 24/7 security monitoring, and gave the brass handle a pull. It didn't open. "Huh. Let me ring her."

As Micki phoned Gina, Jem drifted closer to the shopfront window, distracted as ever by the lure of unusual books. The window's theme was *Alice in Wonderland* by Lewis Carroll, and someone had done it up proper. The focal point was a velvet toadstool cushion, absolutely perfect for young readers, and around it various incarnations of the classic tale were displayed: a well-loved old *The Nursery Alice*, a brand-new Disney picture book, a toddler's chunky board book. Occupying pride of place was a gorgeous antique edition of *Alice* with a jacket illustration from the Edwardian era.

The window's other decorative touches were nice, too. Over an Alice doll's head, playing cards had been affixed to the window, massed like an avalanche poised to fall. From a high shelf, a soft toy version of the Cheshire Cat smiled down on the action with yellow eyes and psychedelic stripes. There was only one sour note: a pink plastic flamingo, lying on its side as if discarded behind the velvet toadstool. Jem wasn't sure what it was doing there, unless it related to the flamingos the Red Queen favored when it came to croquet. Maybe a kiddie had reached into the display and mucked about.

Behind the pink flamingo, a slice of sales floor was visible beneath the partially drawn shade. Jem could see light brown carpet. Upon it sat a single ladies' shoe: shiny, black, abandoned.

"She's not answering," Micki said.

Jem's gaze went from the lonely shoe to the antique *Alice*'s illustrated cover. It depicted Alice during the famous croquet game, her pink flamingo held like a mallet. Behind her loomed the Red Queen, finger pointing, huge mouth opened wide. Jem could almost hear her bellow, "Off with her head!" A chill went up her spine. "Micki."

"Hang on—"

"Micki. Look." Seizing her friend's arm, she dragged her to the *Alice* window. "Look under the shade. On the carpet. See that shoe?"

"Shit." Micki drew in a deep breath. Then she shouted at the top of her lungs, "Gina! Are you in there? *Gina!*"

The cry echoed through the now-deserted lane. Atop the statue of Sir Humphry Davy, the seagull shrieked and flapped away. Inside the bookshop, no one answered. No one made a sound.

"It's only a shoe. We shouldn't assume the worst," Jem said, marveling at her own nerve, since her mind had jumped straight to murder. "Keep trying to get her on your mobile. In the meantime, maybe I should ring 999. Could Gina have collapsed? Does she have any health problems?"

"She's forty-five and healthy as a horse. *Gina*," Micki cried, pounding on the window.

"Is there a back door?"

"What? Yeah, I'm not thinking, of course there is. C'mon."

Jem followed Micki past Tatteredly's nearest neighbor, a vintage shop called Age of Aquarius, and into the long alley that was the flip side of Silversmith Lane. It looked very much as she'd imagined while listening to Tori's tale: a long, dismal parade of wheelie bins, plus mismatched fences of different heights and a few storage sheds, some made of corrugated metal, others ramshackle wooden affairs. Squinting, she tried to see The Siren's extra-large bin, but the lane followed the curve of the bay, putting the gastropub's back lot out of view.

"What are you looking for?"

"I don't know. This place looks like that alley Bruce Wayne's dad marched his family through. A place to get murdered." It was especially true because Jem was currently on a diet of Gold, Silver, and what she called Alloyed Age mysteries, where shady types lurked in alleys, and a single gunshot always went straight to the heart. "At least there's that." She pointed to the CCTV camera mounted over Tatteredly's back door, its dull-glass eye pointed their way. But the red light wasn't on, and the camera gave no click of recognition as they passed within its scope. "Assuming it's real."

"It's not. It's a dummy. Gina's too loosey-goosey to bother with security. Eddie bought a cheap fake and installed it."

Tatteredly's back door, marked RESTRICTED, looked perfectly secure, with strong hinges and a reinforced lockset. As Jem gave the steel handle a tug, unsurprised when it didn't budge, Micki said, "I know where Gina hides the spare."

Running her hands behind the electric meter mounted on the shop's rear wall, Micki felt about until she discovered a magnetic hide-a-key box. From it, she produced the key, passing it to Jem, who opened the door and passed it back. As Micki returned the key and box to its hiding place, Jem entered into Tatteredly's back room.

"Gina!"

No answer. It was quiet and slightly eerie, but not dark. Fluorescent bulbs burned overhead, washing the room in stark light. Part stock room and part office, it was a tight space made even tighter by piles and piles of books.

"Is she here?" Micki asked, the heavy door closing behind her and locking itself with an audible *click*.

"Not sure." Purely from habit, Jem's restless eyes picked up several details, though she wouldn't fully process them until later. An old desktop computer; a positively ancient printer; a hotplate; a mini fridge; a coffee maker. The latter was switched off, but the carafe was full of black coffee. Beside the computer sat a small video monitor of the type used to review CCTV footage. Fleetingly, Jem wondered why Gina had it, if the camera mounted over the back door was a dummy. Then something else caught her eye, ominous enough to command her full attention.

"Mick. The safe." She stepped closer to examine a small

floor safe, about two feet by four. Its heavy bolted door was wide open. Nothing was inside. "That's it. I'm ringing—"

Micki, rigid with alarm, didn't wait to hear the rest. "Gina!" she cried, blazing through the thin red curtains separating the back room from the sales floor.

Jem dashed out in Micki's wake. The shop seemed in good order, at least for a used bookseller. She saw an antique brass cash register, bins crammed with paperbacks, and freestanding bookcases. On one wall, the floor-to-ceiling shelves were accessed by an old-fashioned wheeled ladder. At the foot of that ladder lay a woman, crumpled on her side. One foot wore a shiny black shoe. The other was bare.

"Gina!" Micki dropped to her knees at the fallen woman's side.

"Is she breathing? Check to see if she's breathing."

"Gina!" Micki seized the body by the shoulders and shook her. Gina's head lolled forward, her face dead white apart from some blood pooling along the right side, which had been pressed against the carpet. At her hairline, above her left eye, was a circular red wound. The blow had been so powerful, a divot had been taken where the weapon came away with hair, skin, and blood.

Off with her head...

Jem shuddered, seeing the decapitated mallet in her mind's eye.

Though it was clear that Gina Marrak would never be roused, Micki kept trying, despite her ex-sister-in-law's lolling head and stiff left arm, which seemed frozen into position. That made estimating time of death a bit tricky. Either she'd been dead for a short time, and was only beginning to stiffen with rigor mortis, or she'd been dead for a long time, and was almost released from rigor's transient grip.

There's a full pot of coffee in that back room. We know she came in early this morning to do a special inventory. An inventory for me, Jem thought, wincing at the idea. All signs pointed to Gina being dead a long time, over twelve hours. And another signpost had appeared in Jem's mind, off in the distance but increasingly clear. It was awful, and completely unwelcome, but once seen it could not be unseen: the mallet in her bathroom was the murder weapon, and her sister knew something about it that she wasn't telling.

"Oh, Jem," Micki whimpered, gently lowering Gina's unresponsive body back to the floor. She looked shocked beyond tears. "She's gone. I really think she's gone."

"I know. I'm so sorry," Jem said gently, squatting down for a closer look. In life, Gina Marrak must have been highly attractive, with fine cheekbones, a sensuous mouth, and breezy black curls threaded with gray. The outfit she'd died in, a satin blouse and linen slacks, was unmarked, apart from some blood spatter near the collar. No wounds were apparent except the terrible one on her head.

"I reckon she must've fallen. Don't you think, Jem? She was working alone, climbed the ladder to get a book, and fell. It would've been so early, there was no one on the lane to notice, or even know she was in here..."

Jem was already looking over the sales floor, seeking one very specific item. She didn't want to find it, and hoped against hope that she wouldn't. Nevertheless, a few seconds' searching was all it took for her gaze to fall upon a circle of metal lying between Gina's corpse and the *Alice* window. Without touching it, Jem could see that the metal circle, once shiny brass, was now dark with dried blood.

"Micki. Look at this."

Slowly, as if sleepwalking, Micki rose from her place next to Gina and moved to Jem's side.

"What's that?"

"Remember the mallet I found? How it was bloodied on

one end? Go back and look at the shape of the wound on Gina's head. Really look at it."

Micki returned to Gina's body, leaned close to her, and studied the brutal round divot. She put out her hands as if to touch it, then pulled them back as they began to shake. The tremor rippled across her body like a live current, but she didn't speak.

"That broken mallet came from The Siren's wheelie bin. It's not far—just a short walk down the alley. I think Tori brought the murder weapon home to my flat. It's bizarre, I know, to think I'm mixed up in this, but don't you agree that..."

Jem tailed off. The look Micki turned on her was like nothing she'd ever seen on her face before.

"This is your fault," she said, voice shaking as she straightened to look Jem in the eye. "Yours. Gina was here alone because of you, doing an inventory because of you. Wherever you go, Jem, people die. I wish I'd never brought you here! *I wish to God I'd never met you!*"

8

A SCARF, A BOOK, AND TWO FAMILIAR STRANGERS

Jem sucked in her breath. Micki's words hit her like a fist, but they were nothing to the rage and accusation in her eyes.

"W-what?" she heard herself say, followed by a weak sound, like a pitiful chuckle.

"I said I wish I'd never met you. You're bad news. Cursed," Micki cried. "Ever since I met you, my life's been a shitshow! If I could go back and do it over again, I'd avoid you like the plague. Maybe if I had, Gina would still be alive!"

Dissolving into sobs, Micki whirled and ran for the back room, losing a shoe in the process. The sandal sat alone on the carpet, more or less perpendicular to Gina's lonely sensible heel.

If you draw a line from sandal to shoe to corpse, it makes an isosceles triangle.

That unhelpful thought drifted into Jem's brain from someplace unknown, as jarring as a sparkly balloon floating into a burial service. Such mental non sequiturs afflicted her whenever she was overcome by shock. Her mind, incapable of generating anything valuable, resorted to firing off weird observations, trying to pass them off as normal thoughts like a con artist passing off counterfeit notes.

Right. There's been a murder and I have one job—to ring 999, Jem told herself with determined rationality. Dusting herself off mentally, she looked around for her bag—it was still hanging on her shoulder—and located her mobile. Then for the second time in one day, she rang emergency services. The first time, the dispatcher's detached monotone had irritated her. Now she found it soothing. Something in the woman's uninflected, aloof tone seemed to say, *it's all right, you'll get through this, just follow my lead.*

"Signs of respiration?"

"No."

"Use two fingers, not your thumb but fingers only, and depress the skin of the throat. Can you feel a pulse?"

"No."

"Examine the body for signs of circulation. Is the skin pale or ruddy?"

"Pale."

"Dry or perspiring?"

"Dry. Look. I know you're not allowed to take my word for it, but this poor lady's deceased. Probably for several hours. One of her arms is stiff as a statue."

The dispatcher didn't take her word for it, or comment on her opinion. "Hold the line, please," she said. "Do not end the call. If you need anything I'll be right here. The authorities will arrive in six to ten minutes."

It felt maudlin to crouch over Gina Marrak's corpse, so Jem wandered around the sales floor with her mobile in hand, careful not to touch anything. Micki didn't re-emerge from the back room, but from somewhere Jem heard a toilet flush. She was probably crying behind a locked door.

It crossed her mind to find the bathroom and urge Micki to come out and be comforted, but when Jem tried to make herself do it, something cold and unyielding held her back. Theirs was a new friendship, begun on the spur of the moment in the Kernow Arms only a few months ago, when Jem had been stood up and Micki, the bartender, felt sorry for her. How well did they really know each other?

She doesn't want me to follow her. She doesn't even want to know me, she made that perfectly clear. And I still have one job —to hand off custody of the scene to the proper authorities.

Had it been six minutes? According to her mobile, only three. Biting back a sigh, Jem paced the sales floor, searching for anything else out of place. In a bin full of old paperback mysteries, she spied one of Rex Stout's Nero Wolfe novels: *The Doorbell Rang*, one of the very best. What would Archie Goodwin, Wolfe's man of action, do while he waited for the paramedics?

Make jokes. Eyeball everything. Catch something out of place and pick it up, but only with his handkerchief.

The gods of Alloyed Age mysteries must've taken pity, because they sent her a distraction. Lying atop one of the freestanding bookcases—a collection of children's books with more versions of *Alice in Wonderland*, as well as other classics, on the top shelf—was a lady's scarf. It had a whimsical pattern of tender orange blossoms and teacups, and was the sort of scarf usually worn as an accessory, though it was large enough to tie over the head babushka-style. Jem really wanted to pick it up, but unlike the intrepid Archie Goodwin, she didn't have a handkerchief, since people stopped carrying them at least forty years ago. That left her with one alternative: snap a picture of it with her smartphone.

Top that, Archie.

She found herself compulsively hunting for more clues. Outside of the scarf, everything else was tidy in the shop's rear. Drifting back toward the front, Jem inspected the cash register. Like the safe, it was wide open, a money tray sitting out as if waiting to be filled. Had someone robbed Gina before or after killing her? Or did the empty safe and cash register prove she'd been killed long before the banks opened for business?

There was one more thing out of place, and it was so obvious that Jem couldn't believe she missed it the first time around. Apparently the sight of a corpse had blinded her to the book lying in the middle of the floor. Halfway between the *Alice* window and Gina's body lay an old trade paperback called *Cannabis for Fun and Profit*.

Maybe Gina was carrying it with her when she was attacked. The mallet hit her, the book flew out of her hand, and there it fell.

As with the scarf, Jem resisted the temptation to touch the book by snapping a photo instead. During her career in what she called Library World, she didn't recall running across *Cannabis for Fun and Profit*, but she was familiar with the *Fun and Profit* series of home industry how-to guides. They'd been wildly popular in the late eighties and early nineties, then slowly been forgotten as internet searches and YouTube videos became the dominant sources of practical information.

Jem checked the contents of the nearest shelves. The book was definitely out of place. The closest paperback books were standard-sized and neatly grouped by genre: romance, mystery, thriller, women's fiction, men's adventure, sci-fi, and fantasy. Oversized how-to guides belonged in Tatteredly's dimmest corner, where Jem found several books in the *Fun and Profit* series, packed tight on the shelf between travel handbooks and DIY project manuals.

She checked her mobile again. Eight minutes had passed. Surely the paramedics would be here soon. Her neck and shoulders ached, and after a moment she realized why; she'd been holding herself rigidly, in a sort of living rigor mortis after yet another brush with murder. Shouldn't she be getting used to this by now?

No. And I hope I never do.

Forcing herself to go limp, Jem lifted her shoulders to her

ears, held the pose for five seconds, then dropped them. It was a stress-relieving move her friend Pauley Gwyn, a self-taught yoga enthusiast, had given her, and it worked surprisingly well. As she started to do it again, something near the ceiling, in the corner between the shelves and the *Alice* window, caught her eye. It was another CCTV camera. This one had a glowing red light, so if it was another dummy, at least it was a realistic one.

That monitor in the back room I saw—maybe it's attached to it.

When Gina arrived to do inventory, had Tatteredly's interior video recording system been turned on? Jem wasn't sure anyone would bother to do so while working alone, but then again, it might be habit—enter the premises, fire up the security system. It would be a wise practice, and one that just might send someone down for murder. Given the camera's relation to where Gina had fallen, it would have probably recorded everything.

She heard the siren several seconds before she saw the vehicle pull up. The sound grew louder by the second, and then suddenly it was upon her, absolutely deafening, as a yellow ambulance with flashing blue lights pulled up along the curb. Jem said goodbye to the 999 dispatcher, who surely didn't hear a word of it, disconnected, and put her hands over her ears just in time for the siren to cut off. Then the ambulance's rear doors swung open and two paramedics emerged.

As she let them in, Jem zeroed in on Tatteredly's front door latch. It was a simple thumb-turned deadbolt. No key was required to unlock it from within. That was a relief—the last thing she wanted to do was summon Micki to help her open it—but it was significant in another way. Gina's killer couldn't have left via the front door. If he or she had done so, the deadbolt wouldn't have been engaged. That meant the murderer exited out the back, where the heavy security door would automatically lock when shut.

I wonder if the killer was invited in? Maybe someone called at the back door and Gina let them in. Or maybe she brought someone with her to help with the inventory and they quarreled?

Suddenly another possibility occurred to her. Micki had easily retrieved that hideaway key box from behind the electric meter. Had someone else known where to look, and unlocked Tatteredly's back door to catch Gina unawares?

The paramedics trooped in, kits in hand and pulling a collapsible gurney behind them. Brusquely, they demanded the patient's whereabouts, and Jem obliged them. As they checked Gina's corpse minutely for any sign of life, a panda car pulled in next to the ambulance. Two constables, one male and one female, got out.

From behind Jem, a quiet voice spoke. "I don't know what came over me, Jem. I'm so sorry. The things I said were awful. I didn't mean it, I promise I didn't."

Jem forced herself to turn around and give Micki a little nod. "No worries," she said with deliberate lightness, and gave her attention to the approaching police officers. The male spoke importantly into his shoulder radio while the female marched up to her and demanded, "What happened here?"

Archie Goodwin would say something outrageous to take the piss. Do not be like Archie.

Despite the woman's suspicious tone, which Jem found overwrought and more than a little performative, she answered her questions with calm precision. When she reached the part about entering by using a hideaway key, the constable asked, "Did you touch the key with your fingers?"

"Yes. I lost my telekinetic powers in my last battle with Magneto."

Whoops. Those Nero Wolfe books are a bad influence.

The constable scowled at her. To her male partner she called, "Trev, go and fetch the key behind the electric meter. It may still have usable prints." Turning back to Jem, she asked, "Right. Now. Are either of you related to the victim?"

"She is," Jem said, turning to indicate Micki. "I'm really just a bystander. Now that I've told you all I know, can I be on my way?"

"Don't go, Jem," Micki said, sounding alarmed. "I've pulled myself together. I am sorry, I don't know why I—"

"Hang on, lovely, let's stay focused on the matter at hand. I need to know who you are. Name, address, how you know the victim," the constable interrupted. Apparently still annoyed by the crack about the X-Men, she sniffed at Jem and said, "Yeah, you can be off, I've had plenty from you."

"Gotta get home and check on my sis," Jem told Micki over her shoulder. She was moving toward the exit, eyes on the street, and didn't look back. "Ring me later."

On the walk back to her building, Jem felt like such a heel she twice contemplated turning around and heading back to Tatteredly's. While it was true that she'd only known Micki for a few months, during that time the other woman had always been extremely easy to get along with. She wasn't one to complain, remained upbeat in the face of trouble, and was careful of other people's feelings. Micki was the kind of person who always seemed to give more than she received and looked after her own needs—a low-maintenance friend, in other words.

Maybe that's part of the problem, Jem thought. *Maybe she's so accustomed to never asking for anything that when she really needed support, she expected to get it—still without asking.*

She thought back to Micki's attitude on the phone that afternoon. How she'd asked, "What gives you the right to treat me this way?" and imagined that even the servers at the caff didn't want her around, and were giving her pitying looks.

Some detective I am. She was working herself up to a melt-down even then. Of course she snapped when we found Gina dead. Anyone would.

Even so, Jem found herself viscerally reluctant to actually go back to the used bookshop, or shoot Micki a quick text of support. Something was holding her back, and it wasn't nearly as easy to analyze herself as she could size up the motives of others. Therefore, she pushed her thoughts in other directions, allowing them to run restlessly over the intersection of Gina Marrak and the broken mallet. While answering the constable's questions, it had crossed her mind to launch into the long, strange story of how a bloody weapon, almost certainly the weapon that killed Gina, had ended up in her bathtub. Two factors persuaded her not to bring it up.

First, she suspected the first coppers on the scene were not the correct officers to burden with such knowledge. They were placeholders; as soon as the scene was secured and the basic information collected, the murder squad would be called in. Second, there was no harm in going home to tell Tori what had happened and see if she couldn't shake a bit more truth out of her sister. The mallet was already in police custody undergoing lab analysis, if not at that very moment, then first thing Monday. Assuming DS Conrad and his fellows were on the ball, they should easily connect the dots. And by the time they did, and summoned Tori for a second discussion, maybe she'd be ready to reveal whatever she was holding back.

The evening was cool, pleasant, and peaceful. It was hard to believe someone had died by violence only a short distance away. When Jem reached the intersection of Silversmith Lane and Adelaide Street, the stucco buildings parted to give a view of the sea. Just offshore was St. Michael's Mount, an islet over-looking the famous stone causeway, currently two meters underwater. Atop the mount perched the St. Aubyn family's historic castle, glowing golden above steep paths and stacked garden terraces. According to legend, the islet had been created by the giant Cormoran, who was later slain by the peasant Jack, known thereafter as Jack the Giant Killer. As everyone who'd made the trek up to the castle knew, Cormoran's heart remained on St. Michael's Mount, transformed to stone and trampled by hundreds of tourists each season.

Within ten minutes, Jem was back at her building. The courtyard was lit up, as well as most of the windows. Apparently her neighbors were having a Saturday at home with Netflix or satellite TV. Mounting the stairs, Jem took them two at a time, eager to talk to Tori. She'd just reached the walkway leading to her front door when a man's voice issued from inside her flat.

"Pull the other one!"

He sounded loud and raucous, like a lad shouting at the telly during a football match. Jem started to open the door, then decided to pause on the mat and listen. The insulation of her new-build flat was minimal and through the door Tori's voice issued quite clearly:

"What did you expect me to do, tell the truth?"

Someone replied, probably another man, but too low for Jem to catch the words.

"But they haven't found a body," Tori replied, her higher-pitched voice carrying crystal clear. "That's the saving grace. No body, no murder!"

Jem threw open the door. It gave her a certain amount of satisfaction, after a bizarre afternoon and a truly terrible evening, to scare the hell out of Tori and her two male guests. All three of them goggled at her, wide-eyed, as if caught in a vault with gold bullion in both hands.

"Hi there," she said, looking from face to face. "Let me guess. Josh and T.J., am I right? I heard part of that through the door, about habeas corpus. Guess what? A dead body was just discovered near Silversmith Bay."

9

REASON NO. 342 WHY YOU SHOULD NEVER
TEASE A CAT

Tori, frozen in place with a bottle of Pepsi in her hand and the skeletal remains of an Indian takeaway spread across the coffee table, looked much better than she had that afternoon while lying spread-eagled on the living room floor. Scrubbed pink, with hair still damp from the shower, she was dressed in Jem's old clothes—trackies, fuzzy socks, and a T-shirt with a quote from Edmund Wilson: NO TWO PERSONS EVER READ THE SAME BOOK.

Beside her on the sofa sat a nice-looking young man with a square jaw, high cheekbones, and dark hair that wanted cutting. Apart from the shaggy hair, he was clean-cut and neat right down to his red and white trainers.

In the armchair sat another young man, also attractive, though in a completely different way. Brown hair shorn in a classic barber's #2, which made it perhaps a quarter-inch long, he had a hooded gaze and a mouth that curved habitually into a lopsided, knowing smile.

"Let me guess," Jem said, turning to the clean-cut one. "You're Josh. And you're T.J.," she told the shorn one.

Tori still looked a bit mortified, as if she'd been caught out, but she grinned bravely at Jem and didn't evade her gaze. "See? Live and in person. Between you and the coppers, I was starting to believe I'd imagined them both, but they're real."

"Do they have surnames?"

"Lansallos. Josh Lansallos," he said, looking like he might stand up to shake hands before deciding it might not be welcome. A polite young man, at least. Jem looked at T.J., who said nothing. After an uncomfortable silence, Josh said, "That's T.J. Mallard."

"Wonderful. Thank you very much. But did you lot miss the part where I said a body was found near the bay? I just came from Tatteredly's Bookshop on Silversmith Lane. A woman named Gina Marrak was murdered."

What followed was the lamest example of improv acting Jem had ever seen, and she'd done a little theater at uni. Tori widened her eyes, opened her mouth, and swiveled her head to look first at Josh, then at T.J., as if to say, 'Doth mine ears deceive me?' At least Josh did what he could to meet her halfway, also putting on an expression that suggested utter disbelief. T.J. only shrugged and muttered, "People die every day."

Josh said, "That's terrible about Ms. Marrak. What happened to her?"

Tori said, "Jem, how do you know this? Why do you think—?"

"Know what?" Jem cut across her. "My flat. My questions first. We'll get to yours later."

Snagging a chair from the kitchenette, she dropped it into a position that gave her a good view of the trio's faces. Josh seemed to be striving for a neutral expression. Tori looked like she was bricking it. Only T.J. seemed relaxed and happy, which worked for Jem, because he was the one she hoped to make talk.

"First," she began, "I went by Tatteredly's with a friend to meet Gina because she helped me on a case. She came into the shop early to inventory the rare books and see if any might interest my employer, the Courtney Library. When we knocked, there was no answer—"

"On a case?" T.J. interrupted. "Wait a sec. I know you." There was an avid gleam to his eye, as if he'd hit upon a dirty little secret. "My gran gets *Bright Star*. Reads it out to me over brekkie. You're the Scilly Sleuth, Jennifer Jago."

"Jemima Jago."

"Je-*mi*-ma. How very proper. So you're the Isles of Scilly's answer to Miss Fisher?"

"Something like that."

"Do people pay you to solve murders?"

"I told you, I'm a librarian."

"A hot librarian." T.J. grinned at her. "Didn't know they made 'em like you." As he spoke, he thrust a hand in his hip pocket, digging for something in his tight jeans. As he worked, he flattened himself against the armchair, putting his crotch and thighs on display for what felt like an eternity.

Oh, good Lord, he thinks he's giving me a thrill, Jem realized. On a normal day, it might have been good for a laugh, but under the circumstances, she didn't think she could dredge up even a chuckle.

Finally T.J. completed the operation, coming up with a lighter and cigarettes. Jem said, "You can't smoke in here."

"C'mon. It's just tobaccy. Not wacky." He was trying to look and sound like a charming bad boy, or at least a lovable scamp. The librarian in Jem wanted to call him impudent or impertinent, but she thought if she started down that road, she'd end up shouting "Cheeky arsehole!" in his face.

"It's her flat," Josh told his friend. "You'll just have to wait."

T.J. flicked the lighter, produced a flame, and held it within a millimeter of the cigarette's end. "What will you do if I light up anyway? Ring 999? Report me for giving you cancer in thirty years from secondhand smoke?"

"T.J., be nice or get out." The scowl Tori aimed at him

became a smile when Wotsit the cat, looking well rested and intrigued by the visitors, jumped onto her lap. "Wotsit! You were gone for so long, I thought you'd slipped outside."

"Where's his tail?" Josh asked, but in a kindly tone, as if the little stub crowned with ginger fur worried him. Jem found herself instinctively liking Josh, based only on the briefest of interactions, almost as much as she disliked T.J. How the two young men were mates was beyond her.

"Somebody probably set it on fire," T.J. said, flicking his lighter again. "What do you think, cat? Had a taste of this? Want some more?"

"Tosser," Tori said, stroking Wotsit's mostly white fur. For his part, the cat seemed to regard T.J. with interest. His big paws flexed and his ramped-up backside quivered.

"Come on. Try me," T.J. said, flicking the lighter again.

Wotsit launched himself. His moment of hang time was a thing of beauty; Jem couldn't remember the last time she'd seen an airborne cat who looked so perfectly at home defying gravity. He landed on T.J.'s lap, very near the goods the young man had seemingly put on offer, and tried to settle himself by digging in his claws.

"Hey! It's crazy! Get it off," T.J. cried, or something to that effect. Jem couldn't have provided a transcript of exactly what anyone said or did in that moment, even if it meant the firing squad. She and Tori and Josh were all up and surging toward T.J. and Wotsit in the armchair, all with a shared goal— protecting the cat—while T.J. tried to extract the feline from his lap. Apparently he wasn't a cat person, because he assumed the best way to achieve his goal was to flick the lighter again, directly in Wotsit's face. The yowl that followed was indescribable. Something went flying—the lighter—and T.J. was bowled over backward, armchair and all.

"He bit me!" T.J. cried, sounding like a small boy who'd got shoved in the playground. "The bloody thing bit me!"

"Wotsit," Tori darted for the cat—who moved like lightning —and missed by a mile. "Wotsit, come here!"

"He ducked under the sofa," Josh said, pushing the coffee table aside and getting down on the floor—stretched out flat, Jem noted with amazed approval—to check beneath.

"Is he hurt?" Tori looked and sounded stricken.

"He's not under there now," Josh said, getting to his feet again. "I reckon he just crawled out the other end."

"But what if he's hurt?"

T.J. rolled out of the armchair, which he left on its back like a stranded turtle, and struggled to rise, announcing, "I'm all right."

"Not you!" said Jem, Tori, and Josh in three-part harmony.

Wotsit, apparently deciding that if T.J. had dared to stand up it was time to reassert dominance, strolled back into the living room just as he had moments before, looking as if his fur was freshly pressed and all was right with the world. T.J. clearly hadn't laid a glove on him, or even singed a whisker.

"Put him in a sack and drown him in the river," T.J. said, trying to come across as mean and dangerous. He still sounded like the small boy who'd been shoved off a swing.

Wotsit wasn't bothered. Ignoring Josh's appreciative chuckle and Tori's happy squeal, he veered for Jem. For just a moment she was unsure—he did have massive paws, a full set of pointy-pointies, and the ability to fly when provoked. But something in the cat's green eyes reassured her that he only wanted a cuddle. So she opened her arms and he leapt into them, purring like a swarm of bees.

"Careful how you talk to Wotsit," Jem told T.J. "Need a plaster for your finger? It's bleeding."

T.J. swore and stuck his finger in his mouth. Mortified, he seemed to be looking for a way to exit without anyone being able to say he'd done a legger after being thrashed by a pussy-cat. Jem decided if she was going to ask him Gina

Marrak/bloodstained mallet-related questions, she'd better do it, and fast.

"Anyway, as I was going to say before you pulled out the ciggies, my friend and I found Gina Marrak dead in her shop. It obviously happened some time ago—probably in the wee hours or just before dawn. She was killed by a blow to the head, and the mark looks exactly like it was made by that mallet. You know, the one you three dragged into my flat?"

"You're not a cop. I don't have to tell you anything," T.J. said. He stuck his chest out, which would've been more imposing if he hadn't also stuck his injured finger back in his mouth.

"When I was out on the walkway, I heard you yell 'pull the other one,'" Jem continued conversationally, shifting Wotsit slightly so he could purr against her chest. His short fur was silky-soft, and he seemed perfectly content to remain with her as she stood talking. "It could have been over the gangbangers in black leather, but that was so idiotic, I can't imagine Tori admitted she floated that to DS Conrad. So I reckon you yelled 'pull the other one' when Tori told you her story hinged on the pursuit of your empty wallet."

"Yeah. People who don't know how to lie shouldn't try it," T.J. said. "Last night the three of us had a bit of fun. In the end, that one"—he nodded at Tori—"passed out in my mate Joshie's bed. He was too much of a gentleman to take advantage, and Lord knows I wouldn't touch it on a dare. So I went out to have a smoke, a friend gave me a bell, and off I went. When I came back, it was getting daylight and this great nancy"—he nodded at Josh—"was still tipsy and mooning after his comatose girl. For a laugh I convinced him to go bin climbing. On American telly they call it dumpster diving. I do it all the time. You wouldn't believe what people toss out."

"It's an offense to steal bin rubbish. Even if it came from a pub or a supermarket," Jem said.

"So if you can't get me on murder, you'll get me on nicking stale loaves from behind The Siren?"

"What time did Tori pass out?" Jem asked, looking from T.J. to Josh.

"Three," T.J. said.

"Maybe half-three," Josh said.

"Right. And smoking isn't allowed at Josh's place, so you went out of doors." Jem turned back to T.J., who eyed the purring cat in her arms as if she were cuddling a piranha. "You said a friend rang you. Who?"

He let out a contemptuous laugh. "Shove off."

"Where'd you go? Tatteredly's, by any chance?"

"Yeah. Perfect capper to a night on the town," he said with heavy sarcasm. "Go club a witch in the head."

"Witch?"

"Too right. Ask around. Everyone knew Gina. Everyone who lived or worked around Silversmith Bay hated her, too, but that's another story. I can tell you this much for sure, if I'd used a croquet mallet on Gina, I wouldn't have chucked it in a wheelie bin. And if I had chucked it in a wheelie bin, I wouldn't have asked that great numpty and his new girlfriend to help me retrieve the ruddy thing *in broad daylight*. Much less bugger off afterward leaving it in her control," he added, giving Tori a contemptuous glare. "I mean, really."

Put like that, Jem couldn't argue. But as T.J. spoke, something else had occurred to her—a theory that fit the known facts even better.

"Try this on for size," she said, watching his face. "You went out for the smoke, got called away, and somewhere in the two or three hours you were away from Josh's place, Gina Marrak was murdered. Maybe you had nothing to do with it—but you knew the mallet had been tossed in one of the bins in the alley behind Silversmith Lane. Maybe you got a tip. Maybe you witnessed the murderer dispose of the weapon. But you thought the binmen were coming soon, and you wanted possession of that mallet so badly, you were willing to take help from anyone. Even the tipsy so-called numpty and his semi-comatose new friend."

T.J. didn't answer right away. Instead, he patted himself down, as if suddenly wanting his cigarettes and lighter. He probably thought the action made him seem supremely unconcerned with Jem's theory. It actually only made him look desperate for a quiet moment in which to review his options.

"By the chair," he muttered, and retrieved his lighter and a loose cigarette from the floor next to the fallen armchair. While he was there, he didn't put it back in place, because of course he didn't.

"Okay, Scilly Sleuth," he said at last with exaggerated calm, "if all that's true, why didn't I just ring the police? They could've sent over a team and found it, easy-peasy."

"They could've retrieved the bloody mallet," Jem agreed. "But how could you use it to blackmail the killer if it was in police custody?"

T.J. emitted what he no doubt meant to be a cavalier laugh. "I don't need this. Josh, if you hang with this lot, don't bother ringing me."

To show him she wasn't destroyed by the thought of him walking out, Jem helpfully opened the door. T.J. responded by sticking the slightly bent cigarette in his mouth and lighting up. His mouth twisted up on one side—he was smoking while still two steps inside her threshold—so Jem feinted with Wotsit and gave a fairly realistic *meow*.

T.J. and his cancer stick hopped over the threshold with dispatch. Jem placed Wotsit on the floor, stepped over to the fallen armchair and put it back where it belonged. Then she sat down and regarded Tori and Josh, who both looked a good deal more relaxed with T.J. gone.

"Don't think because I'm finished with him that I'm

finished with the two of you," Jem said, giving them a little Stern Librarian to show them she meant it. "Now you're standing in the dock, Josh. Did you know what T. J. was looking for? Did you know you left Tori in my flat with the mallet that killed Gina Marrak?"

10

OVER TEA AND BISCUITS

Either Josh once had a traumatic experience involving a Stern Librarian, or he was wrung out by it all: a boozy night, a literally trashy morning, missing his shift at The Siren (Jem hadn't forgotten the owner's bleak attitude toward Josh after being left to face the dinner rush alone), and now being interrogated by the Scilly Sleuth. Whichever it was, he deflated so visibly at Jem's throwaway line, "Now you're standing in the dock," she decided to take pity. Tori was allowed to put the kettle on, since it was clear they both badly needed a cuppa, and Jem even went so far as to open the packet of chocolate Hobnobs she'd fully intended to keep for herself.

"If we're getting a treat, Wotsit deserves one, too," Tori said, peering in the cupboard where Jem kept her boxes and tinned goods. "Didn't you pick up any Dreamies when you did the shop?"

"No, I failed in that respect. I got him a litter tray, some kibble, and a tin of tuna in case the stereotype is true, but I didn't remember the Dreamies." Turning to Wotsit, who'd arranged himself on the windowsill and was dozing with his eyes half-closed, she asked, "What's your opinion on tuna fish?"

He yawned, stood up, stretched, and reconfigured himself in loaf mode. The eyes closed completely.

"I think he just wants a nap after showing your friend who's boss," Jem told Josh. "Let's shift to the kitchen table for tea and biscuits. That's where the cops pulled that stupid yarn out of Tori. Which I fully expect she's going to have to correct and apologize for," she added as they took their seats.

Tori, who'd apparently decided the quickest way to get back in Jem's good graces was to be mother, brought her a mug of tea already sweetened to perfection and two chocolate Hobnobs on a little plate. "I know I shouldn't have said all that about the wallet and the guys in leather..."

"Black leather," Jem muttered.

"But bin climbing is a criminal offense." Tori placed a mug and biscuits in front of Josh. "Take sugar?"

He shook his head, gazing into the depths of his tea as if it fascinated him. He didn't seem particularly enticed by the chocolate Hobnobs, either.

"Is that it, Josh?" Jem asked, speaking to the crown of his thick dark hair that wanted cutting, since he didn't seem willing to meet her eyes. "Did my little sis tell a pack of stupid lies to a detective sergeant so you wouldn't get your wrist slapped over playing amateur rag-and-bone man?"

"Jem, I'm standing right here. Don't talk about me like I'm not—"

"No," Josh said, looking up at last. "No, Tori, this has gone too far. I don't want you lying to your sister on my account." To Jem he said, "Tori didn't understand what was really going on until we were back at her place—I mean, your place. By then she'd sobered up enough to realize T.J. and I weren't just rooting around looking for bits of electronic gear or sealed food containers. T.J. knew there was a weapon in one of the bins. He said my aunt Natalie put it there."

"Why did you try and get it back yourself? Why not ring the authorities?"

Josh gave a bitter laugh. "You're kidding, right? With Teej being like he is, and my aunt being like she is, and me not knowing what to believe, and you want to know why I didn't just ring 999 and—"

"Hey," Tori said, breaking in by placing a gentle hand over Josh's. "You're speaking in shorthand, babe, and it's not making sense. Have a sip of tea and tell her slowly, from the beginning, the way you told me."

Josh gripped her hand, let out a deep sigh and nodded.

"The thing you have to understand," Josh said, peering into his tea as if it held all the answers, "is Aunt Natalie's had a rough time of it. How she is... it's not her fault, that's the main thing. No one cares for her anymore, since she fell out with Gina. No one but me.

"She has problems," he continued, pausing to give Jem a quick look, as if gauging her likelihood to empathize. "Mood problems, head problems, that kind of thing. The kind of problems doctors can't fix."

"Has she been in hospital for it?" Jem asked.

"A couple of times. Not for long. She's sort of in between. Able to live alone, at least for now." Josh spoke slowly, as if trying to proceed in a way that was both honest and sensitive. He was loyal to his aunt, clearly, and didn't want to say anything to Jem that was unfair, despite the fact that Natalie wasn't around to hear it. She respected that.

Despite her early impulse to dislike Josh, who'd left Tori holding the bag, more or less literally, the young man gave her a good feeling. He wasn't handsome in the leading man sense, not to her way of thinking, but he had good features: thick brown hair, blue eyes, and the bloom of young adulthood. His red cheeks and luminous skin reminded Jem of the poetic ideal: the athlete crowned with laurel leaves. He was polite and well spoken, which was a breath of fresh air after T.J., but most importantly, he seemed as smitten with Tori as she was with him. It came through, clear as a bell, every time he looked at her. Each time she smiled back, he sat a little taller—as if transforming into a leading man, at least in his own life.

She asked, "Does Natalie live nearby?"

"Yeah. On Weaver Road, just down from me and T.J., in the house she inherited. It's the best place on the street, in terms of how it's situated and built..." He sighed. "Except for how she's kept it up—or not kept it up—over the years. By the time she leaves it, the council will probably decide it has to be knocked down. Only the plot itself will be worth anything.

"She doesn't work and never has," Josh continued, eyes flicking up again to see how Jem received this detail. "That's why my dad—her younger brother—won't have anything to do with her. He says she's part of the parasite class."

"I wouldn't think your dad would be so cruel," Tori said.

Josh shrugged. "You know how it is in families. Aunt Natalie's been on benefits forever. She's fragile. Flighty. Just turning up on time every morning would put her in a state. She likes an early breakfast from Jones's Diner, six a.m., and then she watches her chat shows and posts about them online. *Bright Star* has a web community and she posts there every day. If she misses out because of a power cut or computer problem, she goes into a tailspin."

Jem's face must've revealed some sympathy with Josh's father and his "parasite class" verdict, because Josh added hastily, "I'm just being honest about her coping mechanisms. She has lots. But part of why she has them is because everyone in real life has abandoned her. When I was little, Mum still had her over to the house, and Dad didn't put her down all the time. I mean, she dressed funny and had breakdowns over little things, but she was still part of the community. Now she's an outcast because she's a hoarder. Everyone hates what she's done to her house. But part of why she's a hoarder is because of how they all treat her. It's a vicious circle, you know?"

Jem nodded, watching as Tori took Josh's hand again and squeezed it tight. They'd certainly advanced a long way in a mere twenty-four hours—less than that, if you wanted to get technical. Was Tori responding to Josh's personal charms? Or simply because he was a warm male body who might step into the overlarge place in her life Dave Jago once commanded?

"So, yeah, the thing you have to know about Natalie is, she's had a hard time of it. The thing you have to know about me is, I'm dyslexic," Josh continued. "I've pretty much overcome it, but when I first went to school it was a nightmare. The tutor called me 'densely dyslexic.' Some boys overheard and from then on I was Thickie McDense."

Tori made a noise. "That's horrible! It's a learning disability."

Josh grinned. "Tomorrow we can look up some of my old schoolmates and you can tell them so, all right? Anyway, if they hadn't been on me about that, it would've been something else. Probably Aunt Nat. When she used to wait for me outside the schoolyard, the kids would laugh at her crocheted hats and her plastic jewelry. She always looked like a church fete threw up on her.

"Anyway, I was getting bullied every day. My dad told me to stand up for myself, which was worthless, and my mum cried, which was worse," Josh said. "I reckon they both thought I was stupid and due to get pushed around for the rest of my life. But Natalie didn't think I was dense. Every day after school, she took me to her place, gave me a snack, and helped practice my reading. Someone else owned Tatteredly's then, and she was in and out of the shop constantly, hunting down books I might like. In those days, Gina Marrak was her friend—maybe her only friend—and she helped. They used to talk about buying Tatteredly's and running it together."

"You know Gina Marrak better than I realized. It sounds like she was a friend of the family," Jem ventured.

"Yeah. Gina used to live on Weaver Road, too. She and Natalie were schoolmates, just like T.J. and I were schoolmates."

"Did you like her?"

His mouth twisted.

"Why not? Because she and your aunt fell out?"

Josh shrugged, peering into his mug of now lukewarm tea. "I just didn't get her. She wasn't a bad person," he said doubtfully, as if trying to convince himself. "But when she got money, she changed. Dropped Natalie like a hot potato. Bought Tatteredly's all on her own. Broke her husband's heart—"

"Eddie?" Jem cut in. The thought of Micki's brother led back to Micki, of course, and brought a sudden wave of pained mortification. Why had she just walked out of Tatteredly's when Micki had clearly needed her support? When she'd already apologized and probably would've provided a long—possibly even satisfying—explanation as soon as the authorities cleared out?

"Yeah. Eddie Latham. I know him. Anyone who works near Silversmith Bay knows him. He used to do pipe fitting and plumbing for the marina," Josh said. "But I thought you lived in the Isles of Scilly. How do *you* know him?"

"I mentioned a friend took me to Tatteredly's to meet Gina. That was Micki Latham, Eddie's sister," Jem said. "She didn't seem to have any hard feelings toward Gina. If anything, she made it sound like Eddie was to blame for the breakup. You disagree?"

He shrugged. "Maybe. It's not like I'm his best friend. I just work at my uncle's gastropub, The Siren, on and off, so I've spent lots of times on the row—the line of shops between The Siren and Tatteredly's, in sight of the bay. So of course I know Eddie and Gina and Millie and Toby and—well—everybody.

"Anyway," he continued, again giving the impression of one striving to be fair, "to me and my uncle, Gina seemed like she wasn't willing to give Eddie a chance. He wasn't a qualified plumber, but he'd learned on the fly, and took every job that would have him. Gina used to call him a skiver and a layabout, always spending her money. Like when he said Tatteredly's needed a security system and bought one without asking her. She never used it, never even switched it on, just to spite him."

So much for hoping that ceiling-mounted camera in Tatteredly's recorded the murder, Jem thought. Of course, the police were investigating, and Gina Marrak's death wasn't her case even in the loosest amateur sense. But she still noted the lack of video evidence with a twinge of interest. Gina's murder might turn out to be a puzzler, and she could never resist puzzles.

"All right. So some people think Eddie was unappreciated. By the way, just before we went to Tatteredly's, Micki and I had dinner at The Siren. There was one man doing almost everything—a very harassed-looking man who went out of his way to tell me never to buy a restaurant. That's your uncle?"

At the mention of the harassed, apron-wearing gastropub owner, Josh groaned.

"I'm sure he's cross with me. Uncle Jerry's always boiling over something, but this time he's right to be angry. I really left him in the lurch."

"Hard to work with a bad hangover," Jem said sympathetically.

"It wasn't that. I had to see Tori." He waved a hand, as if interrupting himself. "But I'm getting ahead of the story. Now that you understand about my aunt Natalie, I can explain about last night. It's true that Tori fell asleep—well, passed out—in my bed sometime around half-three. And it's true that me and Teej stepped outside so he could smoke. While we were out there, his mobile rang. I wasn't surprised—it goes off at all hours of the day and night."

"What does T.J. do for money?" Jem asked, thinking she could guess.

Josh looked pained. Clearly he viewed Jem as a bit of an authority figure—perhaps he'd taken her Stern Librarian persona to heart—and he wasn't sure what he could reveal without being a first-class grass.

"I'll give you a hint," Jem said, once again finding herself on Josh's side. "If you harm Tori or put her in danger, you'll wish you never met me. Otherwise, I'm safe to confide in. I won't go running to the police to score points. They don't seem to care for me much, anyway. I'm not an arm of Exeter Police HQ, I promise."

That seemed to work. Slightly more relaxed, Josh said, "Teej sells a little weed, and other stuff if he can get it, and he's always in demand. I wasn't surprised that he took off, and I didn't expect to hear from him again that night—or morning, if you want to be technical. But it wasn't long before he gave me a bell and said get your arse to the alley behind the row, sharpish. He sounded really shaken up."

"What do you mean?"

"Usually he's cool no matter what. He likes to beat about the bush, and tease you, and then come out with something bonkers. Last night, he went right to it. He said, 'Your aunt's really done it this time. She's off to the psych ward for sure.'"

"You mean he witnessed Natalie hitting Gina with the mallet?" Jem asked, wondering if it were possible. Maybe if he'd been inside Tatteredly's when it happened—or standing at the *Alice* window with his nose pressed against the glass.

Josh shook his head. "He said he was cutting through the alley when he saw Natalie with the mallet in her hand. She was walking slowly, dressed in her housecoat and carpet slippers. T.J. said when she passed under a security light, she held up the mallet and looked at one end, which was dark. Bloody. To him she seemed as mad as a hatter."

"Why didn't he ring the police?" Jem asked.

Josh rolled his eyes, then gave a grin to show he meant no disrespect. "That's not a question you'll ever ask about Teej. He doesn't talk to police. Full stop."

"So what did he do? Confront her?"

"Not with her looking like that. Instead he looped around to the bayside, went to The Siren, then slipped down the access road and peeked around the corner in the alley. That was just in time to see Natalie leaving through the gap. She still—"

"What gap?"

"Oh, sorry. A gap in the fences—it's a shortcut to Weaver Road. We all use it. Anyway, she still looked mad, but the mallet was gone. T.J. started hunting for it. He said he looked on the ground and tried in the sheds, but they were all locked. So he figured she must've got rid of it by flinging it into a bin."

Jem digested that. To her right, Tori bit into a chocolate Hobnob, reminding Jem of the biscuits and tea in front of her. If Josh had drunk his lukewarm, she'd forgotten hers entirely, and let it go ice-cold.

"So T.J. comes to tell you this. I get that he wanted the mallet, bad. Did he know it had been used on Gina?"

"No. I mean, he didn't say that. He just reckoned Natalie attacked someone." Josh sighed. "It's happened before."

"Oh." That changed Jem's prior image of Natalie as a some-what tragic figure covered in crocheted doilies to something more sinister. "We'll come back to that. But as far as black-mail... from what you describe, Natalie doesn't sound like she'd have much to give."

"Teej has never had what you'd call big dreams. She gets a little, here and there, from charities and the local authority. Besides, those two have a history. They've been on the outs for months, and I reckon he wanted leverage over her so she'd come crawling back."

"Wait, this part's new to me," Tori said. "Are you telling me your aunt was *seeing* T.J.?"

"No." Josh seemed taken aback. "Aunt Nat doesn't do much for herself. If she goes out, she either has a meltdown or gets into a row with someone, so she likes to send people around on her behalf. It used to be me who did it, mostly, but I'm too busy now. T.J. has more free time to do her bidding. But they quarreled and they've been on the outs ever since."

"All right. So I understand why T.J. didn't ring the authorities and why he wanted the mallet. But why on earth didn't you call the police?"

"Because... because she's my aunt, and I love her," Josh said awkwardly. "And I didn't know Gina was dead. I didn't know anything much, except that T.J. said there was a mallet with a bloody end. Trying to get hold of it seemed like step one to... to whatever came next."

"Right. You mentioned Natalie had a history of attacking people. What happened?"

"It's kind of a legend around Weaver Road." Josh sighed, looking mortified. "A bloke was in her yard, looking for his kid's lost Frisbee. It's a right mess, so of course he was picking things up and moving them around. Natalie hates trespassers more than anything. She crept up behind him and hit him over the head with a hosepipe."

Jem bit back a laugh. "Yikes. He wasn't seriously hurt, was he?"

"No. But he was furious. If she'd been a man, I think he would've punched her. He rang the police and when they came, of course they took one look at all the clutter and were against my aunt from the start. When the PC asked for her version, she told it straight and wasn't a bit sorry. Said she'd do it all over again, except instead of the hosepipe, she'd use a rusty hammer.

Then she'd picked up one nearby and swung it through the air to demonstrate."

"All right," Jem said. "Now we get to the tricky part. Did you tell Tori any of this before dragging her into it? Because if you didn't, you involved her in a crime—some form of obstructing justice—and she's not out of the woods yet."

11

YOUR QUINTESSENTIAL AMATEUR SLEUTH

"I was drunk," Tori said, ignoring the fact that Jem's question was directed at Josh. "I couldn't have understood all that backstory. He said how about a bit of bin climbing, I said sure, and the next thing I knew, we'd taken it way too far. Most of what I told the police was true. By the time the three of us dragged the bags of rubbish to your building, Josh and T.J. were arguing..."

"Yeah," Josh said. "See. There's something else. I told you, Natalie has an early breakfast every day at six. Jones's Diner, every time. I realized I could text her and see if she answered. So as we hauled the bags back, I did. And she answered, but the answer scared me."

"What did she say?" Jem asked.

"That her life was ruined, it was the worst day of her life, and she was better off dead. I know," he said, accurately reading Jem's face. "But again, if you know her, half of that is typical for any day with a y in it. Still, I took it as confirmation something bad had happened. And that meant I needed to protect the bags from T.J."

"But when I let them fill your tub with rubbish, it suddenly struck me that we'd gone round the bend," Tori said. "I panicked. T.J. had already left in a huff. I told Josh to get out, went to bed, and woke up thinking it was all a dream—until I smelled it."

"Can I see the text Natalie sent you?" Jem asked.

"Jem." Tori looked startled. "Don't you trust Josh's word?"

"It's not about trust," Jem said, not adding that she didn't trust easily and considered it a valuable form of self-defense. "Like *Bright Star* says, I'm your quintessential amateur sleuth. I investigate, and that means verifying."

"I deleted the thread," Josh said. "Just in case something like this happened. That there really was a bloody weapon, and someone got hurt. It never occurred to me that it might be Gina. Natalie's oldest friend, before Gina dropped her."

"Right. So when you decided to blow off your shift at The Siren, I take it you wanted to come back here and explain things properly to Tori?"

"Yeah. It all made sense then. We decided to order takeout, get T.J. to come over, and talk through what came next," Tori said.

"In other words, get your stories straight in case the police came back with more questions. Maybe decide on a name for the gangbangers in black leather?"

"Oh, my gosh, will you please get off that?" Tori moaned, sounding exactly like her teenaged self. "I'm not a good liar. Sue me! At that point, I didn't even know what it was all about. I just knew Josh must've had a good reason for doing what he did, and I needed a story that didn't make him look too bad."

"You did great," Josh said, smiling at her. "Better than I deserve."

Jem blew out a sigh. It was hard to be a loveless grinch in the face of these two, but she'd had some practice at grinchery, and managed it anyway. "Tori, one of these days you're going to learn to be a little more circumspect when it comes to trust."

"Why?" Tori asked.

"You have to trust people," Josh said. "If you don't, life just doesn't work. The whole thing falls apart."

"The way you apparently trust T.J.?" Jem asked pointedly. She thought she had him, but he waved that away.

"We were mates in Year One. Back when I was getting bullied every day, T.J. was the only kid who liked me and stood up for me. 'Weaver Road strong,' we called it. So yeah, we're still mates," Josh said. "I trust him as much as I've learned is possible."

"How many times did you get burned?"

"I don't know. There's nothing Teej can do that I can't handle. Like today, he was a perfect arse, and the next time I see him, I'll tell him so. Maybe we won't be friends anymore. But that's down to him, because of how he behaved."

"You can trust anyone if you trust yourself." Tori shrugged. "I've always reckoned the real trouble with people who go around bragging they trust no one is they don't trust themselves."

Jem blinked at her little sister. She wanted to argue with the simple logic of that statement, but she couldn't. Suddenly what Tori saw in Josh, and Josh saw in Tori, became a good deal clearer, even if they'd only just met and were still babes in the woods as far as she was concerned.

"All right," she said. "One more question, Josh. Suppose Tori hadn't tossed you out. Suppose you'd found the mallet instead of me. What would you have done next?"

"I would've taken it to Natalie. Asked her what happened. Told her the best way to avoid getting locked in a secure facility for the rest of her life was to turn herself in."

"And if she said no? Were you afraid the mallet might be noticed at the processing center before it went into landfill? Did you want it so you could do a better job of disposing of it forever?"

"Maybe," Josh said.

Tori looked astonished. "Really?" she asked in a small voice.

Josh covered his face with his hands. "I don't know what I was thinking. I was afraid for her. I told you, I'm the only person in the world who cares about her. Dad washed his hands of her. Even T.J. was only out for what he could get. I thought first, find the mallet. Just find it and put it somewhere safe. Then I could decide what to do next. I'm sorry. If I'd known someone was dead—that it was Gina—I would've done better, I know it."

"Yes, well, you may still have a chance to do better," Jem said. Josh looked up at her hopefully, but Tori narrowed her eyes.

"You can't expect him to grass on his aunt now. Let the police do their job."

"Tors. You wouldn't say that if you'd been with me when I discovered the body. Or had to poke her and prod her and assure the emergency dispatcher there were no signs of life while trying not to look at the gaping wound on her head."

Tori winced, looking a bit abashed.

"Thing is, if we call the police now, we're not actually reporting something we know happened," Jem continued thoughtfully. "We'll just be telling them a lot of hearsay. T.J. says he saw this, T.J. says he saw that. T.J.'s been on the outs with Natalie for months and suddenly he's fingering her for a criminal act. If you were the person telling the story, Josh, that would be good enough for me. But all the important details come from someone who..." Jem tailed off, rummaging deep in her Big Bag of British Understatements for the right phrase. "Doesn't strike me as scrupulously honest."

"So we should say nothing?" Josh asked hopefully. "Let the police do their work?"

"I didn't say that. I know I keep harping on it, but I found Gina dead, and it makes me feel responsible for her. Even if she wasn't your aunt's favorite person, she didn't deserve to die like that. And whoever did it needs to be held to account—whether that's prison or a secure facility or whatever," Jem said.

"So what do we do?" Tori asked. But there was a gleam in her eye that meant she knew the answer.

"I'd like to talk to Gina's ex-husband, Eddie. And I'd like to talk to your aunt, too, Josh. Her text message notwithstanding, do you think she'll be up for her usual breakfast tomorrow at six?"

Josh went for his phone, checked it, and smiled wryly. "She sent this while we were talking," he said, and passed it over. The message read,

Joshie, I need my Jones fix tomorrow so bad. Please? XX OO

"Guess her will to live has returned," he said.

"Good. When you take her breakfast tomorrow," Jem said, picking up a chocolate Hobnob at last, "I'm coming with you."

12

THE OLD FLAME, THE NEW FLAME, AND NUTTY NATTY

Jem's bed was too narrow for two to share comfortably, so Tori volunteered to sleep on the sofa. As they divvied up the sheets and pillows, Wotsit chose that moment to open his eyes and desert his windowsill perch. Following Jem into the bedroom, he leapt onto the duvet, clearly expecting the lion's share.

"Nope," Jem said, scooping him up. She was still wary of being scratched, but apparently their earlier interaction wasn't a one-off. He melted against her, purring loudly, his short coat incredibly soft against her cheek.

"Would you look at that? Barmy bloke's in love," Tori said.

"Considering all the sausage he got, not to mention the over-priced litter tray I bought him, he ought to be." Jem tried to look the cat directly in his green eyes, but the feline turned his head. Not a dog in a past life, then. Still, he issued another vibrating purr, as if to assure her that refusing to lock eyes was a cat thing —standard behavior, nothing personal. She asked, "Should I let him out for the night?"

"He's been inside ever since I got here. I don't know— maybe give him the option?"

Jem carried Wotsit to the front door, set him down, and

opened it. After a leisurely visual inspection of the walkway, he sniffed and turned pointedly away, his puffy ginger not-tail twitching.

"You like it better inside with us, don't you, Wotsit? You're going to be part of the family," Tori said, giving him a between-the-ears scritch.

"Tori." Jem was mildly alarmed. "I don't want a pet. Especially not in Penzance. It wouldn't work. I only came back to finish out the lease. I'll be back on St. Morwenna every weekend."

"Part of the family," Tori stage-whispered to Wotsit, giving him another scritch.

Morning came all too soon. When Jem's mobile chimed, she was so deeply asleep, she first mistook the alarm for part of her dream, then felt certain the phone was going off by mistake. But then she remembered Gina, and the bloodstained mallet, and her promise to meet Josh outside his parents' house on Weaver Road at ten minutes till six. That gave her an hour to caffeinate, ponder how she planned to approach the interview, and deal with the previous night's texts and voicemails, which were legion.

Still in her sleep shirt, Jem arose, stretched, and carried her mobile to the kitchenette. After getting the coffee started, she sat down, took a deep breath, and looked over her six missed calls and seven text messages. She expected at least half of them to be from Micki. Not one of them was.

"That cow!"

From inside a pile of bedclothes on the sofa, a sleepy voice issued. "You okay?"

"Yeah. Sorry, love. If you're coming along to meet Aunt Natalie, you'd better get up."

"I want to," said the pitiful voice from under the covers. "But it's so early..."

"No worries. Go back to sleep."

I shouldn't be surprised that Micki didn't blow up my phone with a dozen more sorrys. She tried to apologize. I walked out. The ball's in my court.

The coffee was ready. After doctoring it with milk and sugar, Jem had her first glorious taste, mind still full of Micki. Until yesterday, she'd been loyal, cheerful, endearing, and fun. Getting to know her had changed Jem's life. If Micki hadn't broken through Jem's shell and nudged her on, it was entirely possible that all that came after—including reconciling with Pauley and Rhys—would never have happened.

So why did she say all that stuff? It didn't sound like she thought it up on the spot. It sounded like something she's been holding back. Maybe for a long time. If we do patch things up, how will I ever trust her again to...

She stopped. Suddenly she knew exactly why she'd walked out of Tatteredly's instead of sticking by her friend, who absolutely would've stuck by her, no matter what sort of poisonous outburst she spewed during a moment of extreme pressure. She'd walked out because she didn't trust Jem Jago to handle breaches of trust, including the inevitable ones that arose in any friendship.

Jemmie, it's time to grow up. To try to, anyway, Jem thought, realizing she'd drunk half her mug while leaning over the sink. After a refill, she returned to the table to tackle those missed calls and text messages.

The first missed text was from Rhys. It was a picture of Crescent Beach taken from St. Morwenna's highest point, the observation deck of Tremayne Lighthouse, which he'd inherited from his father. Down on the beach, the rollers were capped with froth, the white sand gleamed, and the late afternoon sky was fiery red. Below the picture he'd sent:

I miss you, and you're missing this.

Jem smiled. The truth was, she missed him, too, and it had only been a day. When she'd announced her decision to return to Penzance and ride out the remainder of her flat lease, Rhys hadn't complained. It would've been unreasonable anyway, given how much it would cost her in fees to break the lease. Besides, the flat was only a brisk ten-minute walk to the Courtney Library. Next year she might very well try commuting from St. Morwenna; Pauley Gwyn had invited her to live at Lyonesse House as long as she wished. Still, travel time between the Isles of Scilly and Penzance Harbour was two and a half hours by boat.

So there'd been no massive guilt trip from Rhys. He'd only said, "I had twenty years' practice missing you. It ought to be a piece of cake. It *ought* to be, but it probably won't be."

If the universe keeps up its wicked ways, Jem thought, preparing to tackle the next message, *the next one I open will be from Hack. Or Ignatius Hackman, as we now know him to be.*

The message *was* from Hack. As she opened it, Jem shook her head in amazement. Every time her thoughts veered toward getting serious with Rhys, the universe cleared its throat, swinging the spotlight away from the old flame—Rhys—to the new flame—Hack.

His text read,

> *Had a cryptic message from the rockpile that walks like a man. I'm astonished Conrad took the time and energy to look into a discarded weapon. He rarely stands up without the guarantee of at least one corpse. I wouldn't mind hearing the whole story. Ring me sometime.*

An open-ended invitation was typical of Hack. Like Rhys, he'd made it clear that he wanted more than casual flirtation. Also like Rhys, he seemed determined not to crowd her—more so, in fact. Forty-something and once divorced, Hack didn't seem inclined to jealousy; if any first rodeos awaited him, they had nothing to do with romance. Well aware that Jem and Rhys had been teen sweethearts, he seemed resigned to Rhys having the inside track. That didn't mean he'd dropped out of the race. Whenever they ran into one another, he went out of his way to be charming, and of course needed no special effort to be sexy. She had the sneaking suspicion he thought she needed time to get Rhys out of her system, and was determined to wait it out.

Next came a voicemail from PC Kellow. It had arrived around the same time Jem was hanging on the line with the emergency dispatcher, waiting for the authorities to take charge of Gina's corpse. PC Kellow was just touching base to inform Jem that according to preliminary lab results, the blood and hair on the broken mallet were human. Therefore, Jem and Tori were not to leave Penzance for any reason, including boat trips to the Isles of Scilly, without prior clearance from Exeter Police HQ.

After that came another voicemail, this time from Kenzie DeYoung, Jem's thirteen-year-old friend from St. Morwenna:

"Oh my God, Jem, I can't take it anymore. No one treats me like a woman." (Suppressed screech.) "I am so tired of being jerked around like a little baby who doesn't know which end is up. My mum is a witch and Rhys is worse. He grounded me for drinking half a cider with one of my friends. Half a cider! Everybody I know gets wasted on weekends, but when I try one little taste, he goes into orbit! I want to live with you." (Another suppressed screech.) "Rhys can't ground me. Call me the second you hear this. I mean it!"

Grinning, Jem moved on to the next voicemail, which unsurprisingly was from Rhys. The short message was delivered in a flat, emotionless voice, like a kidnapper issuing an ultimatum.

"Just so you know, I've hogtied Kenzie and stuffed her in a sack. She is not a human child. She is a Tasmanian devil. When

Hackman bangs me up for it, never mind about bail. Just feed my dog." *Click.*

That message, along with the coffee, cheered Jem up so much she suddenly felt ready to tackle the day, even if it was still pitch-dark outside. Rhys and his kid sister, Kenzie, had a twenty-one-year age gap between them; it made the eight-year gulf between Jem and Tori seem negligible. Lissa, Kenzie's irresponsible mum, had chosen not to tell her daughter the truth about her parentage, with the result that most people assumed Rhys was her father. Certainly he served as a parental figure, bossing Kenzie as much as he indulged her. Lately Kenzie had started testing the bounds of their relationship in a bid to learn how much authority over her he really had. They were heading for a showdown, sooner rather than later. She decided to text Rhys back.

> *Sorry I missed it. Yesterday was beyond bizarre. Did you hear about the dead shopkeeper in Penzance? I found the body. Yes, me. Expect fallout. The police read about me in* Bright Star *and don't seem impressed.*

After she hit SEND, she realized it had been ludicrous to ask Rhys if he'd heard about Gina Marrak. If he hadn't when he went to bed, he'd know as soon as he read his mobile's push notifications. The news would've ricocheted around the West Country by night and would surely have bounced all the way to the Scillies by daybreak.

She moved on to the next message, a text from Pauley.

> *Micki's in a state. She didn't mean it. Call me.*

A few minutes later, also from Pauley:

> *I mean it. Don't dig in your heels. Call.*

And ten minutes after that:

Fine. You know what? Where there's a Bart, there's a way.

Jem sighed. Pauley knew precisely who she was dealing with, and had misinterpreted Jem's silence—when she was meeting Josh and T.J., performing a series of interrogations, and then heading to bed in anticipation of an early morning—as her broodily refusing to answer her oldest friend's texts. Knowing Pauley as she did, there was no doubt what her last message meant. Pauley was coming to Penzance via Bart the Ferryman's converted fishing boat, *Merry Maid*. She probably intended to bring Micki to Jem's doorstep to work things out or know the reason why not. For a second, Jem resented it, but there was no use ringing Pauley to say no way. Pauley never hesitated to call bullshit when she thought Jem needed it. And there was something wonderful in having friends who knew you that well and still thought your friendship was worth the bother. She texted a quick reply:

I'm heading out early this morning. Probably will be back to the flat in the afternoon. My little sis Tori is here. Can't wait for you to meet her.

Jem vaguely remembered Weaver Road from her teen years in Penzance. The terraced homes were interesting in their variety, with cream stucco beside red brick and sky-blue paint next to slabbed granite. That morning, however, it was still dark when she reached the Lansallos house, and everything was just a conglomeration of shapes. It was a brisk morning with a stiff wind off the harbor and dark clouds on the horizon. Jem regretted leaving her mac behind on St. Morwenna, and hoped the sun came up soon. She'd worn a T-shirt and jeans, which was overoptimistic as far as the temperature went; she wished she'd put on the sweater that Tori said made her look like a great blue sheep.

"Good morning," she told Josh, who awaited her under a streetlight. "I didn't expect to find you empty-handed."

"I had a think. I've decided the best way to introduce you is to do it while she's waiting for breakfast," he said. "That way she can't retreat into the house with the excuse that you're disturbing her meal. Sometimes she likes to hide out. But she'll be expecting me at six and will come to the window."

"Window?" Jem asked.

"You'll see. Last night, when I was explaining about her— did I tell you what they call her?"

"I don't think so."

"Nutty Natty," Josh said grimly. "Keep that in mind if she gets a little—challenging."

13

"IF YOU'RE NOT A COUNCIL BUSYBODY OR A
SEX FIEND, WHO THE HELL ARE YOU?"

The sky was just beginning to lighten up as Jem and Josh followed Weaver Road east toward a granite-faced detached home. It occupied a premium spot, real estate-wise, that might originally have been a smith's yard or a small farm. Unlike most private homes in Penzance, the front door was reinforced with a steel security door. On that forbidding barrier, red letters on a white sign read:

PRIVATE LAND

NO PUBLIC RIGHT OF WAY

DO NOT TRESPASS

I guess if that doesn't put you off, the rest of the front garden might do it, Jem thought.

Even in the predawn gloom, it was a dispiriting waste of space. Like many neighborhoods in a seaside town, this area was mostly houses, pavement, and the odd tree. But Natalie Lansallos, finding herself with a goldmine of a comparatively huge lot, hadn't planted a thing. Rather, she'd dumped a truckload of gravel on it, thick enough to kill any grass with the temerity to try and grow. Dark masses of weeds had managed to get a toehold around the old stone fence enclosing the property. The most ambitious specimens stood eight feet tall or more.

"We're going around the back to the bedroom window," Josh said. "Keep in mind, things are worse back there. Please don't start in on her about how she lives."

No, I'll just ask her very nicely if she's a murderer, Jem thought. But despite her mind making a quip, she found Josh's protective attitude endearing.

The sun rose on Natalie Lansallos's backyard, which was the stuff of antisocial behavior complaints, gas safety violations, and quite possibly mental capacity hearings. Jem suffered a stab of pity as well as revulsion. The poorly patched roof, cobwebby eaves, and windows covered with tinfoil were bad enough, but an assortment of plastic kids' toys was piled all over the gravel-choked yard. According to Josh, his aunt had never married, had no children, and had always lived alone. So why she felt the need to collect and retain so many toys, faded by the sun and ruined by disuse, Jem didn't know. But the sight of them made her sad.

One window wasn't entirely covered in tinfoil. There was a viewing slit, perhaps two inches by two inches, near the bottom. It seemed that Natalie had been watching their approach through that slit because as they drew closer, she flung open the window, leaned out, and called, "And where's my breakfast?"

"I'll be off to fetch it in just a minute, Auntie," Josh said. "I want you to meet someone first." Having stopped about ten feet from the window, he didn't seem inclined to go any closer. Following his lead, Jem tried to make out Natalie's features from there, but the gloom made it impossible. She was definitely rather large, though, filling up the window so completely no light from the bedroom spilled out.

"Are you a social worker?"

"No," Jem said.

"Are you one of those God-bothery types?"

"No."

Natalie leaned out a bit more. "Are you interfering with my nephew Joshie? Some kind of cougar robbing the cradle?"

"Auntie!" Josh laughed in a way that Jem almost found insulting. She decided to take it as a show of loyalty to Tori rather than a slight against her ability to lure him from his crib.

"If you're not a council busybody or a sex fiend, who the hell are you?"

"My name's Jem Jago," she said, feeling slightly ridiculous as the day dawned slowly around them. "I'm a librarian. Also—"

"Also the Scilly Sleuth. Good heavens. Approach."

Jem looked at Josh.

"Approach," Natalie bellowed.

Jem had been expecting more of a shut-in, but Natalie Lansallos seemed robust and hearty, with excellent lung capacity. Her second queenly demand sent Josh hurrying forward, so Jem again followed his lead. Beneath the bedroom window was a makeshift platform composed of produce crates. Josh climbed up on them, putting him at the right level to converse through the window. Jem, feeling like a fool, did the same.

Natalie withdrew back into her room, shifting her bulk so the interior light revealed her features at last. She had a round face with a stubborn jaw and an upturned nose permitting a direct view into each nostril. Her curly hair was more salt than pepper, and if she'd brushed it in the last week, Jem couldn't tell.

"Tall one, aren't you? You could almost just stand on the ground," Natalie said. "How's the light? Can you see behind me?"

"A little."

Natalie shifted so Jem could see more of what turned out to

be her bedroom/command center. "I read in *Bright Star* that you're a Special Collections librarian. I'm something of a bibliophile myself. How do you like my collection?"

"It's—amazing," Jem said, and meant it.

The room was first and foremost a shrine to the written word. It had been modified by someone, perhaps Natalie herself, to have floor-to-ceiling bookshelves on three walls. Jem's expert gaze took in every sort of book: paperbacks, hardbacks, trade-sized manuals, coffee-table books, atlases, and a whole shelf of children's picture books, their spines a riotous rainbow of colors. Jem couldn't see into every nook and cranny, but what she spied of the floor was literally covered with books.

"You could make your own lending library."

"Never. I love my books too much." Natalie's bed was pushed up alongside the window. Arranging herself so her chunky legs stuck out in front of her, she shifted her laptop off the nearest pile of books and balanced it on her thighs.

"This is my inner sanctum." Her gaze, lively and rather shrewd, darted to and fro, from Jem to Josh and back again. "My favorite spot, where I attend to the business of the realm. Now. Joshie. Where's my brekkie?"

"I promise I'll be off in just a minute. But Auntie—did you hear about Gina?"

The change that came over Natalie's face was hard for Jem to characterize. She rolled her eyes and tapped a finger against her lips, as if struggling to recall some esoteric fact.

"Gina. Gina. Where do I know that—? No, sorry. Doesn't ring a bell."

"Auntie..."

"She's dead to me," Natalie screeched, making Jem jump. "She's been dead to me for years! It's not my fault the world only just caught up!"

"Auntie, don't talk that way. Please," Josh said, glancing around to see if any early risers had been attracted by his aunt's booming voice. "The news says she was murdered in Tatteredly's yesterday morning. Police are investigating. Anyone involved will be in trouble."

Natalie raised both eyebrows at her nephew. For a moment she regarded him silently. Then she said, "If you want me to confess to murder, love, just promise me breakfast. I'm starving to death." Shifting her gaze to Jem, she asked, "Is that why you're here? Someone got whacked and here you are, going door to door in Penzance, eliminating suspects one citizen at a time?"

"Not quite," Jem said, trying for a tone of sweet reason. "If you read about me in *Bright Star*, you know how I was doing a job at a private library on St. Morwenna when I ended up suspected of murder. I solved that case to clear my own name, and then a few weeks later someone else died—"

"And you're obviously killing these people yourself for attention, is that what you're saying?"

"Erm, no, not at all, just lucky I guess, or unlucky, depending on your perspective. Anyway, my employer is in Penzance, so I came back yesterday, and I wasn't looking for another case, but this one seemed to reach out and grab me. The murder weapon was found in my home."

Natalie let out a startling hoot. "You totally did it. Confess, girlie. Your desire for fame and fortune has turned you into a serial killer."

"Not much fame, no fortune, and this time the police don't suspect me. But I wonder if they might soon have reason to suspect you."

Natalie, who until that moment looked as if she was having a fine time, pressed a hand to her ample bosom. Then she dissolved into loud shuddering sobs.

"Auntie," Josh cried, shooting Jem a look of betrayal. "I'm so sorry. No one suspects you. It's only—"

"I'm going to the big house," Natalie wailed, covering her face with her hands. "I'll die there. I'll never breathe the free air again!" Sobbing even harder, she cried, "I'll have to marry the woman with the most cigarettes!"

"Josh," Jem hissed in his ear. "For heaven's sake, go get her breakfast. Maybe I'll do better alone."

She expected Josh to argue, but apparently he, too, thought it might be a good time to do a legger. "I'm off, Auntie," he cried, leaping off the produce crate and jogging away from the house. Jones's Diner was a ten-minute walk away, so Jem thought she might have a half-hour with Natalie. Assuming, of course, she could drag a sensible word out of her.

As soon as Josh was out of earshot, Jem turned back to see Natalie, eyes dry and face calm, looking at her with frank curiosity. Running her fingers through her untidy curls, she blew out a sigh.

"Lord. Sometimes the Nutty Natty routine wears me out. Sorry about all that. What exactly would you like to know?"

14

"SHE CAST AWAY PRICELESS, IRRETRIEVABLE THINGS"

Jem was so startled, she laughed—not a real laugh, but a nervous titter she immediately wanted back. Natalie scowled.

"Oh, dear. I didn't take you for a lightweight, but now you sound like one. Did you really solve those crimes like *Bright Star* says? Or is scampering about playing Nancy Drew just your con?"

"My... con?" Jem repeated stupidly.

"Con. As in, deception. As in, the art of a confidence man." Natalie's mouth pursed. "I was trained as an English teacher, though I never worked as one. You do speak English, don't you?"

"Oh, give the attitude a rest. You're the one running a con," Jem snapped. It felt good to let go after those first agonizing minutes of walking on eggshells. "I had to promise Josh I'd treat you with kid gloves. He was worried to death I'd work you into a state. But it's all an act. Why? Afraid Josh wouldn't bother with you if you gave up the bonkers routine?"

"Don't try to psychoanalyze me." Reaching for a nearby cola bottle, Natalie treated herself to a huge swig of the fizzy stuff. From the look of her sheets, she ate every breakfast—and possibly all her other meals—in bed. "If you want to ask questions, ask them.

"Fine. First question," Jem said briskly. "How long did you know Gina Marrak?"

"All my life."

"And you were close friends for most of that time?"

"Close until she lost her first husband. A great deal of money came to her, and she changed," Natalie said, eyes on her laptop screen and fingers working as she rapidly toggled through what looked like a message board's comment threads.

"How did she change?"

"She didn't want to share. Got greedy. Oh! Someone replied. Hang on."

Natalie was a fast typist. As the keys clicked, she chuckled to herself, becoming more visibly amused as she typed. From Jem's angle the sentences weren't readable, but there were a lot of capitalized words and emojis.

"Trying to win an argument?" Jem asked.

"Always. People are idiots. It's up to me to tell them." Natalie banged out a few final words, then hit ENTER with a flourish. "What was I saying? Oh, yeah, Gina the Greedy. That's who she became after hubby number one dropped dead. Had a seizure at the breakfast table and was gone just like that. Could've been poison. There's a real mystery for you to dig into, if you want a hot tip."

"Maybe later. I understand Gina used to live on Weaver Road. I suppose she used some of the money to move away?"

"To Alverton Street. Where the quality people live."

"And then she bought Tatteredly's?"

"Yes, but Tatteredly's was my idea. I should have been half owner. I was the one who suggested running a bookshop to Gina. She never had an original thought in her life. Even her precious *Alice* window was my idea. She never would've read the ruddy thing if I hadn't loaned her *Alice in Wonderland* all those years ago. Gina was nothing without me. No wonder she ended up dead." Natalie flashed a smile at Jem, bright and revolting.

"Did you know someone saw you on Saturday morning, in the alley behind Silversmith Lane, carrying a bloodstained croquet mallet?"

Natalie sat up straight. "What?"

"You heard me."

"I think you made that up. But whether you did or not, it doesn't matter because it didn't happen."

"All right. Where were you on Saturday morning, between five and seven a.m.?"

"I was here. Asleep until a quarter to six. Fired up the laptop and checked my sites and played my games." At the mention of games, she minimized the message board, filling the screen with digital solitaire. Her laptop's volume was cranked up, and each time she shifted a card from tableau to foundation, the move was accompanied by a decisive *thwack*.

"What about breakfast? Did you miss it, or was it so terrible you decided you were better off dead?"

Natalie's mouth tightened with obvious displeasure. "Joshie," she said, putting the jack of spades on the queen of diamonds, "should know better than to share my private communications with publicity-seeking snoops."

"You frightened him. He thinks your Nutty Natty routine is for real. You really do it just to string him along, don't you?"

The ace of hearts *thwack*ed into the foundation slot, but Natalie, jaw working, didn't answer.

"I wonder if that's what came between you and Gina."

Thwack. Thwack. Thwack.

"I'm sure it will all come out soon, what with the murder weapon in the hands of the police and—"

"Hah! I win. I always win," Natalie declared. Cards from the tableau and pile began migrating automatically into the foundation stacks. The game concluded with the usual winning animation—an explosion of dancing, fluttering cards all over the screen. She watched for a while, then shut her laptop with a snap.

"All right, little miss librarian. Here's what I can tell you about Gina Marrak. It wasn't just the money that changed her. It was Eddie Latham. He was the first true wedge between us."

"Why? Didn't you approve of him?" Jem asked, remembering how Micki had called Gina the best thing to ever happen to her brother.

"It wasn't that. There was a powerful attraction between me and Eddie. A sexual energy that couldn't be denied."

Jem saw that Natalie wasn't joking, and determinedly kept a straight face.

"The fact is, I could've taken Eddie away from Gina anytime I wanted. He loved talking to me. He adored my way with words and found my habitual déshabillé and my general sophistication, especially compared to Gina, quite intoxicating." Natalie spoke with absolute sincerity, as if she wasn't being interviewed through an open window in her hoarded-out house. "And, yes, that tension helped destroy our friendship. But the final and irrevocable reason Gina and I fell out was because she was an interfering *cow* who trespassed. I cannot abide trespass."

"Meaning what, exactly?"

"She came into my home under false pretenses and stole my things."

"What kind of things?"

"What do you think? Books, obviously. *Librarian.*" Natalie shook her head. "Gina dealt in used, antique, and rare books. My collection used to rival the lost Library of Alexandria. One day she said she was going to Plymouth for a bookseller convention and would I watch Tatteredly's for her? I said certainly, anything for a dear friend. I sallied forth, dressed to the nines, to sit behind the cash register and serve customers. Do you think she actually went to Plymouth? No. She came here, to my home, when I wasn't around to defend it."

Jem nodded. Natalie's color was rising, her wide nostrils deepening. This emotional reaction wasn't an act. Her pupils had dilated, and she was beginning to tremble. "She used her spare key and two accomplices to haul away my things. To steal them under the pretense of organizing my living room. I have it on good authority that she took away truckloads of books and filled up two skips with what she called rubbish. Can you believe that? And do you imagine for one minute that some of those books didn't go into her personal collection? Or that the rest went to Tatteredly's so Gina the Greedy could sell them?"

"That must've felt like a complete betrayal," Jem said with a bit of genuine sympathy. Whether or not the details were accurate, Natalie's depth of feeling was clearly genuine. "Were any of the books from the *Fun and Profit* series?"

"Why?"

"I saw a lot of them in the shop," Jem said, recalling *Cannabis for Fun and Profit* lying in the middle of the sales floor, far from its proper shelf.

"Maybe. I don't know, I never had an exact inventory. The point is, she broke into my house. She stole my possessions. She cast away priceless things, irretrievable things. I cried, I raged, I complained to the authorities, I tried to get her arrested, and no one cared. Why do you think I hit the next person who trespassed over the head with a bloody hosepipe? To defend what little I have left!"

"And you're not worried the police might think you decided to do the same thing to Gina?"

"No, because Nutty Natty is innocent as a lamb. No one likes to deal with a hysterical, borderline psychotic, confabulating woman, and I can play that role in my sleep. Nutty Natty has saved me from all the worst irritations of life. Police come nosing round? No worries, they're scared witless of Natty.

Church people? Same. And the last time I staged one of my very public breakdowns, you know what it got me? A reduction in my council taxes, that's what." Natalie looked past Jem and brightened suddenly. "There's Joshie with my breakfast at last. So I have no more time for you, Scilly Sleuth, though I'm flattered you came to accuse me of murder."

Turning, Jem saw Josh crossing the yard—which took a certain amount of sidestepping and detouring—with a takeaway box in his hands. It was yellow Styrofoam and looked familiar.

"So takeaway from Jones's Diner comes in yellow boxes?" she asked.

"Erm, yeah," Josh said, too polite to ask her if she needed her eyes checked.

"You'll never put one over this one," Natalie laughed. "Hand it over, Joshie. Oh, thank goodness, it's still warm."

"Did I mention I came home to find a murder weapon in my bathtub?" Jem asked. "In a bag of rubbish from behind The Siren?"

Josh looked nonplussed. "I explained all that to my auntie..."

"My cat was poking around in the mess. There were a couple of Jones's Diner breakfasts that had been tossed out. Probably around the same time as the mallet," Jem continued.

Natalie paused with a sausage halfway to her mouth. She seemed about to say something, then chose to take a bite instead.

"I wonder, since there were two breakfasts," Jem said, the notion coming to her as she spoke, "and they were both complete before Wotsit got to them, if the killer dropped by Tatteredly's with breakfast for himself—or herself—and Gina. The morning took a turn, Gina ended up dead, and so the food and the mallet went into the bin."

"Flimsy," Natalie said, though her eyes were narrowed.

"Ring the police and float that theory. They'll tell you to go read Agatha Christie."

"Maybe," Jem said, intrigued by the other woman's reaction. "Those yellow Styrofoam boxes are still under my bed, where my cat hid them. I think it might be a good idea to ring PC Kellow at Exeter Police HQ and tell her."

"Sure, annoy the authorities with harebrained scenarios, that's a good way to get them on your side," Natalie said. Seeming to suddenly recall her nephew's presence, and perhaps realizing she was still in rational Natty mode, she announced in a ringing voice, "I have seen... *a vision.*"

"It's too early to get worked up, Auntie," Josh said warily.

Ignoring that, Natalie squeezed her eyes shut and put both hands to her temples like a funfair psychic. "Jem Jago. Go to Silversmith Bay and ask around the shops. Every single shopkeeper despised Gina. A word is coming to me. Livingston's... yes... Livingston's. The sale that went sour. Ask them about the sale that went sour."

Now that Natalie was back in character, there was no sense remaining, so Jem said goodbye to Josh and started home to see if Tori was awake yet. The news about two binned breakfasts had certainly provoked a reaction. As for the last-minute tip about the shopkeepers and a sale that went sour, Jem didn't know if it was purely a distraction, or a real bit of information that might lead somewhere. She was turning the idea over in her mind when she realized she'd twice referred to a certain tailless feline as "her cat."

15

JAM DOUGHNUTS AND HAIR CLIPS

As Jem walked back to her building, the sun climbed higher in the sky and the wind off the water didn't feel so cold. Most of the dark clouds were scudding out to sea. It might be a pretty Sunday after all.

The thing about a deal going sour was interesting. A better angle than Natalie's supposed mutual attraction with Eddie. I'll need to talk to him, too, as soon as I can swing it. But Sunday on Silversmith Bay could be a good time to check out the shops—and feel out the shopkeepers.

After her visit to one of Penzance's prettiest neighborhoods, Jem's building, put up by an outside investor catering to single professionals and young families, looked more like an eyesore than ever. Penzance was composed of mostly one- and two-story buildings, generally gray stone and white stucco, with charming accents like bay windows and bright blue doors. The streets were narrow, the cottages had names like The Owls or Thornhill Place, and many front gardens were only two feet across, overflowing with spiky greens and lush tropical blooms that spilled onto the pavement. The nicest part of Jem's building was the courtyard, and it only had a bench and a couple of saplings.

I should be grateful I'm not coming back to another rubbish heap. Hopefully, Jem thought as she entered her flat.

Tori, predictably, was still under a blanket on the sofa, but the telly was on and she was watching something with half an eye. Wotsit, perched on her chest, jumped down when he saw Jem and crossed the room. She was about to praise him for this almost dog-like devotion—hurrying to greet the mistress—when he stopped, wet a paw, and began casually grooming an ear. His attitude seemed to be, *Oh, are you here? What a coincidence. Just decided it was time to freshen up.*

"Wotsit, you are such a cat," Tori said.

He stopped grooming, looked at her, then strolled the remaining few inches to Jem and brushed her leg with the faintest accompanying *purr*. With his formal greeting of Jem accomplished, he headed off to see what was happening in the bedroom.

"Josh texted me," Tori said. "He says his aunt denies T.J.'s story and thinks you're a fraud. Also, her breakfast was cold and you owe her a hot one."

"Good luck collecting on it," Jem said. "Speaking of food, all I had this morning was coffee, and I'm starving. How do you feel about going out in search of Sunday brunch?"

Tori's blanket was on the floor and the TV went dark. "Give me five minutes to put some clothes on," she said, already halfway to the bedroom. Then, from inside: "I forgot, all my stuff is dirty. Can I borrow more of yours?"

The quickest route to the bay was along Clarence Street. Jem set a brisk pace, hoping Tori was still too sleepy to catch sight of The Buttery. As the sign proclaimed, the restaurant was perfect for morning coffee or afternoon tea, but it could wait for a leisurely weekend. Today, Jem wanted to eat within sight of Tatteredly's and mix with potential suspects.

"You're walking too fast, flamingo legs," Tori said.

"Sorry." Jem didn't slow down. "Keep up and there will be pastry and a latte at the end of the rainbow." At least she hoped there would—it all depended on what kind of Sunday hours the shops kept in mid-September. Fall and winter were hard for tourist towns, especially in the present economy. But with any luck the merchants along Silversmith Bay would still be keeping summer hours, intent on squeezing out every last bit of the season.

Out on the bay, it could've been June; the water was gentle and boats were everywhere. Residents and emmets strolled along the promenade, a mile-long walkway that snaked along the shore. Farther out to sea, Jem's sharp eyes saw a catboat—a traditional sailboat with a four-sided sail—cut through the waves as the Cornish flag flapped over the stern.

Silversmith Lane was bustling. Plenty of shoppers were on the hoof and most businesses were not only open, they had their doors propped wide.

Tori clutched Jem's forearm in a death grip. "Oh! Jem!"

"What?"

"Warren's Bakery! They have jam doughnuts. And the best coffee. Please, please, you owe me a doughnut after leaving me flat on the floor yesterday."

"Well, I wouldn't say no to one, if I'm being honest," Jem said, studying Warren's sign, which proclaimed it the world's oldest Cornish pasty shop. "The smell coming out of there is amazing. But it's a really long queue."

"Of course it is. That proves it's worth it."

Jem couldn't argue with Tori's hungry logic, and her stomach was already rumbling at the mere thought of a fresh, sugar-encrusted pastry, so they diverted into Warren's. It took several minutes to get through the queue, and by the time they did there were no seats left, so they ate and sipped coffee just outside the bakery, leaning against a low stone wall. As Jem mulled over the interview with Natalie Lansallos, Tori watched the pedestrians across the street.

"Oops. Dropped something," she muttered.

"Who did?"

"That funny little bloke across the way. He dropped— Oh, he's going. Oi!" Tori shouted, loud enough to make a nearby lady drop her paper napkin. "Behind you! Yeah, you! You dropped something!"

The man in question was shorter than average and dressed all in black—black T-shirt, black trousers, and a faded black apron studded with what looked like elongated black buttons. At first he frowned at Tori, probably thinking he was being heckled by a stranger. Then, seeming to process her words, he spun around to look behind him, patting himself down at the same time. Bending, he retrieved something lying on the pavement—was it one of the elongated buttons?—straightened up and waved at Tori.

"Cheers, love!"

It was the voice Jem recognized, not the bald head, protuberant brow, or rosebud mouth. Twenty years had changed her former schoolmate, Toby Smithfield, almost beyond recognition, apart from his diminutive stature and boyish, piping voice.

"Toby!" she called. "Hiya!"

"Jemmie?" He lit up, the smile making his moon face almost attractive. "Look at you. Haven't changed a whit. Still got that long hair, haven't you?" He was crossing the street as he asked, looking both ways with the unconscious self-assurance of someone who knew the area well. As he drew close, she saw that the black things attached to his apron, which she'd first taken for long black buttons, were actually something else.

"Why all the hair clips?"

"I'm a stylist," he said proudly, brandishing the item he'd

dropped. To Tori he said, "Thanks for the heads-up. Some of these gator clips are losing their bite. I'll need to buy a new lot soon. Or not," he added, as if remembering something. "My life's a bit up in the air at present."

"Why's that?" Jem asked.

"Oh, dear, how long have you got? There's been a murder just down the row from my shop. It has everyone in an uproar. I hoped it might draw a few extra bodies, but they're just gawking, not spending."

Jem tossed her coffee and crumpled pastry wrapper in a nearby bin so she could give him her full attention. Back at St. Mary's School, she and Toby had been in the same year, but barely on nodding acquaintance. He'd been quiet and a bit of a loner, constantly teased for his unconventional interests. Pauley had tried to befriend him—he was the only other person she knew who took fashion seriously and spent hours in the library poring over *W* and *Vogue*—but for some reason, they hadn't hit it off. As for Jem, she hadn't given Toby Smithfield a single thought since leaving the islands, but if he owned a business near Tatteredly's, she was eager to keep him talking.

"Which place is yours? Age of Aquarius?"

"Nah, that belongs to Millie Ambury-Taylor. Sweet girl. No chance of making it," he said, glancing up and down the lane as if double-checking to ensure no one who knew Millie had overheard. "I'm not being unkind. I'm as underwater as she is, maybe more so. I own Hair Today, Gone Tomorrow. A topic I know a little bit about, as you see," he added, touching his round pink scalp. "Attended the London School of Barbering."

"Jem used to live in London," Tori offered.

"Manchester location," Toby said with a cough, as if he hated making the distinction. "I originally planned to study fashion design, but the industry's so cutthroat. All about who you know. I didn't have the killer instinct, and, as you might remember, I had loads of blond hair, so I enrolled in a hair course. I did so well, I continued my training at the London school, then came back here and opened my own salon."

"You did have loads of blond hair," Jem said, thinking it wasn't such a shame that nature had taken it away. As a boy, Toby had been overwhelmed by the shaggy mop, which had contributed to making him a figure of fun. As a bald man, he now possessed a certain gravitas that would've been pleasing, if not for his piping voice and continually pursed lips.

"And you have twice as much hair as you need, if you'll forgive my saying," Toby announced, tutting at Jem's double bun. "I'll bet it falls all the way to your waist. Be honest—it's nothing but split ends, am I right?"

"I trim them. Plus there's such a thing as conditioner. Don't even think about it. You're not touching my hair."

He waved that away. "I should've known. When a woman gets to be your age and still has hair that long, it's not a style choice, it's a way of life. Nothing your friendly neighborhood barber says will change it. Anyway," he sighed, "I should get back to the salon, but I don't know what good it will do me. I've opened early every day for the last two weeks, trying to bring in anyone who needs a cut—late-shift workers coming home, binmen and street sweepers on the job, you name it. It's a lost cause."

"Did you open early yesterday?" Jem asked, trying to sound casual.

He nodded.

"Only... well, you're not going to believe this, but I'm the one who found Gina Marrak's body." Jem gave him a quick rundown of the circumstances. "It seems like she was working alone in there when someone attacked her. Did you notice that Tatteredly's was closed all day, even though it was Saturday?"

"Nope." Toby shrugged. "I never paid the slightest attention to what Gina did or didn't do."

"Doesn't sound like you cared much for her."

Folding his arms across his chest, he managed a thin smile. "She cost me a quarter of a million pounds."

"What? How?"

"Well, not just me," Toby said, lowering his voice and once again glancing up and down the lane to see who might be listening. "All of us along the row—me, Millie, Jerry, Fred, Krish—we all would've cleared about a quarter of a million, easy, if the real estate deal had gone through."

"Oh, yeah, Livingston's," Jem said wisely, hoping he would say more. So Natalie's parting suggestion hadn't been total bollocks.

"You heard about it? I'm not surprised. Rich Richards at Livingston's took us all out to dinner, including Gina, and walked us through the benefits of selling out. He had a buyer lined up to completely renovate that section of the lane. It was going to be a boutique hotel and spa overlooking the bay. Of course, they needed all of us to sell. Tatteredly's is the biggest plot, and would've been the cornerstone. But Gina just said no."

"Wow." That was a motive for murder if Jem had ever heard it. Natalie was right; Toby and every other shopkeeper had ample reason to despise Gina. And now with Gina out of the way...

"Maybe there's a silver lining," Tori suggested, mind going to the same place as Jem's. "Whoever inherits Tatteredly's might be willing to sell."

"You think?" Toby asked hopefully. "I shouldn't even think it. I can't bear another disappointment. I'm so skint I can't even buy hair clips that aren't half-sprung. If Eddie was inheriting, it might all come right, but I'm sure Gina changed the will when she divorced him."

Oh! There's another possibility, Jem thought.

Toby was still talking. "...after she tossed him out, maybe she wrote a new one. Penciled in her skeevy little boy toy or similar."

"Boy toy," Tori repeated, giggling. "I never heard that one."

Toby blinked at her. "How old are you?"

"Twenty-five. And it sounds a bit slut-shamey, don't you think?"

"Speak as I find," Toby said more coolly.

"I heard Gina got a new boyfriend after she and Eddie split up," Jem said, trying to keep the gossip flowing as long as possible. "I don't suppose you know his name?"

"Sorry, no. Really, I'm just repeating what I've heard from Millie and Krish. I wasn't kidding when I said I paid no attention to Gina Marrak. She was an infuriating woman and the world's a better place without her." Looking a bit startled at his own declaration, he added, "That *is* a good smell from Warren's, isn't it?"

"If you want a late breakfast, I give it five stars. Would recommend," Tori said.

He shook his head. "Already ate. I'm a creature of habit. Breakfast every morning at the same place. If I missed a day, they'd alert the media. Well." He sighed in a way that seemed to indicate the conversation was over. "It's good to see you again, Jem." To Tori, he added, "Thanks for giving a shout," and tapped one of the clips clinging to his apron. "Must be off."

He took the pedestrian walkway toward the top of Silversmith Lane. Because it was the same direction Jem intended to go, she decided to hang back for a little while. Toby had seemed slightly nervous, and she didn't want to make him feel like he was being tailed.

"I think he's a suspect," Tori declared. "He sounded pretty bitter about the money."

"He's definitely a suspect. Why don't we try the vintage shop?" Jem asked, indicating Age of Aquarius only a few meters away. "He said the owner was underwater. Maybe she'd be willing to tell us how she felt about Gina's putting the kibosh on the deal."

16

A BOHO PRINCESS AND TWO SCARVES

Millie Ambury-Taylor could've been PC Kellow's sister, except for her style, which was a far cry from a uniformed officer of the law. Her long blonde hair, parted in the middle, hung on either side of her pretty face in what people sometimes called "beachy waves"—meaning they were slightly crispy, as if she'd recently emerged from salt water. Her paisley floral dress, in shades of sea green and rust, swirled around her as she moved. Its loose bodice was unlaced, showing the cream-colored chemise beneath.

"Everything I'm wearing is for sale," she announced by way of welcoming Jem and Tori into Age of Aquarius. "Dress, sandals, rings, earrings, everything. Make me an offer for this"— she flipped back the beachy waves—"and I just might chop it off and hand it over."

"I'm shopping for a friend," Jem said, thinking that in an otherwise empty shop with an eager proprietor, making a small purchase was the best way to elicit goodwill. "She loves scarves."

"I'll need a little more," Millie said, coming around the counter eagerly. "How would you describe her vibe? Take me, for example. Some people call me a hippie, but I prefer boho princess."

"Oh, that's easy. She's a goth."

"Industrial goth? Vampire goth? Perky goth?"

"Definitely perky."

"Maybe something in pink skulls? They have hair bows. Who says dead can't be darling?"

"I usually stick to black and burgundy. Those are her favorite colors."

"Of course. Follow me."

Fortunately for Jem, who'd already spent too much in the last twenty-four hours when you combined Tesco Express, dinner at The Siren, and breakfast at Warren's, the prices at Age of Aquarius were quite reasonable. It seemed clear from the numerous struck-through prices and red sale tags that Millie's business fared no better than Toby's salon. Jem selected a black organza scarf patterned with roses for the bargain price of four quid. She was searching for the best way to bring up the murder next door when a familiar pattern caught her eye.

"This is pretty," she said, picking a scarf with a whimsical pattern of teacups and orange blossoms. She didn't have to consult the camera roll on her mobile to know it was an exact match to the scarf she'd seen lying as if forgotten in Tatteredly's.

"You mean for you, right? No self-respecting goth would wear it," Millie said. "It's on final markdown. Last of the lot, so if you want it, now's your chance."

"Actually," Jem said, deciding this was as good an opening as she was likely to get, "I think I've seen it somewhere. Have you sold lots?"

"I sold one," Millie said. "Exactly one, to an estate agent. Her name's Keeley Jin—" She stopped. "Sorry. I can't think of her real last name. One of the other shopkeepers called her Keeley Jingle-Jangle because of her charm bracelets, and pretty soon we were all calling her that. She tinkled whenever she moved. I'm not being nasty," Millie added hastily. "I like musical ornaments. Only some of the other folks along the row seemed to think she was a bit of a joke."

"Oh, yeah, an estate agent," Jem said, trying to sound in the know. "Was she working with Rich Richards? On that deal to build a hotel and spa overlooking the bay?"

Behind Millie, Tori's head jerked up from the fluttery dress she was inspecting. From the look on her face, she was impressed by Jem's rapid deployment of information so recently gleaned from Toby.

"Yeah." Millie sighed. "I'm still not over the loss of it. None of us are, really. How do you know about it?"

"I sort of knew Gina Marrak. Not as a friend. More a friend of a friend thing," Jem continued, still in an offhand manner, as if the various scarves before her were just as interesting. "Believe it or not, I found her. Last night, after hours. I reckon she'd been dead inside Tatteredly's all day."

"I *know*." Millie pressed a hand to her heart as if deeply shocked. "Can you believe it? I always fancied myself a little bit psychic, if you want the truth, but I didn't sense a thing. I guess her leaving this plane of existence didn't cause much of a ripple."

"Did you think it was odd when the shop didn't open yesterday?"

"Oh, Gina wasn't one for schedules. Or letting people know what she might do next. Or giving a damn what any of us thought," Millie said lightly, as if striving to paper over a much stronger emotion. "I thought she was home counting her money. She was rolling in it, you know. Unlike the rest of us. If this place doesn't make bank, I don't eat. Gina ran her bookshop for a lark."

Jem nodded sympathetically. "I've heard she changed after she got the cash. I didn't hear where it came from, though."

"Oh. Her first husband. Some kind of workplace accident.

The company was at fault and had to settle," Millie said. "When I first opened up, I did everything I could to make Gina my friend. Us businesswomen have to stick together, you know? But it was all one-sided. By the time she decided to say no to Rich Richards, I'd already written her off." Millie took a deep breath, held it, and then released it as an explosive sigh. "I honestly never thought she'd ruin all the rest of us with a smile on her face, but she did it."

"We ran into Toby outside Warren's," Tori announced. Apparently she was incapable of letting Jem's fact-finding mission proceed without trying to get her share. "He felt the same way about Gina. I said there could be a silver lining to her death. The sale might be on again, depending on who Gina left the shop to."

Millie nodded as if she'd already considered that. "We reckon it's Eddie. But who knows? They were quits. It would've been like Gina to will her place to someone else with the stipulation that they never, ever sell it in the next fifty years, just to be sure the row is never renovated."

"Was she that spiteful?" Tori asked.

The boho princess suddenly realized she was veering dangerously out of her friendly workplace character. "Oh, no, never mind me. I can't stand here speaking ill of the dead. It's sure to be bad for my aura, and I just got my karma cleansed. Would you like to try on that dress, love?"

"She would," Jem said firmly, giving Tori a stern look that said, *Go to the dressing room and keep still till I finish this interview.*

"So," she said to Millie as Tori disappeared inside the curtained alcove that served as Age of Aquarius's dressing room, "you reckon Eddie's going to inherit? You've already discussed it? You and the rest of the shop owners on the row, I mean?"

But Millie's willingness to discuss the matter had dried up with the word spiteful. "Seriously. I light a candle every night to banish negativity. If I keep gossiping about Gina, I'll have to burn a case of them. Now about the scarves—do you want both, or just the black organza?"

Still mindful of her budget, Jem bought only the black organza. When she and Tori were back on the lane in the bright noon sunshine, Tori said, "Sorry about that. Maybe someday I'll learn to shut it."

"Quit torturing yourself. Millie told us quite a bit. Just don't break in if you see I'm getting somewhere. Let's try New Day Electronics Repair."

They did, but it was a total bust. After Toby, who'd filled in the details about the lost real estate deal, and Millie, who'd not only confirmed it but also identified the likely owner of that teacups and orange blossoms scarf, Jem's appetite had been whetted for much more. Instead, the electronics shop owner, Krish, was cool to the point of rudeness, and every subsequent interview was a dud.

"I can't believe things went cold so quick," said Tori, who seemed to have jumped head first into amateur sleuthing. Jem wasn't surprised; she'd seen a similar reaction from Pauley. In the age of true-crime TV and addictive podcasts, it was easy to get wrapped up in real-life murders.

"Did you notice how Krish put down his mobile, quick, as we walked in the shop?" Jem asked. "Notice how he didn't even try to make a sale? Just went right on dusting like we didn't exist?"

"Oh. Yeah. The guy in the jewelry place did the same. I figured he was just more interested in whoever he was texting than us."

"I wouldn't be surprised if Krish was texting Millie. Same with Mr. Jewelry," Jem said.

Tori turned to regard Jem with fresh respect. "I'll bet you're right. They're thick as thieves, aren't they? Think Gina's murder will turn out to be like *Murder on the Orient Express*?"

"What, meaning they all did it?" Jem laughed. "Pretty sure that's just in books."

"It's a movie," Tori corrected her wisely. Before Jem could launch into an extemporaneous speech on the classic novels of Agatha Christie, her mobile chimed. It was Rhys.

17

"HE LOOKED IN A MIRROR ONE DAY AND SAW AN EEJIT LOOKING BACK"

"Hiya," Jem said, moving into the space between New Day Electronics and The Siren and steering Tori with her so she could talk without obstructing foot traffic. There were plenty of potential customers out and about, but most of them seemed to be eating or window-shopping rather than buying.

"Hiya, Jemmie. You pulling a Sunday at the Courtney, or working the case already?"

"Oh, wow, the Courtney." She'd managed to put her first day back to work completely out of her mind. "Nope, this is amateur hour. Me poking my nose where it doesn't belong."

"Not according to *Bright Star*. Ten people emailed me the link. In the Scilly group, it's been reposted a dozen times. You're famous."

"Lucky me. What about you? Decide to release Kenzie from the sack?"

"She said she hates me and ran home to Lissa. I don't get it. She knows I started drinking in my teens, and she watched me hit rock bottom. I might never have quit if she hadn't begged me to stop. And now she wants to go out and get pissed on Saturday nights when she's not even of age?"

"Don't look for it to make sense. It won't," Jem said.

Tori had leaned in close enough to listen in. Elbowing her sister aside, Jem continued, "I might not be a mum, but I vividly remember being Kenzie's age. She probably wants to fit in with her mates. If they drink cider, she wants to drink cider."

"I reckon. Or maybe she's goading me. Like she expects me to say, 'I'm your father and I'm putting my foot down.'"

"No kid wants to hear that."

"She does. Lissa and I left it too long. When we tell her the whole truth, she'll be crushed."

"Well. Maybe. But we'll all be there to help her through it. And you never know, Rhys. She may like you better as a big brother." Aware that Tori was still eavesdropping, Jem said, "I'd better let you go. I'm working my way along the row, meeting all the people who disliked Gina. When I'm done, there's a real estate place called Livingston's I need to check out."

"Today? They're sure to be closed. And you never said where you were."

"By Silversmith Bay. Just came out of New Day Electronics. Planning to try The Siren. The owner's a bit of a pill, but maybe I can pry something out of him."

"All right. Good luck. Don't do anything stupid."

Jem laughed. "What a lovely sign-off. Bye! Don't do anything stupid," she said gaily, and disconnected.

"Who was that?" Tori wore an expression of smug interest that reminded Jem of Wotsit.

"No one."

"You sort of glowed when you heard his voice. It was gross."

"You have the nerve to say that? After the way you simpered around Josh?"

"Hah! So, who is he? A policeman? DS Conrad hinted that you were seeing a copper."

"He's not a copper. He's someone I knew before. That I've known forever."

Tori waited. When Jem didn't continue, she said, "Fine. I *will* find out. You're not the only Jago who can crack a mystery."

From the other side of the lane a voice carried clearly out of the alley: "You bastard! You're killing me!"

That got them moving. Darting through the gap between New Day and the gastropub, Jem and Tori burst into the long alley behind Silversmith Lane. There, a small white delivery truck was wedged in the narrow space between The Siren's back door and the fateful wheelie bin that once concealed a bloody mallet. Josh's uncle Jerry stood with his fists balled on his hips, feet planted wide and face bright red. He looked ready to scream, cry, or both. Facing off with him stood a fat man in striped overalls with a cigar clamped between his teeth. If he was the person who'd just been shouted at, the expletive seemed to have bounced off him.

"Is everything all right?" Jem asked, feeling slightly foolish.

The man in striped overalls removed his cigar, blew out a plume of smoke, and grinned at her. "Sure and it is," he said in a soft Irish accent. "This dryshite's just unhappy because he looked in the mirror one day and saw an eejit looking back."

"A Saturday delivery on Sunday is useless," Jerry exploded, waving his fists in the air. "Worse than useless. It's bleeding sabotage, that's what it is!"

The man in overalls puffed his cigar. "If you don't want it, just say so."

"Of course I don't want it!"

"Mind you, the delivery fee is non-refundable."

Jerry shuddered as if literally restraining himself from attacking the man. "If you charge me... for a late delivery... of what was to be my Saturday-night special..." he said, pausing for breath at intervals, "I will see you in court."

The man in overalls removed his cigar, studied it, and then turned to Jem and Tori. "I don't suppose I can interest you ladies in fifteen Angus fillets, twenty top-quality white baking potatoes, two large caramel cheesecakes and a complimentary vat of ranch dressing?"

Jem shook her head. She was careful not to smile at his cheerful insouciance, and hoped Tori would show no amusement either. She wanted Jerry to feel like they were on his side, or he might refuse to speak to them.

The man in overalls wasn't crushed by their refusal. "Alas," he said lightly. Popping his cigar back in his mouth, he climbed back into the little white delivery truck, threw it into reverse, and backed out of the alley.

"These people are killing me!" Jerry shouted at the cloudless blue sky. As if itching to take out his rage on something, he glanced around The Siren's service area and rounded on some empty crates. With an incoherent yell, he kicked them, yelped in pain, stumbled, and sat down hard on the steps leading up to the gastropub's back door.

"I'm so sorry to intrude," Jem said, venturing forward. "I don't suppose you remember me from yesterday?"

Jerry looked up, still red-faced, eyes shining. He *was* on the verge of tears, she realized. "Lady, I don't remember an hour ago. It's a minute-to-minute struggle." Passing a hand over his eyes, he looked from her to Tori and said, "If you've come back here to gawp at the crime scene, it's still taped off. I've rung the police twice to scare off lookie-loos and I'll do it again. Don't test me."

"No," Jem said, "we certainly didn't come to stare at the place where Gina died."

That brought him up short. "You knew Gina?"

"Only by proxy. Last night I was supposed to meet her. A friend called Micki Latham brought me to Tatteredly's—"

"Latham? Is she kin to Eddie? I know there's a bloody billion Lathams..."

"Yeah. His sister," Jem said. "Anyway, believe it or not,

Micki and I discovered the body. Such an awful shock. I can't imagine who would have done such a thing."

Jerry rose heavily to his feet. "Come to think of it, maybe I do remember you. Did you eat here last night? With a tall bird, lots of curly hair, rushing you to get on?"

Jem nodded. "When we mentioned Tatteredly's, I thought you were going to say something. Then you sort of clammed up."

He nodded.

"Or maybe you said something..." Jem suggested, watching his face.

He shrugged.

"Something like 'I wouldn't be caught dead in there.' Kind of ironic, considering."

Jerry shrugged. "If you must know, I was going to say the place was closed. That it hadn't been open all day. Then I thought, it's none of my affair. She never gave a damn about us. Why should I warn off customers? Maybe if you went and found it locked up, you'd be so disappointed you'd never come back, and that would serve her right."

Tori said, "We're getting the impression folks didn't like her very much."

Jem could've kicked her. Jerry had seemed on the verge of speaking freely, like a person desperate to unload to any semi-sympathetic ear. Tori's remark—maybe ham-fisted strategy, maybe just a way of putting her oar in—stopped him short and put his guard up.

"Nothing but good of the dead, that's my motto," he announced, dusting himself off. "Right. That's enough of me taking the air. Time to get back to it."

"Could I ask you just one thing?" Jem asked in a hopeful tone.

He looked at her sidelong, clearly on his guard.

"The last time you saw Gina—when was it? What was she

like? Did she have reason to be afraid of anyone? A boyfriend, or a customer, or maybe a former friend? Like Natalie Lansallos?"

He groaned. "Don't bring that one up."

"You're related, aren't you? You're Josh's uncle and she's his aunt."

"By marriage. She's my sister-in-law. My name's Berry. Jerry Berry. People who hear my name smile and say I must be a jolly bloke. Do I look jolly?"

Jem wasn't sure what answer he was hoping for, so she pressed on. "I met Natalie, early this morning. She really despised Gina after that surprise clean-out at her place."

"That's Nat, isn't it? Someone does her a good turn and she's furious for months. I wonder if she's sorry she didn't try and make up sooner, now that Gina's gone."

"Oh. So Natalie was trying to patch up their friendship?"

"Sure. That's what she said. She took our side on the sale because she's crazy, but she's not that crazy, and thought maybe she could be peacemaker. Nothing came of it, of course."

Jem tucked that item aside for future consideration. "And Gina's new boyfriend? What was he like?"

"How would I know? She was coy about it. Whoever he was, I imagine he was squarely under her thumb. Some sad little bugger to jump when she said jump. That's why she tossed Eddie out—he wasn't snapping to attention anymore." Jerry's tone became more than a touch personal. "You'd think a woman would prefer a man, a respectable, responsible man, but there's no accounting for taste."

"Are you sure you don't know his name?" Tori asked baldly, putting her oar in again, and Jerry suddenly seemed to realize he'd been chatting in some depth with a pair of strangers. Before he could decide whether or not to answer, The Siren's back door swung open, nearly smacking him in the rear. Out peered Josh, who said, "Uncle," before spying Tori and goggling at her.

"Tors!"

"Hey, babe." She spoke as if they'd been an item for ages.

"Why aren't you covering the front?" Jerry demanded.

"I am. I need you on the grill," Josh retorted. "Where'd the truck go?"

"Back to the place that spawned it. Hell, I shouldn't wonder. How do you know these ladies?"

"Oh. Well. That's my— Tori," Josh said, as if not quite sure he could say "girlfriend" but unwilling to settle for much less. It was adorable—and frustrating, since the interruption came just at the wrong moment—but still adorable. "And that's her big sister, Jem Jago." Perhaps more instinctively discreet than Tori, Josh refrained from saying they'd spent the wee hours standing on produce crates outside his aunt's bedroom window.

"Please come back on the grill, Uncle Jerry," Josh said. "Before we lose what little lunch crowd we've got."

"Heaven forfend," Jerry muttered.

Josh had time to give Tori a searching lovelorn look, the sort of Romeo and Juliet stare that needed rose petals and a full orchestra. Then Jerry Berry waved a mute goodbye and disappeared inside The Siren, shutting the back door in their faces.

"I'm going to marry that man," Tori said dreamily.

"You nauseating fetus."

"Now, now. Don't talk to your little sister that way. This is her, isn't it?" asked Pauley Gwyn, who'd entered the alley at some point during the exchange with Jerry. Beside her was Rhys Tremayne and Micki Latham, looking miserable.

"Surprise!" Pauley said.

18

A PARK, A PYRO, AND A PERSON OF INTEREST

Pauley Gwyn really was a perky goth, from her dark magenta smile to her black lace parasol. That day she wore a black lace top, a ruffled black skirt, black leggings, and chunky black heels. All that inky darkness complimented Pauley's alabaster skin and purple-red hair. Though she wore no skulls, pink or otherwise, she was anything but emo. Beaming at Tori, she said, "Seriously, Jemmie, introduce us."

Jem turned to her sister, who was gazing at Rhys as if suddenly granted sight after years of blindness. It was a common reaction to her tall, blond, handsome old flame, currently in the best shape of his life. If Tori even knew Pauley and Micki were present, she gave no sign.

"Tors, hon, close your mouth. Didn't you just vow to marry Josh? Everybody, this is my little sis, Victoria Jago, aka Tori. Tori, this is everybody—Pauley Gwyn, Rhys Tremayne, and Micki Latham." Saying her name meant fully acknowledging the other woman before her. When she met Micki's gaze, the other woman began nervously, "I know you don't want to see me, but—"

The rest was lost as Jem threw her arms around Micki,

hugging her tight. For the first second or two it was awkward—Jem wasn't a hugger and Micki stiffened as if she were under attack—but then they both relaxed into it. By the time they broke apart, Micki was smiling and Tori, Pauley, and Rhys were chuckling.

"I'm sorry I walked out on you," Jem said. "I... I flashed back to the old me for a second. I'll try not to let it happen again, okay?"

"It was my fault. I don't know why—"

"This is off to a great start, but the reek of those bins is heinous," Pauley announced. "Let's take a walk. How about Morrab Gardens?" Pauley made it sound more like a directive than a suggestion.

"It's a bit of a walk," Jem said, wondering if they shouldn't all go into The Siren for a pint and try to get more out of Jerry Berry in the process.

"It's five minutes. Besides, there's a method to my madness," Pauley said. "You'll see."

Jem knew Morrab Gardens well. When she first came to Penzance to live with Kenneth, Wendy, Tori, and Dave, the Morrab Library had been her refuge. The walled garden, which dated from the 1840s, was a green haven of subtropical trees and shrubs, with a smattering of late flowers still blooming here and there. On such a lovely Sunday, it was no surprise to find plenty of locals enjoying the park, some reclining in deck chairs, others picnicking on blankets spread over the lawn. Perhaps because the day was mild, no one had claimed the large covered bandstand.

"Perfect!" Pauley cried, twirling her parasol in delight. "Let's talk in there."

Inside the bandstand it was cool and breezy, with no chairs or benches. Rhys, who was six foot four, chose to sit on the steps, giving him room to stretch out his legs. Pauley showed off her yoga-earned flexibility by gracefully easing into a cross-legged position on the bandstand's cement floor. Tori plopped down beside her and Jem chose to lean against the octagonal stage's wrought-iron railing. Looking far better than she had when she first appeared in the alley, Micki joined her.

"Seriously, Mick, how are you? Finding Gina was such a shock, even to me, and I didn't even know her. How are you holding up?" Jem asked.

"I'm all right. I don't know if I've really processed it yet, I've been so worried about Eddie. But first," Micki said determinedly, as if her need to explain her harsh words was a physical pain she was desperate to relieve, "I want to show you something. It's not an excuse. It's... it's something I tried to keep secret, but now I know I have to come clean. I thought confiding in Clarence would be enough," she added, referring to her cousin on St. Morwenna. "But obviously I needed to tell you guys, too."

Withdrawing a folded sheet of paper from her bag, she handed it to Jem. It was a short article that had been printed off a local website called *All Things Penzance*. At the top was a small black-and-white photo of the Minack Theater, one of the West Country's best-known landmarks. A spectacular open-air theater that harkened back to the dramas of Greek antiquity—though it had actually been constructed in the 1920s—it was a hugely popular venue for plays, TV programs, movies, and concerts.

Jem read,

Tommy and the Knockers at Minack a Complete Collapse

By Lemmy Beaglehole, *All Things Penzance* Associate Editor

September 17th

Porthcurno

Don't knock it until you try it, they say. Well, I tried Tommy and the Knockers, the Cornish folk band, and I wish an obliging ghost had rapped on the walls to warn me away. This critic wasn't the only music lover to go away feeling cheated. The gig was half an hour shorter than promised, beset by sound issues, lighted so poorly the band was in shadows, and featured the inauspicious debut of their "songbird," Micki Latham. Tommy and the Knockers is a six-man band, but Ms. Latham, their guest for the evening, drew the brunt of the unhappy crowd's ire.

Tommy and the Knockers' front man, Monty Clarke, is something of a folk virtuoso, at least according to his résumé. He plays guitar, banjo, fiddle, and mandolin, and sings in an acceptable light baritone. However, with an amplifier on the blink and some sort of wiring problem, Mr. Clarke frequently had to make do with mere acoustic guitar. Though the magnificent Minack has famous natural amplification, modern audiences don't like to strain their ears, especially not for a listless rendition of "Black and Gold."

The show, twenty-eight minutes late in starting and never made up, limped along to the midpoint, when Ms. Latham appeared. It is perhaps fortunate that she is an attractive woman, and wasn't too ridiculous in the sort of dripping chiffon number that should be worn by no one but Stevie Nicks. Midway through her set, during an obscure ballad arranged for minor key, she attempted a high note. If only the failing sound system had gone on the blink just then! The way her voice cracked was mortifying. Naturally, the audience had a good laugh. Ms. Latham stopped singing, tried to begin again, croaked out another sour note and fled the stage. Monty Clarke and his band carried on bravely till the end, it must be said, but by then the crowd was down to a third of what it had

been. A sorry night at the old Minack, knocked for six by a
strictly amateur band.

Jem's eyes stung by the time she reached the end. Generally she wasn't much of a crier, but the review's brutality wounded her for Micki's sake. Only recently had Micki expressed her desire to sing before live audiences. Her voice was sweet and true—a once-in-a-blue-moon cracked note notwithstanding—and she was gifted with wonderful timing and sensitivity, qualities that probably could not be taught. The only reason Micki worked as a bartender instead of a full-time singer was her crippling stage fright. Even a highly successful gig could drain her emotional energy and stir up her deepest fears. With this vicious review secretly weighing on her, it was no wonder she'd snapped.

She didn't know what to say, but fortunately Pauley came to her rescue. "Beaglehole, eh? His name gets it half right. What a tosser! That site's only good for a laugh. All the reviews are rubbish."

"Take it from me," Rhys said, "the guy's a failed musician. People who fail at a profession always turn around and write poison-pen reviews. You wouldn't believe the crap I get over my sunsets." He shook his head. "Nasty anonymous comments from people who probably have fifty unsold paintings tucked in a crawlspace."

Micki nodded, trying hard to look as if she agreed, but Jem could see that nothing was penetrating. Lemmy Beaglehole's diatribe had confirmed all her worst fears. She'd taken his words and engraved them upon her heart.

"Mick, I could've looked this rot up on my mobile. Why are you carrying around a printed copy?"

"Ah, see, Micki my love," Pauley said. "Didn't I ask you the very same question?"

"I know why," Rhys said, rising from the steps to come and

meet Micki's gaze. "It's your talisman now. A negative talisman. Proof you got hurt and you deserve it. I don't know why creative people do things like this, but we do."

Pauley regarded Rhys with frank amazement. "Do you realize that actually made sense? You said something wise."

His reply would've been unfit for print, even for Lemmy Beaglehole.

"Oh, take the compliment." Pauley turned back to Micki. "You know what? I've done it, too. Years ago, I broke up with my first boyfriend, Kevin Weymouth. He was crushed, and I felt terrible about it. For Valentine's he'd given me a locket—a tacky brass thing that might've come from a vending machine. For a whole year I made myself wear it as punishment for being mean."

"Kevin Weymouth? You were moping over that wormy little zero?" Rhys frowned. "You should've said. I would've had a quiet word with him."

Pauley rolled her eyes. "I just said it was my fault. Besides, every guy who ever looked my way was already scared shitless of you. If I'd sicced you on Kevin, I couldn't have bought another date."

"I have a negative talisman, too," Jem admitted. Pulling off her trainer and sock, she showed Micki the scar, pink and raised, on her right ankle. Pauley and Tori had seen it, of course, but Rhys gaped at it, surprised.

"How'd you do that?" he asked, bending down for a closer look.

"A souvenir from back in the day. You know. The accident."

"Oh. Wow. The doctors did a lousy job, eh?"

"No. They dressed the wound and told me to follow up. Only I didn't. After Gran died and I came to live in Penzance, I hid it from everyone."

"I remember that," Tori said. "You were limping for a month. It must've hurt all the time."

"It did. That was what I wanted," Jem said. "And you see what good it did," she added, looking meaningfully at Micki. "It was pointless, and self-destructive. I was wallowing in pain instead of processing it."

"I guess so. We've looked at this long enough," Micki said, folding the paper as if to put it away.

"Nope. Give it to me," Rhys said firmly.

Wide-eyed, Micki handed it over. "Why? What are you going to do?"

"What you should've done, but can't. I'm going to vaporize it." Reaching in the pocket of his jeans, he pulled out a cigarette lighter.

"You smoke?" Jem asked.

"No, I paint. This is for heating up the oils when they dry out and get sludgy. I also use it for things like this." Holding the poison-pen review by one corner like he might lift a dead rat by the tail, he flicked the lighter and set it alight.

"Hey!" Micki cried.

"Oi! Don't be a pyro, mate!" someone yelled from the lawn.

Leaping to her feet, Pauley shifted automatically into caretaker mode. "You drop that this minute! Stamp it out!"

Grinning, Rhys danced away from her, into the center of the bandstand, still holding the paper as yellow flame ate it from the bottom corner up. Jem had to admit there was something cathartic in watching the cruel words turn black, curl up, and crumble into nothing. When the flame touched his fingers, Rhys dropped the last flaming bit, grinding it under his shoe until it was nothing but a black smear.

"I should call the authorities. It's an offense to set fire in a public place," said a stern-faced mum with a baby on her hip. She'd walked all the way to the bandstand to deliver this warning to Rhys, who responded by giving her a dazzling smile.

"You're right. I'm sorry. I got carried away supporting a

friend." He slid the lighter back in his jeans pocket. "No more hot stuff, I promise."

"Oh. Well. See that you don't. But no harm done," the mum said, no longer stern. Nervously pushing a strand of hair away from her face, she smiled at Rhys, lingering a few seconds before turning away.

"You man-whore," Pauley muttered.

He shrugged. "It's a gift. So, Micki—how do you feel?"

"Much better," she said, and burst into hard, racking sobs.

"It'll be okay," Jem said, wrapping her arms around her yet again. "Everything's okay."

"I shouldn't have taken it out on you," Micki gasped when she was able to speak again. "Clarence says I always do this, and he's right! I try too hard to keep everything on an even keel. To smile no matter what. To never let them see me sweat. But I can't keep it up. The pressure builds and builds until I explode. I'm famous for it. You pushed me to sign up for all those concert dates with Monty's band. It was my choice really, but I told myself the disaster at the Minack wouldn't have happened if you hadn't encouraged me. Then when we found Gina dead, and it turned out the weapon was somehow in your flat, I... I..."

"Needed someone to blame," Jem finished for her. "I get it. Until now, I reckoned you were more evolved than us," she said, gesturing to include Pauley, Rhys, and Tori. "We shout, cry, storm off, and do it all over again, day after day. Now I see you're different. You save it up till you melt down."

Micki nodded. "Yeah. I'm so glad you understand. And now I need your help. With my brother Eddie, I mean."

"You mean, he wants me to find out who killed Gina?"

"Yeah. Or just prove to the police that he didn't," Micki said. "Gina has only been gone for a day and they're already hounding poor Eddie. They said straight up that he's a person of interest. It's because of our name," she added fiercely. "We're Lathams, and the authorities blame us for everything!"

19

THE ROADMAN

"Didn't I tell you there was a method to my madness?" Pauley asked, leading the group out of the park by way of a narrow side street. "That's why I picked Morrab for a place to talk. Eddie's nearby."

"Is he?" Jem glanced around their surroundings, impressed. This area was a gorgeous mix of new-build townhouses and old stone cottages. The lane Pauley now led them down was bracketed by six-foot stone walls with green vines and leafy trees swaying just above. Here and there, a wooden door in the wall marked the entrance to a back garden, looking secretive and romantic, like the hidden gateway to another world.

"He's staying with a friend," Micki explained. "Renting a furnished bedsit until he can find something permanent. Gina tossed him out almost a year ago, and he's been on the back foot ever since. Is that number fourteen? No, it's that one," she said, indicating one of the wooden doors. "I'll just ring him to let us in."

When Jem had pictured Micki's brother she'd imagined a male version of her friend—slim and tall, with dark skin, striking features, and a cloud of curly hair. The Eddie Latham who opened the garden door to admit them was none of those things. But he was certainly one thing: a roadman. Dressed in a black Nike wind runner with the hoodie up, he wore a coordinating Nike bum bag and black Nike trainers bearing the silver swoosh. Around his neck hung a thick gold chain, both ears bore flashy studs that Jem thought must be CZs, and his wristwatch was more crystal than metal.

"Hiya, darling," he said to Micki, going straight in for a hug. He barely came up to her shoulder, his light brown face buried somewhere against her chest. A sob seemed to escape him as he gripped her tight, but when he pulled back to look up at his sister, Jem saw only freckles dotting his cheeks. No tears. Maybe he was more of a verbal crier. Or maybe, like Nutty Natty, he was just pretending.

"You look like you're dealing," Micki said disapprovingly, flicking his hoodie back to reveal close-cut reddish hair. "Please tell me you're not back in the biz."

"Nah, girl, that's ancient history. I'm legit. I still do odd plumbing jobs around the bay, but it's hard when you're not qualified. I also have an eBay store now, very up-and-up. Clean as a whistle," Eddie said, looking over the group as he spoke. His hazel eyes widened as they landed on Rhys. "Copper," he declared, pointing a finger.

"Artist," Rhys countered, pointing a finger at himself. "Rhys Tremayne. Dragged along by these ladies for moral support."

"Big bloke like you? I reckoned you're their bodyguard. To protect these delicate flowers from a murderer like me."

"Eddie, don't joke about it. I can promise you the police won't," Micki said. "This is Jem Jago, the one I told you about."

"Hiya, Jem." Eddie shook her hand—too firm, too fast, and accompanied by a stare that was much too intense. He seemed to be intent on winning her over as quickly as possible, which always struck Jem as the mark of a conman.

"I'm very sorry for your loss," she said, reminding herself

not to prejudge him before she even got through the door. "Can we come in and talk to you about Gina?"

"Sure. I'm afraid I don't have much room. I didn't expect so many people."

"We'll make it work. This is Pauley," Jem said, deciding to make the rest of the introductions. "She's my—"

"Special assistant," Pauley cut in, shaking Eddie's hand.

"And this is Tori, my—"

"Mentee," Tori supplied, offering her hand as well. "Jem's having so much success she's taking on assistants."

"I for one soon hope to be paid," Rhys said, and the five of them followed the roadman through the paved back garden. It was full of potted plants, mostly hardy exotics: agaves and aloes, myrtles and magnolias.

"This is lovely, Eddie." Micki sounded nakedly suspicious. "How much longer can you stay?"

"Oh, I was meant to be out yesterday, as a matter of fact," Eddie said as he led them into the house. "But, of course, when Colin heard the awful news about Gina, he gave me another extension. Now I hope to be gone a week from tomorrow. I've worn out my welcome."

"That you have," called a voice from another room where a television was playing low. "What's with the stampede?"

"It's only my sister and her friends. We're going upstairs to talk about Gina. The funeral, and so on," Eddie said.

"I'm having someone over at five o'clock. See that your lot clears out well before then."

"No worries!"

"Eddie. I mean it," said the voice, presumably Colin, with what sounded like exaggerated patience.

Eddie flashed a grin at Micki, Jem, and the others. "I do understand, Colin, I promise. Thanks, mate. You're the best."

That was met with a snort. The volume on the TV shot up, indicating the exchange was over.

"He's a lovely bloke, our Colin," Eddie said as he led them up the narrow carpeted stairs. "A lifesaver when I needed him. Someday I'll repay him. One day my ship will come in, and all will be made right."

Jem looked sidelong at Micki. Judging by the other woman's expression, she'd heard her brother make such declarations thousands of times, to the point where it had become so much noise.

Eddie's bedsit was nice enough for a single man, though spartan to the point of coldness. There was a futon, a coffee table, a laptop that apparently doubled as a TV, an electric kettle, a mattress on the floor covered by a cheap duvet, and one of those rolling garment racks used in retail. It was loaded down with the bulk of Eddie's earthly possessions—more matching black tracksuits, chiefly, plus some odds and ends that could be mixed to make a couple of dodgy suits.

"Hard times," Eddie announced, grinning again. "When Gina chucked me out I said it's all right, I'm not bothered. I'll be back in her loving arms again soon. Can't keep a good man down. And, as you see, I didn't try to make this place a home, didn't burden myself with highboys and lowboys and all that rot, all the stuff Gina kept that would soon be mine again. I said to myself, Eddie lad, live simply, do your time in the wilderness, let her feel the pinch of loneliness. That's how it works, yes? Absence makes the heart grow fonder?"

Jem resisted the temptation to say, "Out of sight, out of mind." Eddie was a remarkably fast talker, gaze roaming from face to face, hands waving and always grinning, or at least showing plenty of teeth. He seemed to pepper his statements with stock phrases and clichés to give the impression of easy sincerity, but she suspected the fillers were there for another reason—to give him a beat to ascertain whether his audience was still with him. Definite conman.

"Anyway, sit, sit, listen to me run on. Some people weep

when they grieve. Others go silent. I talk. Talk, talk, talk," he said, still grinning, as he snapped the laptop shut and put it aside. "I'm sorry there aren't any chairs..."

"No problem. The floor will do for most of us," Pauley said, sitting down on the carpet to prove it. Tori, Rhys, and Micki followed her lead, which left the futon for Eddie and Jem.

Wishing she was equipped for taking notes, Jem hoped four extra pairs of ears would retain any details she missed. It was rare to have a second willing interviewee in one day—usually she gleaned information by misrepresenting herself, as she had with Millie at Age of Aquarius. It was almost daunting to have Eddie's freckled face and widely spaced hazel eyes looking back at her, waiting for her to fire away.

Jem said, "First, let's talk about you and Gina. When was your divorce finalized?"

"It wasn't."

"Oh. So it was still being hammered out?"

"Gina and her lawyer handled that," Eddie said, waving a hand. "Not me. No thank you."

"Eddie," Micki groaned.

"I didn't want the divorce, so why should I participate in it? When I promised to love her and stay with her for life, I meant it. I swore it before God, and I take my vows seriously," Eddie said with conspicuous virtue. "Like I told you when this whole thing started, I wouldn't set foot in court except in leg irons, and I wouldn't sign one bloody piece of paper. I kept to that."

"I didn't realize you could opt out of your own divorce," Pauley said.

"You can't," Micki said quickly, probably to head off Eddie's next avalanche of words. "You can be obstructive and intransigent. Isn't that what the judge called it, intransigent? But you can't just refuse to recognize a lawful petition."

Eddie shrugged.

"So you really did it. You dragged your feet for so long, you ran out the clock." Micki shook her head in disbelief.

"That's right. I'm legally her widower. As I should be. I'm devastated." He gestured to himself, as if anyone could see how racked by grief he was.

Micki looked away.

Jem asked, "When was the last time you spoke to Gina, face to face?"

"Last week. I came by Tatteredly's during shop hours. It was the only way I could see her."

"Were you welcome there?"

He grinned. "You tell me. Gina said I wasn't to come in, that it was her shop and I was barred, but she never gave me written notice or served an order of trespass. So it was all part of the dance. I made a move, she made a move. She said, don't come to my place or I won't open the door. I said, fine, I'll see you at Tatteredly's. And I did. She never rang the police. Mind you, I was never anything but polite and appropriate, so even if she had complained, they couldn't have touched me."

"Eddie, you sound like a stalker," Micki said.

"And you sound like a certain detective sergeant. Scary bloke with a face like a slab of clay. He came right out and accused me of doing Gina in. Me!" His eyes roved from face to face, still reading the room, checking to see if his audience was with him. "Me, who loved her the most, he accused of killing her. Me, who would've done anything for her."

"Except give her a divorce?" Rhys suggested.

"He speaks!" Eddie looked amused. "You ever been in love, mate?"

"Love my dog."

"It's not the same. When you love a woman you can never let go."

"So even if the divorce had gone through, you wouldn't have

let go?" Jem asked. "Would you have rather seen her dead than with another man?"

He looked shocked. "Of course not. Where there's life, there's hope. I would've worn her down. But some sick, evil, cruel person took her away."

Jem wasn't sure if she believed him or not, so she pressed on. "How long were you married to Gina?"

"Six years."

"You were her second husband, right?"

He nodded.

"What happened with the previous marriage? She was widowed, correct? And there was a legacy or settlement?"

"A settlement. The bloke died under strange circumstances. Somebody messed up." For the first time since they'd begun talking, Eddie folded his arms and looked uncomfortable.

"Somebody messed up how?"

"I don't know. He worked with dangerous chemicals. Even though he died at home—fell over dead at breakfast—Gina said he must've been exposed in the workplace. She got a solicitor and won a big judgment."

"Do you know his name?"

Eddie thought about it. "Richard something. Or something Richards."

"Like the real estate guy?" Tori asked a split second before Jem could. Little sis was getting her oar in again.

Eddie paused to consider. "Yeah. No. Maybe that's who I was thinking of. Sorry."

"Speaking of Rich Richards, I've heard a lot about the real estate proposal. Buying up all the shops from Tatteredly's to The Siren," Jem said. "Gina was dead against that, wasn't she?"

Eddie nodded. "She loved the shop. It was all she ever wanted. She told the others they could sell with her blessing, but her plot was the most valuable, because of how it overlooked the bay. She knew the deal couldn't happen if she said no."

"Did you get involved at all? Offer an opinion?"

"Of course." Eddie goggled at her as if it were a trick question. "Gina always had plenty of money, but selling out would've taken us to the next level. No more iced-out watches for Eddie," he said, holding up his wrist to show off the CZ-laden piece. "We would've rolled in diamonds and pearls. Like my man Prince sang, God rest his soul."

"I'll go way out on a limb and say Gina didn't care for your opinion on the matter?" Micki asked archly.

"She didn't. Not that you or anyone else in my family lifted a finger to make her see sense," Eddie retorted, his words sharper than his tone, which was still amiable. To Jem, he added, "My own family was on Gina's side one hundred percent. Would've traded me in for her in a London minute."

Micki didn't deny it, though the look she gave Eddie was very much that of a big sister, fond and exasperated all at the same time.

"When you say Gina always had money—how much was she worth?"

"I couldn't say. Gina wasn't good with numbers, or details. I'm much keener on all that, but she wouldn't let me take control, even when we were first married," Eddie said, sounding as if the lack of trust still hurt. "I reckon she was worth half a million, easy. Maybe the full mil."

"Wow. So." It went against the grain for Jem to ask the next question, but if she wanted to be an investigator, she'd occasionally have to ask the cringiest questions. "Do you happen to know who inherits it all? Her house, her money, and Tatteredly's?"

Eddie grinned, then un-grinned, and seemed to be reaching deep inside himself for a very specific expression—reluctant gratitude, perhaps. "I can't say for sure, of course. But unless she had her will updated—I reckon it all comes to me. Including Tatteredly's."

"Will you sell out to Rich Richards, if the offer is still good?" Tori asked. Jem gave her a repressive stare, but Tori pretended not to notice.

"I might. A lot of people would be counting on me, wouldn't they?" Eddie said. "Gina was different. She loved the shop. All she ever wanted was to mess about with books all day long, and Tatteredly's let her do it. But now that she's gone— why not sell, if it will make so many people happy? And set me on my feet again," he added, as if his own bottom line was merely an afterthought.

"All right," Jem said. "Well. Now. This is awkward, but just so I can say I asked—where were you yesterday morning between four a.m. and seven a.m.?"

He pointed at his bed. "Just there. Asleep."

"Was Colin at home? Does he support your alibi?"

Eddie shrugged. "The police talked to him. He told them he was asleep in his own room and couldn't vouch for my whereabouts either way. It would've been aces for him to back me up. To say I must've been in bed, because he would have heard the back door creak open, or the neighbor's dog start to bark if I slipped into the garden, but of course Colin didn't think of helping me. He just said he was asleep and left it at that."

"Eddie. He's just supposed to tell the truth," Micki said.

"Listen at you! Cozy with the coppers, now that your friend solves murders?"

"No." Micki looked startled, as if he'd lobbed a particularly nasty insult. "I'm on your side, you know I am. But you shouldn't be surprised if Colin only said what he knew for sure and left it at that."

Eddie shook his head. "Never thought my big sis would side with the law. They'll take away your Latham card."

Jem wasn't sure what that was supposed to mean, but she could see Micki would've appreciated an interruption. Moreover, something Eddie said earlier had stood out, and she wanted to circle back.

"You said an evil, cruel, sick person took Gina away from you. Did you know of anyone, like a customer or a supplier, who had a grudge against her?"

"Well. Every shopkeeper on the row was cross with her, but I wouldn't think they'd get physical. Much less kill. I don't want to make accusations—especially to the law..."

"Just to me," Jem said. "I'm not in authority. I have no right to harass anyone or make life hard for them. But if you know of someone who might be mixed up in this, I can do a bit of legwork. See if it's worth tipping off the police."

"She has a friend. Used to have a friend," Eddie said with a sigh. "Her name is Natalie Lansallos..."

20

DEEP FRIED CRAB CLAWS AND WYATT THE WALRUS

For a late lunch they stopped by the Sea Palace. Loading up on several boxes of Chinese takeaway, they brought it back to Jem's flat, where they could eat and endlessly talk about murder without scandalizing an entire dining room. Rhys and Pauley ate in the kitchenette while Jem, Tori, and Micki occupied the sofa. The food, spread across the coffee table, was excellent, and Jem saw that Tori was eating with a vengeance, as if the morning's jam doughnuts and coffee had long burned away. Meanwhile, Micki had been picking at the same deep-fried crab claw for five minutes.

"He just seemed so *guilty*," she burst out, not for the first time.

"You said yourself Eddie would never hurt Gina," Jem replied, also not for the first time. "You told us he fell apart when he heard the news."

"I thought he did. Maybe he was having me on. Acting a part. He certainly seemed to have a spring in his step when we talked to him today, didn't he?" She shook her head. "I don't know, Jem. Maybe all this amateur sleuthing is making me paranoid. Twice now you've snagged a murderer who struck me as normal and innocent right up to the moment they ripped the mask off. Obviously I have no radar. What if I'm blind to Eddie? The whole time we were talking, I kept thinking, why is he smiling like that? Why doesn't he shed a tear, or choke up, or seem like he really gives a damn?"

"You can't go by demeanor," Jem said, putting aside her chow mein noodles. Delicious as they were, she couldn't eat another bite. "Not by demeanor alone, anyway. And right after a murder, most people are still in shock, whether they know it or not. Sometimes the screaming and crying comes later. It's different for everyone."

"Has Eddie always been a fast talker?" Rhys asked from the kitchenette.

"He could talk the bark off a tree," Micki said.

Pauley nodded. Unlike Micki, she'd made short work of her allotted crab claws and was finishing up some beef with cashew nuts. "A lot of it sounded like nerves to me. Wanting to be liked. Not wanting to seem guilty. As long as he has no history of violence, Micks, I don't see any reason to fret so much."

Sighing, Micki dropped her half-nibbled crab claw like she might never eat again.

Jem and Pauley exchanged glances. "What?"

"Right. Well. First, I've never talked about this, but I'd better tell you now," Micki began unhappily. "You know there are beaucoup Lathams in Cornwall and Devon. I mean, *lots*. But I've never told you about our reputation. Ask a copper or magistrate about us, and you know what they'll say? 'The Lathams? They're all alike, half of them look alike, and none of them can be trusted.' I've heard that song all my life. It boils down to this: in the eyes of the law, we're legion, and we're bad news.

"I'm not saying we're blameless," Micki added, sounding as if she'd rather discuss anything else. "I don't want to run anyone else down, but as far as I'm concerned, I've done plenty of stupid things and been held to account. You know—cutting school, trespassing, five-fingered discounts. But all that's behind me. Since I turned nineteen, I've been on the straight and narrow. Worked for everything I've got. But the fact is," she continued sadly, "there are plenty of inmates and parolees called Latham. In lots of places, you can't put that name on a job application without being shown the door. You know about that, don't you, Pauley?"

"A bit, since I went into business with Clarence," Pauley agreed. "At first I thought he was just unlucky. Then I realized being called Latham was bad for business."

"Yeah. One of the reasons I was drawn to you, Jem," Micki said, turning to her, "was because you'd been away for so long, you'd completely lost touch with the local gossip. If you check, you'll probably find a whole list of Lathams who are barred from every library in Cornwall."

"Why?" Tori asked.

"You name it. Fighting. Hooking up in bathrooms. Watching porn on the public computers, that sort of thing."

"I've heard rumors about the Lathams," Rhys volunteered. "But I had the impression there were two branches. The West Country Lathams, who own a chain of warehouses. And the, erm, other ones..."

"The St. Ives Lathams. *My* Lathams," Micki agreed. "Clarence is from the West Country branch. The most shocking thing he ever did was move to the Isles of Scilly and open a B&B that almost flopped. Clarence's people aren't used to failure. My people—it's a given."

"So for Eddie, a bad reputation comes as standard. But did you say violence?" Jem asked.

"Afraid so. Of course, you know, I have to defend him," Micki said. "Eddie's the baby of the family. It happened years ago, when Eds was barely out of school. He and his girl got into a fight. They both drew blood, and they both ended up serving a few weeks' time. She cut him with a steak knife—he needed twenty stitches. He tried to hit the knife out of her hand, and popped her in the face instead. Broke her nose."

Rhys gave a low whistle, shaking his head in disgust. Pauley and Tori, while not precisely thrilled by the story, seemed to take it better. Both of them appeared to believe that if you lunged at a man with a steak knife and drew blood, you might get smacked in the face. Rhys, who'd been over six feet tall since his fifteenth birthday and was bigger and stronger than most men, found the idea of breaking a woman's nose abhorrent.

"I know, I know, you're thinking he's a beast. But you've met Eddie. You saw he's not the most imposing man that ever walked the earth," Micki said. "Give me just a sec."

Micki brought out her mobile and started tapping. After what seemed like an eternity sorting through files and checking various social media accounts, she found what she was looking for. "Here's Eddie with the girl who got him sent down," she said, passing the phone to Jem.

It seemed that before Eddie Latham had been a roadman, he'd been very into Burberry camel check. In the photo, he wore a navy tracksuit, white trainers with Velcro fasteners, a thick gold chain, and a ballcap made of his favorite fabric. Attached to him was a very tall, broad-shouldered, athletic-looking young woman with a blonde ponytail. Spray-tanned to the brink of orange, she loomed over Eddie, squeezing him like a funfair teddy bear.

"Yes, he accidentally broke her nose," Micki said as Jem passed the mobile around so Tori, Rhys, and Pauley could see. "But as I said, he ended up with a scar and did seventeen weeks inside HMP Dartmoor, so he paid his debt. And he never raised a hand to a woman again. Certainly not Gina. But the coppers won't see it that way. They've already fixed on him as a person of interest. They'll look at how he behaved during the divorce, and his prior conviction, and decide he must be guilty."

"If you don't mind my asking," Pauley said, "why did Gina

want out of the marriage? Not to speak ill of the dead, but she didn't seem to have many friends. Eddie is the only person who was trying to stay in her life no matter what, and she threw him out."

"Well, I was her friend," Micki announced loyally. "I mean, I didn't know her as well as I know most of you, but when she came into Eddie's life, he went from living like a nomad to a beautiful house on Alverton Street. I never worried about him getting in trouble with the law while he was with her. And she donated hundreds of books to charity every year. She did *Alice*-themed parties for the neighborhood kiddies and sent every child home with a free book."

"So the *Alice* window at Tatteredly's wasn't a one-time thing?"

"No, she reverted back to it every few months," Micki said. "Remember when I corrected you about the story—that the Red Queen played croquet with flamingos? I knew because Gina used to have a mallet with a plastic yard flamingo stuck to it, so the kids could hold it and pretend to be Alice."

Jem's mind flashed back to the *Alice* window. It had been lovingly devised but for one discordant note—a pink plastic flamingo lying on its side.

"I'm pretty sure that was the murder weapon," Jem said. "Whoever killed her reached into the display, pulled off the flamingo, and hit Gina with the mallet. It probably wasn't premeditated. Someone just boiled over with rage, took the closest thing to hand, and attacked. I think I'll get my notebook and make a list of—"

"Hang on," Pauley said. "I'd love to stick around, but look at the time. Any of us who want to sleep at home on St. Morwenna need to get back to the docks. Kit Verran's ferry is due at five o'clock sharp, and he won't wait more than a couple of minutes."

"Kit Verran?" Jem asked. "His service is up and running?"

"Yes, and it's quite nice. Sun-shaded seats, piped-in music, and complimentary bottles of water."

"I loved it," Rhys said. "Bart the Ferryman's eating his heart out. He'd better step it up or Kit will get all his business."

"To be fair, we did try Bart first," Pauley said. "I meant it when I said where there's a Bart, there's a way. But he canceled on us because of a Wyatt the Walrus situation at St. Martin's. The big buffalo got into another boat and sank it. Lucky for the owner, it was empty at the time."

"But I thought Wyatt problems belonged to the RNLI and the divers' association and all that."

"The lifeboaters and divers have made an appeal to the public for assistance."

"Walrus?" Tori asked.

Pauley explained about the young male pinniped, nicknamed Wyatt, who'd started making appearances from Ireland to the Scillies to Wales and back again. In the beginning, tourists and locals had been delighted. A ham for the spotlight, Wyatt lolled on docks, begged for handouts near quays, and followed boats around. This was far outside a walrus's natural behavior—he belonged in Arctic waters—but young Wyatt was developing some very bad habits. His new penchant for climbing aboard small vessels, either for fun or in search of fish, was now wreaking havoc. Conservatively, he weighed a ton, and was still a growing boy. Worse, he'd become completely at home around people and boats. Property damage was bad enough, but if Wyatt kept this up, sooner or later someone could be hurt or killed.

"Anyway, the new strategy is to run off Wyatt with air horns," Pauley continued. "Bart rigged his boat with a new sound system. I reckon he wants to swoop in, blast that poor animal with a super-amplified air horn, and be the hero."

"Good grief. I hope he doesn't hurt Wyatt," Tori said. She'd gone from not knowing who or what he was to being staunchly on his side.

"Me, too," Pauley said. "Ordinarily I'd figure Wyatt is big enough to look after himself, but you know Bart. Anything for five minutes of fame. He'd better watch his step. Kit's a very attractive alternative."

Jem grinned at that. Kit Verran, a recent transplant to the Isles of Scilly, was just the sort of competition Bart needed. Like Bart, he owned his vessel outright, was a solo operator, and offered both a circuit of the islands and occasional jaunts to the mainland and back. Unlike Bart, his boat was clean and well maintained, and his service was smoothly professional. No doubt Bart, who suffered from an inflated view of his boat, his service, and his personal charms, really was eating his heart out.

"All right, if everyone has to go, I understand," Jem said. "My bed's a single and Tori's already got the sofa. But if anyone wants to save a few quid by sleeping on the floor, or maybe in the bathtub, you're more than welcome."

"I may be limber, but if I spend an entire night on the floor, I'll be in hospital by morning," Pauley said.

"I can stay," Micki said. "If you're helping Eddie, sleeping on the floor is the least I can do."

"There's no need, Micki. We can come back tomorrow. We've barely started the investigation," Pauley said. "What time should we be back here, Jem?"

"Wow." Tori looked impressed. "Don't any of you have to work?"

"I do," Jem cut in acidly. "I have to be at the Courtney by nine o'clock and put in at least a couple hours' face time. Especially if that *Bright Star* story has started making the rounds. Everyone will probably be buzzing about the murder. If I go AWOL, they'll know why, and my boss will be texting me all day long." Mr. Atherton was naturally suspicious of Jem's activities; he'd never forgiven her for briefly being arrested on suspicion of murder.

Micki told Tori, "I took a week off from the Kernow Arms to sulk over that bad review. Never thought I'd need the time to try and keep Eddie out of police custody, but there it is."

"As for me, I'm an entrepreneur, darling," Pauley told Tori, grinning to let her know she was mostly kidding. "What I really mean is, except for Clarence's B&B, I'm sort of between things at the moment. And I love snooping—I mean, sleuthing. Jem's a bad influence."

Tori looked at Rhys. "What about you?"

"Live off my looks."

"That's why I have to loan him money all the time," Pauley said, getting to her feet.

Because she was hardwired to be responsible and shone the most when other people needed help, Pauley refused to leave Jem's flat before she'd helped put away the leftovers. Then she gathered her things, texted Kit to tell him they were on the way, and motioned to Micki and Rhys. "Shall we get on?"

Rhys was still lounging in the kitchenette as he had been throughout her flurry of activity, chair turned away from the table and long legs stretched out in front of him. "I thought maybe I'd stick around to help Jem sort through the clues so far. All the rest of you have had a share in the investigations. I've always been on the sidelines—except when I was a prime suspect. And if Eddie's innocent, and DS Conrad's determined to fit him up the way he fitted me up, well... I'd enjoy tossing a spanner into the works."

"How do you know it's Conrad?" Pauley asked.

"You heard Eddie. A scary guy with a face like clay. There can't be two of them." He looked at Jem. "You don't mind if I help, right?"

"Of course not. Let me say goodbye properly to Pauley and Micki, and then I'll fetch my new journal and we'll have at it."

"You might as well say goodbye to me, too," Tori announced. "Josh just texted to ask if I'd like to meet him for a pint."

"Booze again so soon? Yesterday you were on the living room floor," Jem reminded her.

"I'll risk it to help with the investigation," Tori said loftily. "I think if Jerry Berry knows who Gina's new boyfriend is, Josh might know, too. Maybe he didn't like being under her thumb and picked up that mallet. But, Jem, if he asks me what you think about his aunt, what should I say?"

"Tell him she's still a suspect. Oh—this is important. Remember those takeaway breakfasts Wotsit dragged under my bed? They're from Jones's Diner—the same place Natalie orders from every morning. I mentioned them to her. Floated the idea that maybe she tried to patch things up with Gina by stopping by Tatteredly's with a peace offering. Then things went wrong and it ended in murder."

"Whew. What did she say?"

"She changed the subject—put me on to the real estate deal with Livingston's. If I'm being honest, Tors, nothing we saw or heard today has changed my opinion that Natalie's the killer. Jerry even volunteered that Natalie was making friendly over-tures to Gina again. I know T.J. doesn't seem like the ideal witness, but maybe he was telling the truth, and it all unfolded exactly as it seems."

"I'm not telling him all that," Tori said. "I wonder if he'll ask me if the takeaway boxes are definitely from Jones's Diner. Should I snap a pic before I go?"

"Why not?" Jem said. "I need to think it through, but if nothing happens to change my mind, I'll probably ring PC Kellow and spill it for her. I'm not sure it's the sort of evidence that could ever hold up in court, but that's not my call. If I know something for sure, I'll have to tell the police."

Tori went to the bedroom, took a picture of Wotsit's yellow

Styrofoam boxes—prompting an angry *meow* from their feline owner—and then picked up her bag and headed for the door. "Bye! I'll be back before midnight," she added, glancing speculatively from Jem to Rhys. "So, erm, keep that in mind."

After Pauley, Micki, and Tori departed, Jem told Rhys, "Let me grab that journal. I'm glad you want to help, but I warn you. Fooling around with murder can be addictive."

He shrugged. "Story of my life. I have an addictive personality. Look how long I've been after you."

There was nothing Jem could say to that—nothing that wouldn't have taken the evening in an entirely different direction—so she only smiled, turned, and retreated into the bedroom.

Tori will be back before midnight, eh? I guess that's a good thing—but right at this moment, I'm not so sure.

21

THE CATERPILLAR, THE MAD HATTER, AND THE MOCK TURTLE

"That's fancy," Rhys said doubtfully. "Possibly mental."

"It's simply gorg, and as an artist you should be able to see that," Jem said, smiling at the journal she'd placed between them on the kitchenette table. "The cover is a reproduction of the original *Olive Fairy Book* by Andrew Lang. I adore Art Nouveau," she added, tracing the fairy's graceful golden lines.

"More of a Fauvism person myself," he said mildly. "You have such a good memory, I'm surprised you need to take notes at all."

"It's not really about jogging my memory. It's about making connections. Sometimes I can't see how things relate until I put them on paper," she said, uncapping a gel pen that wrote in a glorious forest green. "Pen to paper makes the synapses flare. Statistically speaking."

His eyes narrowed. "I don't think that's a statistic."

"Maybe not. To quote Archie Goodwin, 'There are two kinds of statistics. The kind you look up, and the kind you make up.'"

"Who's Archie Goodwin?"

"A detective in a book series I'm reading. Of course, his life is easy. He has a quip for every situation, and when worst comes to worst, he works for a genius who can't be outsmarted."

Rhys smiled. "You make me wish I was more of a reader."

Jem smiled back, struck by the crinkles around his dark blue eyes. He was handsomer now than he'd ever been. A little seasoning made all the difference. "You make me wish I knew what Fauvism is, so I could prove that Art Nouveau is better."

He leaned closer. "Did Jem Jago just admit she doesn't know something?"

"Why do you think I became a librarian? If you can't know it all, you can at least stay near to the repository of all knowledge." Being so close to Rhys, alone in her flat with no potential distraction except Wotsit, who was snoozing on the windowsill, sent a ripple of nervousness through Jem's belly. Best to open the journal and crack on.

Starting a page with the name GINA MARRAK, she wrote beneath it,

Grew up on Weaver Road
Schoolmate and friend for years to Natalie Lansallos
First husband died at home, supposedly poisoned in the
workplace
Financially secure due to settlement
Second husband, Eddie Latham
Had a boyfriend Toby called a "boy toy"
Tatteredly's was a labor of love
Apparently disliked/hated by the other shopkeepers on the row:
Toby, Millie, and Jerry for sure, others wouldn't speak about her

"Toby," Rhys said. "You don't mean Toby Smithfield from St. Mary's School?"

"Yeah. He runs that salon. Hair Today, Gone Tomorrow."

Rhys scowled, automatically running a hand through his still-thick blond hair. "Why would you ever name a place that?"

"He's bald now."

"I know. I ran into him years ago, at Noughts & Crosses." Rhys sighed. "Whoops. There's another missing piece of Step Four."

"What do you mean?"

"I have a vague memory from my drinking days. I don't think I hit him—he's always been a wee fellow—but maybe I intimidated him. Pretty sure I should drop by his place and say sorry. If I don't, my sponsor will insist on it, next time I'm in Penzance. Of course..." He tailed off, smiling at Jem. "I reckon that will be more often, since I was fool enough to let you move back without kicking up a ruckus."

"I was coming back no matter what you or anyone else said. I couldn't stomach spending so much money every month on a flat no one lived in," Jem said. "Besides, I need to try working on the mainland five days a week and coming back to St. Morwenna on weekends. If I find it difficult, the reverse will be almost impossible."

"There's a library on St. Mary's."

"Rhys. First of all, that location already has a librarian. Second of all, I'm a Special Collections Librarian. There's a difference."

He nodded, though he didn't look happy about it. "You forgot something about Gina."

"Do tell."

"Her favorite book, judging by how often she featured it in the shop, was *Alice in Wonderland*. And the person who killed her used a prop from the *Alice* window."

"Right. They boiled over with rage, grabbed it, and acted."

"Yeah, but... I mean, the bookshop is full of hardback books, right?" Rhys asked. "A dictionary or a thick reference book would have made just as good a weapon. The killer had to reach into the window, pull off the flamingo, and swing the mallet at her head. Act it out," he urged Jem. "Compare it to just grabbing a heavy book and clobbering her a few times. Using the mallet is not only more complicated, it takes more will."

Jem sat back in her chair to consider his perspective. "You're right. I didn't look at it that way."

"Because you haven't attacked anyone. That's a good thing," Rhys said. "When I drank, I went to some dark places. And thank God, I never hurt a woman, far as I know. But the only way I can imagine using a mallet that way is if I'd been fantasizing about it. If cracking Gina on the head had been the plan for a long time."

"Off with her head," Jem murmured. "Yeah. I think you're right. I'm not sure it brings us any closer to the murderer, though. But, maybe. I mean, the real estate deal is huge. It could still be the one and only motive. But killing Gina the way the Red Queen threatened to kill Alice is personal. Deeply personal."

"Nothing more personal than a husband or boyfriend," Rhys said.

Jem sat with pen hovering over the journal's next blank page. "You like Eddie as the killer?"

He shrugged. "I don't like him at all. I thought he was a little creep. Don't tell Micki I said so. Still, history of violence or not, I can't see him murdering anyone himself. He'd put someone else up to it, don't you think? Impose on a friend, the way he's imposed on Colin?"

"You could be right." On the page, Jem wrote EDDIE LATHAM, followed by:

Past conviction for domestic violence against female partner
Micki initially convinced he was being fitted up
Disappointed by his upbeat demeanor
Admits he tried to slow or prevent Gina divorcing him by
obstructing the process

Technically Gina's widower; may inherit Tatteredly's plus
Gina's assets
Was sympathetic to the other shopkeepers who wanted to sell out

"Don't forget to add that he's apparently DS Conrad's pick, which is a strong vote for his innocence," Rhys said. "If that copper did a jigsaw puzzle of Big Ben, it would have empty spots all over and a picture torn out of a magazine pasted in. I wish you'd ask your friend Hackman about him, since they're ex-colleagues. Ten quid says Hackman called Conrad on his methods and got packed off to the Isles of Scilly for revenge."

"That's the nicest thing you've ever said about Hack." Jem drummed her pen against the tabletop. "I wish Eddie had an alibi. If he does turn out to be guilty, Micki may go to pieces again."

"Don't take her meltdown too much to heart," Rhys said. "I've thrown tantrums like that, too, I'm sorry to say. It's part of being an *artiste*. The stupid part."

"I can't imagine you agonizing the way she does," Jem admitted, studying his face as she tried to picture it. "You've always been so ruddy confident."

He chuckled. "Of course. And you're fearless and wise and have great hair. C'mon, Jem. I'm as insecure as anyone else when you get down where I live. When I was a kid, I thought I could hide it. If I fooled you then, surely you can see through me now."

"Working through a murder mystery might be easier," she admitted. "I was never wise, but I used to be fearless. Now it seems like I'm scared of everything. Including the same stuff that scared me as a fourteen-year-old."

"Oh, yeah, you're terrified," Rhys said, raising an eyebrow. "By the end of this thing you'll be confronting another killer, with the police swooping in or me kicking down another door.

Five minutes too late," he added archly. "At least Eddie isn't physically imposing. Who else do you have?"

Jem labeled the next page T.J. MALLARD

Grew up on Weaver Road
Sells weed and who knows what else
Schoolmates with Josh
Smokes a lot
Claims he saw Natalie Lansallos holding the bloody mallet early
Saturday morning, right around the time Gina was killed
Did not see her put the weapon in the wheelie bin but believes
she must have
Wanted possession of the weapon to hold over Natalie's head
Used to run errands for Natalie but they fell out

"I wonder if she was one of his customers," Rhys said.

Jem blinked at the idea. "Maybe so. If Natalie was Gina's schoolmate, she would be the same age, around forty-five or so. She might be a regular pot smoker."

"All this talk of *Alice in Wonderland* has me picturing T.J. as the Caterpillar. Hookah, toadstool, and all."

Jem chuckled. "Wasn't the Mad Hatter short? I suppose that could be Toby. And Wotsit over there can be the Cheshire Cat..."

"No, the Cheshire Cat is Eddie. That grin," Rhys countered. "Which one was late for a very important date?"

"The White Rabbit. I don't reckon we have one of those yet. We do have a Mock Turtle, though," Jem said, suddenly remembering a character her younger self had found quite amusing. "Poor Jerry Berry. I can imagine him getting misty-eyed and saying, 'Once, I was a real Turtle.'"

Grinning, she wrote on the next page, JERRY BERRY

Owns The Siren and seems to bitterly regret it

Josh's uncle and boss
Wanted to sell
Seemed a little miffed by Gina's taste in men

Her mobile *chirrup*ed, which was just as well, because apart from Toby and Millie, she wasn't sure who else to add to her list. It was Mr. Atherton, requesting a FaceTime chat.

"Oh, no. I have to take this. Do you mind?"

"Nope. I'll stretch my legs."

It turned out that her boss was calling to give her a Monday-morning pep talk on Sunday night, which he probably thought was a very slick and subtle way to prime her for the working week—ask if she was glad to be back, then casually tell her everything that was going wrong at the Courtney, and how much of it he expected her to fix. At first Jem was afraid he might be calling about the Scilly Sleuth story, but Mr. Atherton would have led with that if anyone had clued him in. She knew he wouldn't have got it from *Bright Star* himself, in the same way she knew Dracula wouldn't show up at midnight with a deep, dark tan.

When the call was done, Jem headed outside. She found Rhys standing in her building's courtyard, watching the sunset.

"Do you still need to study them for inspiration, after painting so many?" she asked, coming up behind him.

"Nah." He turned. "Lucky for me, I like them." He slipped an arm around her waist, smoothly, just as he had when they were teen sweethearts on St. Morwenna. "How's your boss?"

"Bossy." Slipping out of his grasp with a mischievous smile, Jem darted for the stairs, sprinting up them two at a time. Rhys was right on her heels, but Jem threw herself into her flat just ahead of him. She made for the sofa, but he caught her by the waist again, so strong he needed only one hand to overcome her. Pulling Jem close, he cradled the back of her head with his other hand, just under the weighty double-bun. Then his mouth closed on hers. The first kiss was soft, just on the lips, but the next one was searching, passionate. It was the way he always did it, ever since the first kiss they'd shared in a crumbling castle on Tresco— shot, then chaser.

"Rhys..."

"You want me to let go?"

She didn't answer. The feel of his body against hers was intoxicating. She wondered what it would be like to undress him. But kissing Rhys was like standing on an unguarded precipice. The plunge was profound and inevitable—and it came with the territory, if she let herself go forward.

"I want... to pretend like we're still kids," she said, wondering if he'd understand.

"Nothing easier. I never grew up." Leaning back against a throw pillow, one leg on the floor and the other dangling over the sofa's armrest, he beckoned for her to slide on top of him, into his arms. Even with both of them fully clothed, in the middle of the living room and with one of his feet on the floor, Jem felt like she was blushing all over. As they kissed, her hair slipped out of its bonds—his fingers were to blame—and the scrape of his beard stubble against her lips burned, tantalizing. Time dissolved into the pure pleasure of kissing Rhys, of being in his arms. At some point there was a sound—the scraping of metal on metal like a key in a lock—but Jem was too caught up in his kisses to notice.

"Right! Never mind. Going out again," Tori announced. She slammed the door, which broke Jem's concentration completely. She would've fallen off Rhys if he hadn't held onto her. He was grinning, eyes bright.

"Busted again."

Through the door, Tori called, "Look at me on the walkway, checking my messages. Five minutes should do it. Five minutes, then I'm coming in!"

22

ANOTHER MURDER

Groaning, Rhys let go of Jem, who struggled to mentally reassemble herself. Heaven only knew how far it would have gone if Tori returned closer to midnight, as her words implied, rather than now—barely an hour later.

"I'll be in the shower," Rhys announced. In record time, the bathroom door closed and the pipes rumbled, followed by the sound of water beating down.

Jem covered her face with her hands, took several deep breaths, and felt like laughing. She couldn't remember the last time she'd been so happy.

Tori rapped smartly on the door, then flung it open. "Are you decent?"

"Get in here. I thought you said midnight."

"That was the plan. I figured after we had our pint Josh and I could head back to his place for a little bit of what you and big blondie were up to." Tori glanced around the living room. "Where'd he go? Out a window?"

Jem pointed behind her, in the direction of audible splashing. "Didn't you tell me I wasn't the only Jago who could crack a mystery?"

"I didn't mean your man's cold showers." Tori grinned with cheerful malice. "Oh! Look at that. You drove Wotsit into hiding, poor kitty."

The tailless white cat with curling ginger markings oozed out from beneath the armchair. It sat close to the floor, so he really had flattened himself to an amazing degree to secrete himself beneath it. He *did* look disgruntled, as if recent human behavior on the sofa had left him wondering what sort of outfit he'd joined up with.

"Sorry, fellow," Jem said, amused by his slitted eyes. Impulsively, she scooped him up as if he was a dog.

"He might claw you," Tori warned.

Wotsit's whiskered face came at her like a shot. He licked her nose, then drew back to check her reaction. She laughed, delighted.

"Nose kisses! Wonderful." She sat him back on the floor with a pat. "Let me debrief this junior detective and then you shall have a treat."

"There's not much to tell." Tori sighed. "The minute I showed my face in The Siren, Jerry Berry told me to get out. Not in so many words—he wasn't an ogre about it—but he said the dinner rush was over and he was closing early for the night. I said, no problem, Josh and I can find a pub somewhere, and that's when Josh said he couldn't make it."

"Why didn't he text you?"

"I don't know. I was texting back and forth with him the whole way over," Tori said. "I sent him the pic of the takeaway trays, then told him a little about our afternoon—Morrab Gardens, jam doughnuts, and all that. Not who we interviewed or what they said," she added scornfully. "You were really about to ask me if I did that, weren't you?"

Jem shrugged. "I'm glad you didn't. How'd he react to the Jones's Diner breakfast trays?"

"He said half the row eats breakfast there. It's the only diner in Penzance that stays open all hours. And it's cheaper than most."

"So if Josh suddenly couldn't spend the evening with you, what was he doing?"

"He said it was family stuff. His uncle and his mum and dad. He didn't get specific."

"Natalie's family," Jem said. "Do you think they might go and talk to her? Ask her to come clean and turn herself in?"

"Maybe." Tori brightened. "That would be the best thing, don't you think? Natalie confesses, the murder is solved, Eddie joins the sale, Jerry and the other owners get to sell out, and there's a fancy new hotel overlooking the bay. Everybody wins."

"Everybody but Gina."

"True. I don't mean to sound uncaring. Only—I like the idea of this case not being solved by the Scilly Sleuth, you know? I wouldn't want Josh and his family to think of us that way. As the people who got Natalie locked away for life."

"I know," Jem said. "But even though you two barely know each other, it's obvious that Josh thinks you're something special. If something I do or tell the police gets Natalie put away, I can't believe he'd hold it against you."

The three of them turned in early—Jem in her bed, Tori on the sofa, and Rhys in the bathtub, which he preferred to the floor. Around midnight, Jem's mobile went off, startling her out of a frustrating dream: arguing folksonomy versus taxonomy with Mr. Atherton. For a confused, pulse-pounding moment, she didn't know whether to be irritated or relieved. Then from the living room, Tori's mobile went off, breaking into the chorus of something by Dua Lipa. Tori, being harder to wake, only groaned as the chorus played out, paused, and started over again.

"Tori!" Jem bellowed, momentarily forgetting Rhys in the bathtub.

As if on cue, Rhys's phone began to sound inside the bathroom. Now all the phones were going off, but his ringtone, the sound of a classic 1950s BT landline, was obnoxious enough alone and at regular volume. In a tiled echo chamber, and as part of a trio, it was unbearable.

"What is happening?" Jem heard herself shout. The confusing racket had turned her into the old *Poltergeist* meme.

"Hello?" Rhys answered his mobile, voice carrying clearly through the closed bathroom door. "Micki... slow down..."

Now fully awake, Jem looked at her own mobile. In her bleary confusion, what had seemed like one endless call had actually been three; Micki ringing, disconnecting, ringing again, disconnecting, and finally leaving a short, frantic voicemail.

"Jem, they've arrested Eddie! He asked a woman at the station to ring me. He came in late from the pub and found Conrad and some others waiting on his doorstep. The charge is double murder! The woman wouldn't tell me who the victims were. Gina, of course, and somebody else. I guess it happened today—yesterday, I mean. Call me when you hear this. I'll try Rhys."

"*Dead?*" Tori cried from the living room. "What do you mean, dead?"

Throwing aside the duvet, Jem hurried out of bed and down the short corridor. Switching on the overhead light, she found Tori on the floor between sofa and coffee table, tangled in bedclothes, mobile in hand. Wotsit glared at her from the windowsill, deeply offended by the sudden upset. From Tori's mobile, Josh said via speakerphone:

"It happened earlier tonight. I would've called sooner, but there were so many people to talk to... so many questions... my dad's taking it hard... Anyway, we had a family meeting. I guess you cottoned on to that. Not with my aunt—the rest of us. I told them about what T.J. said he saw, and how we dragged the rubbish to your sister's place, and all the rest. I showed them the picture of the takeaway trays, too. I'd already forwarded it to my aunt to get her reaction. She texted back to ask, even if she was a killer, wouldn't I stand by her? That wasn't the denial we were all hoping for.

"Uncle Jerry said he'd ring the police first thing in the morning and lay it all out. My mum and dad agreed. But I felt bad about it, and decided to go give Aunt Natalie a heads-up. To apologize in advance, even though I knew she might never forgive me.

"I rapped at her window, but it was closed. No lights were on. I got worried straightaway, because it was only ten or so—too early for her to be in bed. I used my key to get into the living room... pushed my way through the boxes and rubbish and whatnot... and there she was in bed, sitting up. Somebody had... they had..." Josh broke off, weeping.

Jem's heart turned over. Josh had been the one person left who still loved Natalie and was willing to overlook her peculiarities, real and put-on. Yet for some reason he'd been chosen by fate to discover her brutalized corpse.

"Babe. I'm so sorry. What happened to her?" Tori asked when Josh seemed to recover himself.

"Hit over the head. A dozen times, a hundred times, I don't know. She... her body... it's too awful. Her hands and arms, too. Like all she could do to defend herself was throw her arms up, but it wasn't enough. *Someone beat her to death*," Josh cried, suddenly raging. "They beat the life out of her, and for what? Because her house was always in a state? Because she didn't behave the way people thought she should?"

"Guess you've already heard." Rhys spoke softly, entering the living room wearing only his boxers, phone in hand.

"I wonder why they arrested Eddie," Jem said. "Do you think they had any real proof? Or was Conrad afraid of being tried in the press? You know—two murders but no arrests, why are the police failing us, that sort of thing."

"Knowing Conrad, it's all about looking like he's taking decisive action. Anyhow, Micki and Clarence are on it. Calling on all the Lathams—St. Ives and West Country—to pool their resources and get him legal help, stat. Unless someone filmed him committing a murder, he should still be released on bond before long." He regarded her curiously. "Do you think he did it?"

"I hope he didn't," Jem said. "But he did go out of his way to point us to her as a likely suspect. To hear Natalie talk, she and Eddie practically carried on a clandestine affair under Gina's nose. Maybe Eddie's feelings for Natalie were quite different than what she believed. All I know is this—it seems pretty unlikely that Natalie killed Gina. Maybe our snooping yesterday made someone nervous. And maybe they thought Natalie might say or do something to shift the focus to the real killer."

23

INCOMING CALL FROM THE UNIVERSE

Jem got back to sleep around two o'clock, which meant six a.m. came much too soon. Tori, who apparently spent most of the night on the walkway having a mobile heart-to-heart with Josh, returned to her sofa nest much later, and didn't stir under the blanket when Jem turned on the kitchenette lights to make coffee. In preparation for doing a fry-up, Jem accidentally dropped the skillet on the cooker with a bang. Tori still didn't wake, but the noise penetrated the deep slumber of Rhys, whose moderately loud snoring had echoed off the bathroom's tiled walls all night. Awakening with a snort, he called, "What bloody time is it?"

"Six o'clock," Jem replied, belting a robe over her nightshirt before opening the bathroom door. "Murder or no murder, I have to show my face at work. And I'll have to turn up early if I want to justify knocking off around two."

"Fascinating. Why are you telling me this?"

"Because I need you to get your arse up and give me the shower."

"Librarians are so hardcore," he muttered, rising like a zombie coming out of the grave. "Is there coffee? I don't want to sound ungrateful, but I didn't sleep too well in your bathroom, Jemmie. Noise kept waking me up. I think maybe you snore."

By half-nine that morning, back at her old desk at the Courtney, Jem knew the truth: her long summer of independence on St. Morwenna had spoiled her for the workaday world. Of course, she would always love being a Special Collections Librarian, and not just for the pay. Should several million pounds ever fall from the sky, dust itself off, and politely request that she take it home, she would've done so—naturally—but still continued her career in some form. Preferably one that allowed maximum flexibility whenever a murder mystery crossed her path.

Back in the saddle, she revisited all the projects that needed her attention. Like her proposal for a UNESCO partnership to create a new museum exhibit about copper and tin mining. Cornwall and Devon's defunct mines comprised a World Heritage Site, and for weeks Jem had been making a list of resources to loan such an exhibit: land surveys, mineral treatises, and a rare report from the Ministry of National Insurance, which had compiled shocking statistics on the types of brutal injuries and diseases risked by eighteenth-century miners.

After beavering away at that for a couple of hours, she took a break to drink some tea and ring Micki.

"How are you and the family holding up?"

"Not bad," Micki said, sounding surprisingly chipper compared to her frantic midnight voicemail. "The Lathams always come together when one of us is banged up. We've already hired a solicitor for Eddie. He's arranged for me and Mum to visit him at three o'clock. And he thinks the CPS will recommend against charging Eddie, unless DS Conrad coughs up some hard evidence soon."

"Good. Would you mind asking Eddie a couple of questions for me?"

"Sure," Micki said. "But in case you don't know, it won't be a private meeting. At least one guard or police officer will be present. And my mum has never been able to keep a secret."

"Oh, these are amateur detective questions. I doubt anyone would take them seriously besides me," Jem said breezily. "Ask him again if he has any idea who Gina's new man was. That person is potentially as good a suspect as Eddie. Well," she amended, "I doubt he stood to gain anything financially, but the romantic partner is often a sure bet, especially if we can dig up proof the relationship was volatile."

"Gina's new man. Got it. Anything else?"

"Yeah. This will sound strange, but try to phrase it exactly as I do. I know Eddie likes to tell people what they want to hear, so I don't want to give him any clues on what I'm looking for," Jem said. "Ask him what Gina liked to eat for breakfast on workdays. And however he answers, ask him if she ever ate it in the shop before opening."

"Oooh, I'm intrigued. Can you tell me what you're after?"

"I will once you have the answers. And don't get too excited. It's probably a wild goose chase, but I'm grasping at straws. Or do I mean feathers?"

With that murder-mystery detour accomplished, Jem went back to work. A lot had accumulated during her Isles of Scilly sojourn, and she was wondering how she could justify ducking out early when Mr. Atherton announced he had a headache and went home. It was just after two o'clock. Jem gave it another quarter-hour, then made her escape. Once she was safely out of the Courtney and into the bright afternoon sunlight, she rang Tori.

"Are you still on the sofa?"

"Nope. I'm in the kitchen. Rhys and I split a pot of coffee, and then he went off to look up some old friends," Tori said, pausing to yawn.

"Sounds like the coffee hasn't kicked in."

"Oh, it did. You should've seen me before. Josh and I talked most of the night."

"I thought you were out on the walkway a long time. How's he doing?"

"You know. It'll take time," Tori said, with a maturity that surprised Jem. It was easy to think of her little sister as a child, but she was a grown woman, albeit a young and free-spirited one. "I was afraid he'd spend today brooding, but no dice. About an hour ago, he rang me to say the police were coming to interview him and his uncle Jerry about Natalie's murder. Then a few minutes later, he texted to say they were going to Exeter Police HQ."

"That sounds pretty routine. Are you worried?"

"About Josh being the murderer?" Tori shot back, incredulous.

"No. About Conrad coming after the two of them the way he went after Eddie." *And Rhys*, Jem thought, recalling the long days he'd spent locked up for a crime he didn't commit.

"Josh said he reckoned the police were after dirt on Eddie," Tori said. "To build a case on why he might have done in Natalie as well as Gina. Natalie told a lot of people that she and Eddie were practically having an affair. Someone told Conrad, and now he wants more."

"Seems like he's forgotten all about your idiotic gang-bangers-in-black-leather sighting. Lucky you."

"Yeah. By the way, Rhys snores like a freight train. Other than that, I fully approve."

Jem made a disdainful sound.

"What? You felt free to comment on Josh. I'm commenting on Rhys."

Jem's mobile *chirrup*ed, indicating another call was coming through. She glanced at the screen to see who the requested FaceTime session was coming from.

"Sorry, Tors. I have to take this."

"Who is it? Rhys?"

"The universe." Jem switched over. At the sight of Sergeant I. Hackman, she demanded, "What the heck happened to you?"

24

WYATT THE WALRUS AND HACK THE HAPLESS

At gone two in the afternoon, Hack should've been in uniform and either completing desk work at St. Mary's Police Station or out on the water, patrolling the Isles of Scilly. He *was* outdoors, possibly on the deck of a boat, but everything else was wrong. His hair was slicked back wet, his nose was swollen, and his specs with the hot-rod-red earpieces were gone. He wore a white T-shirt so cheap and thin, his dark tan showed through the fabric. All in all, he was still a nice-looking man in his early forties, and while his black hair, razor-edged sideburns, and neat goatee always gave him a faintly piratical look, today he appeared to have gone full buccaneer.

"Oh, no, you've chucked in the job and taken to the high seas," she said. "Please tell me you didn't crash another boat."

"No," Hack said, "and damn you for even asking. But we did suffer a sort of nautical disaster. I went in the drink. Lost my specs, as you see, and got soaked all the way through. It was almost RIP to the RIB."

Jem goggled at him. The IoS PD's new rigid inflatable boat, or RIB, was their pride and joy. They cherished every opportunity to take it out on the water and ride about, looking very stern and professional, like they were busting up nautical smuggling rings instead of what they were actually doing: cautioning reckless pleasure boaters and checking personal watercraft permits.

"So it's all right?"

"Yeah. We got lucky. Bart turned up and saved the day."

"Bart the Ferryman?"

That coaxed a faint smile from him, though his eyes were tired, as if he'd been through the wringer. "There's only one Bart around the Isles of Scilly."

"Yeah, I just never thought I'd hear the words 'saved the day' in conjunction with his name. Where are you?"

"On *Merry Maid*, as it happens, about five minutes from Silversmith Bay."

"Wow," Jem said, wishing she had a customer service number for the universe, or even just an address to send a sternly worded letter of complaint.

"Wow as in, yes, I'd love to grab a pint and an early dinner? Or wow as in, my big blond ex is at my place and three's a crowd?"

Jem blew out a sigh. "I don't know that Rhys is at my flat, but if he isn't, he'll be back soon. Yesterday it was the whole gang, but Pauley and Micki went home on Kit Verran's ferry. They'll probably be back to help us brainstorm about the Gina Marrak case this evening."

"You trying to solve the Marrak murder was a given. Involving Fred, Daphne, Shaggy, and Scooby was a given, too. But—"

"Are you saying I'm Velma?"

"Draw your own conclusions. But I don't think Pauley and Micki will be able to get a ferry to Penzance until tomorrow morning. There's too much activity on the waterways."

"What's happened?"

Hack looked embarrassed. "Well, a couple of hours ago, Newt and I took the boat over to Annet to have a chat with some teenagers. They'd rowed over on kayaks and apparently didn't grasp the concept of 'Landing Strictly Forbidden.' I had something on my mind, and was in a bit of a mood. I thought I might overreact with the kids, so I stayed with the RIB and told Newt to disembark and issue the warning. It was no big deal. We just wanted the kids to say sorry, promise not to do it again, climb back in their kayaks, and go.

"Anyway, I was sitting in the boat, thinking about the best way to murder another copper without getting nicked—"

"What?" Jem cut in.

"You heard me. I'm not saying I'd do it. But when I've just about had it with the job, the powers that be, and a certain detective who shall remain nameless, I like to sit down and work out undetectable ways to kill him and get away with it. It's a pleasant little thought exercise. All coppers do it."

"I refuse to believe PC Newt has ever done such a thing."

"All right, almost all of us. Anyway, there I was in the RIB, minding my own business, when there was this bellowing. Earthshakingly loud. End-of-the-world loud. Dead close and totally unexpected. I looked over my shoulder and there he was. How I ever let him get so close without noticing, I don't know. But there he was in all his glory. Wyatt the bloody Walrus. Did you know those things have bad breath?"

"Can't imagine he brushes his teeth too often." Jem giggled helplessly at the idea of Hack, alone on his boat and thinking dark thoughts—surely about his old enemy DS Conrad—only to be jolted back to reality by the bellowing of an enormous sea mammal. "What did you do, throw yourself overboard in terror?"

"Ha ha. I tried to start up the RIB, of course, and get away. That's the latest directive handed down from the powers on high—don't engage. Wyatt has no fear of humans and has come to see all boats as his personal property. If a boater tried to stand his ground and I don't know, fire a flare at Wyatt or beat him off with an oar, they'd be up on charges for abuse of marine life. So I tried to run for it, but I wasn't quick enough. Wyatt flopped his great bloody bulk onto the RIB—directly onto the engine and right into the seats."

"I would've dove in."

"I didn't have to. It was like a bouncy castle. Wyatt pushed the boat down and I went flying. First up, then down into the drink."

Jem clapped a hand over her mouth but didn't succeed in holding back her mirth. Hack watched her with sour resignation; he knew laughter was inevitable, and most of it would be in his face.

"What happened next?"

"Wyatt couldn't seem to get comfortable. He was crashing around on the RIB, bellowing and rocking to and fro. I don't reckon he could've really sunk it, but I swear he was doing his best. The marine experts say this weather's too hot for him. He's meant for colder waters—I don't know why he doesn't go find them, and leave the Scillies alone."

"Sometimes animals are like people. They wander off the beaten track and end up sticking with a life that makes sense to no one but them."

"Apparently. Anyway, that's how I lost my specs. Lucky I can see so-so without them, or I'd be on desk duty until I can get a new pair."

"Is that why you're coming to the mainland? For a new prescription?" Jem asked.

"No. I was always coming. I had a one o'clock appointment with some Devon & Cornwall representatives. Two guys from the IOPC," he said, meaning the Independent Office for Police Conduct. "Plus a lawyer, and a retired chief superintendent from Scotland Yard brought in to oversee the matter. The IOPC guys wanted to reschedule, but the retired chief heard what happened to me and said if I was willing to come, he would wait. And not to worry about my attire because it wasn't black tie."

"So if he waits, the others have to?"

"Pretty much. He's a living legend type. Also a baron, believe it or not."

"Well, he sounds like he might have a brain. Maybe even a heart."

"I'll reserve judgment until we have the hearing—or should I say, conversation. No one likes to admit this is a hearing to either reinstate me to Devon & Cornwall or keep me in the Scillies forever."

Until that moment, Jem had deferred her questions about Hack's abrupt transfer to the IoS PD, a comparatively tiny staff and station, after years with a metropolitan murder squad. Of course, many coppers would consider it a dream posting: light duty in paradise. But Jem knew that for Hack, it was a punishment. And because he ran a tight ship—unlike his predecessor—and because he enforced the law equally without regard for fear or favor, he'd already made a few enemies. Unkind people assumed he'd made a colossal blunder at Devon & Cornwall and been exiled to a peaceful spot where he could do no harm. Jem didn't buy that theory for a minute.

"Hack. I know it's none of my business, but I'm just going to ask. Why were you sent to the Isles of Scilly? You said it wasn't your choice. That you almost walked away from the job rather than go."

He sighed. "Ever heard of the code of silence?"

"Sure. Coppers don't grass on each other, even when they go out of bounds. Like schoolkids. Or doctors."

"Or convicts," he agreed. "If one officer swears out an official complaint against another officer, especially a senior officer, it's all meant to remain confidential. But the problem with internal review units is that they're composed entirely of human beings. Some of the reviewers even have friends who are human beings. And that means whispers, and gossip, and vengeance. It's the kind of thing that can get a scapegoat transferred to a little archipelago. He can't be sacked outright—that would kick off a second investigation—but he can be relocated to the UK equivalent of Siberia."

"As an adopted Scillonian, I ought to be offended. But I get it," Jem said. "Should I assume the officer you officially complained on was Conrad?"

Hack nodded.

"All right. You know I'm here for you when you want to spill the entire story. But I won't try and badger it out of you." Jem paused, wishing very much that he would volunteer the rest on his own, but he didn't. Taking one last indirect stab at it, she asked, "Is that why he calls you The Saint? Also Saint Ignatius."

He swore an oath so surprising, not to mention physically unlikely, that Jem dissolved into giggles. When she could speak, she said, "I don't think that's even possible."

"It might be, with enough grease. I'd like to hold a gun on Conrad and make him try it. Anyway, he was calling me 'Saint' long before the complaint happened. He threw in 'Ignatius' after my poor old honest mum came to the station, bringing me a birthday prezzie. I was out on a call, so he intercepted her and asked why on earth she'd named her baby boy after the letter I. She told him the truth—that it was meant to be Ignatius, because a psychic worked out the numerology and said Ignatius held great power."

Jem nodded soberly, not a trace of a smile on her lips.

"Oh, go ahead and cackle, I know you want to. I think I once told you my mum loves the metaphysical stuff. Not my dad, he was the practical sort. And he wasn't too keen on the name Ignatius. He thought he'd give her a sort of cooling-off period to pick something else. So when he made out my birth certificate, he just put down an I and a full stop, thinking that would do for the moment. But Mum said it had to be Ignatius, and Dad never did agree. He also never got around to putting in the fee and the effort to legally correct my name on the document. So I and a full stop it remains."

Jem *did* feel a cackle rising, but she kept it down. "I'm surprised you don't correct it. Just pick a name you like and be done with it."

"I like I with a full stop. I like how it worries people who ought to be focused on something significant."

"Contrarian! I knew it. Like those cowboy boots of yours." Ever since Hack's arrival, Jem had watched him trip over uneven cobbles and slide on mucky shingle, yet still refuse to trade his mainland footwear for something boat- and island-appropriate. "You'll never give them up."

"That's where you're half right." Hack shifted his mobile down, showing off hairy legs, cargo shorts, and violent-green flip-flops. They were the type perpetually found in the Island Gifts bargain bin, which was probably where the cheap T-shirt had come from.

"Oh, no! You lost your boots?"

"I lost one boot. I kept the other one, thank you very much. I don't know what use it will ever be to me, but I refuse to give it up." The mobile's screen jumped, giving Jem a quick view of the water and buildings along the bay. Then Hack's face reappeared. "We've arrived. Bart's tying up."

"Oh! Bart." Jem had been so distracted by the conversation's many twists, she'd forgotten that the walrus encounter story was unfinished. "How did he save the day?"

"Right. So I mentioned Wyatt was sort of fretful and cross, wallowing around on the RIB and bellowing fit to break your eardrums. I could barely hear Newt shouting my name from the shore, but I could see him running along the waterline, waving his arms to try to get Wyatt's attention. The kayaking teenagers were watching, too. Also pointing and laughing, naturally.

"I started to swim for shore, but Wyatt wasn't having it. I reckon he thought I was a boat accessory. So he belly-flopped back into the sea after me. Talk about a cannonball. The wave swept me under. That's when I lost my boot, I think—thrashing around, trying to get away from the daft beast.

"While I was underwater, I heard this sound. Like a long musical note. I came up for air, and there was *Merry Maid* chugging toward us fast as it could go. The note sounded again, broadcast over the boat's PA, and then... well, Bart started singing to Wyatt."

"Beg pardon?"

"Singing. It was the maddest thing I ever heard. I thought maybe I'd hit my head on a rock and was dreaming the whole thing. But it was real. Bart was singing his heart out."

"And how did Wyatt react?"

"He seemed to love it. Forgot all about me. Stopped thrashing about, abandoned the RIB, and started following *Merry Maid*. Bart led him to St. Mary's, where the marine blokes have put out a special pontoon for Wyatt's use, to try and tempt him away from commandeering boats. Once it was safe, Newt borrowed one of the kid's kayaks, rescued me, and recovered the RIB."

"What was Bart singing?" Jem asked in wonderment. If Hack hadn't been telling her this *sans* specs and cowboy boots, while wearing a pair of bargain-priced flip-flops, she would've sworn he was having her on.

"Something about a rose..."

A long musical note issued from behind Hack, making him jump. Bart appeared on screen, waving at Jem.

"Hiya, Scilly Sleuth. I hear there was another murder. Be honest. Are you doing them yourself so as to solve them?"

His tone suggested no judgment. A big fellow, well over six feet with enough flesh on his bones for two men, Bartholomew Bottom, aka Bart the Ferryman, had a perpetually scrubby beard that served mainly to give a suggestion of chin; otherwise, his face melted into his neck. Loud, boisterous, and prone to promising things he couldn't deliver, he cheerfully lived a life of endless scrapes with police, local authorities, and creditors.

"If I were going to murder anyone for a lark, I'd start with you," Jem said lightly. "What kind of instrument is that?"

Bart held up the silver disc for her inspection. "A pitch pipe. All your proper *a cappella* vocalists use it before a performance. And through experimentation and careful observation, I've determined that Wyatt's favorite song is 'The Last Rose of Summer.'"

Blowing into the pitch pipe again, Bart broke into the traditional air. He had a decent bass baritone range, a bit wobbly in spots, but not hard on the ears:

> Tis the last rose of summer left blooming alone
> All her lovely companions are faded and gone
> No flower of her kindred, no rosebud is nigh
> To reflect back her blushes and give sigh for sigh

"All right, all right, she gets the idea," Hack broke in. "Bart, you're a great daft beast, just like that walrus," he added, not without affection. "Have you stopped to think Wyatt's become fixated on you? That maybe he's in love with you?"

Bart blew the pitch pipe at Hack. "You're green with envy. Same color as your flip-flops. Because I've discovered my soulmate of the sea and now you're in my debt."

Hack tossed Jem a look of resigned despair. "So that's my day. Thrown overboard, rescued by Bart, Newt, and a lot of ruddy awful teens. Lost my specs. Lost a boot. Now I'll go sit in a room looking like a derelict and let the great man from Scotland Yard tell me Conrad's absolved, my transfer can't be rescinded on grounds of retaliation, and that's that."

"I hope it goes better than you think," Jem said, still fighting back laughter.

"Uh-huh. Anyway, once it's done, I'm heading straight back to St. Mary's. A word to the wise. While you're nosing around the murder, keep out of Conrad's way. He'll bang you up for obstruction and manufacture evidence to make it stick. It's just who he is."

"What about PC Kellow?"

Hack blinked. "Stacy?"

"I had a feeling you knew her. I don't suppose she's an ex, is she?"

He nodded slowly.

"She's the officer who visited me when I called about the mallet in my bathtub. Conrad came along and made sure to introduce me as The Saint's new sweetheart."

Hack made a noise. "One of these days, things will be arranged in such a way that he'll answer for being a right royal pain in the arse. One of these days. Mark me."

"But is Kellow liable to bang me up for obstruction and manufacture evidence to make it stick?"

"Stacy? No, never. She's a straight arrow. She won't appreciate an amateur gumming up the works, but she won't say no to real information, either. If you think you're closing in on the killer, or you come across potential evidence, give her a bell." Hack drew a breath, then added, "I mean it, Jem. No solo heroics. Turn over whatever you find to Stacy and let her help."

"Are you going ashore or not?" Bart demanded.

"Ashore. And now, Ms. Jago," Hack concluded in a trenchant voice that made her giggle again, "as I've entertained you as best I can, I'll be signing off."

"I'm sorry I can't stop laughing. I'm so glad you weren't hurt. But I won't pretend I don't wish I could have seen it."

"Oh, but you will soon enough," Bart announced. "Those kayakers filmed the whole thing on their phones. Got it from different angles, and plan to splice the footage together to make a little movie. They reckon once they get it up on YouTube, it will go viral. We'll be superstars!" he cried, clapping a massive arm around Hack. "Well, Wyatt and me will be superstars. You'll still just be a sad, tragic wreck of a man, won't you?"

25

A NEW PRIME SUSPECT

Jem arrived at her flat just ahead of Rhys, which was lucky for him, or he would've been left sitting on the walkway waiting for her or Tori to turn up and unlock the door.

"You're not going to believe what's happening back home," he said, meaning the Isles of Scilly.

"If it has to do with Wyatt the Walrus, I've already heard. I talked to Hack, and not long after that, Pauley rang to say she and Micki were stuck on St. Morwenna for the night. Kit Verran is busy running TV cameramen here and there, and Bart the Ferryman's being interviewed by all sorts of reporters. Apparently he's a human interest story."

"That should make him happy. Where's Tori?" Rhys asked, heading straight for the kitchenette to put the kettle on. One night in her bathtub and he was already right at home.

"Oh. She texted to say she was off to meet Josh. He and his uncle Jerry spent four hours at Exeter Police HQ being questioned by the rockslide that walks like a man."

"If they walked out as free men, they did well." With water heating for tea, Rhys was peering into cupboards. "What do you reckon for supper?"

"Are you cooking?"

"Not if anyone wants to enjoy what they eat."

"Don't look at me. I was never much of a cook, and living with Pauley spoiled me completely. I was expecting her to whip up a gourmet meal."

"Then it's takeout." He pulled out his mobile and began consulting takeaway menus. "God, the mainland's spendy. I'm a bit skint just at present. Can we go halfsies? Or split it three ways, if Tori comes back to join us?"

"She's even more skint than you are. I could do spaghetti, if you don't mind boxed pasta and tinned sauce."

He gave her a chef's kiss. "I'll set the table. I may even do the washing-up after."

Jem had just dished up two plates of spaghetti and meat sauce—no garlic bread and no shaved parmesan, alas, which were oversights Pauley Gwyn would never have stood for—when Tori barreled into the flat, bright-eyed and bursting with news.

"Guys. I got something sleuthy. Wanna hear it?"

"Have you met me? Sit down at the table. Want some pasta?" Jem asked.

Tori waved that away. "I had lager and some pig snacks with Josh. He needed a pint to steady his nerves." Plopping down at the table's third chair, Tori said to Rhys, "You said you were looking up old friends. Was that extracurricular, or were you working on the case?"

He looked amused. "A little of both. Years ago I used to come here every weekend to surf at Gwenver Beach. Then we'd do a pub crawl and sometimes end up around Silversmith Lane —Noughts & Crosses, to be precise. You know it?"

She groaned. "Been flung out of it. Proceed."

"I figured if Gina ever went dancing or took a bloke out for a drink, it might be at Noughts & Crosses, since it's so close to Tatteredly's. I used to know the barkeep pretty well, so I stopped by and chatted her up."

"You're all right with that? Going around clubs?" Jem asked. In the past, she would've hesitated before so much as implying in front of Tori—or anyone not in Rhys's inner circle— that he was in recovery. But he was remarkably candid about it, so she followed his lead.

"For a legitimate purpose, it's all right. If I sat around just watching other people drink, like my dog Buck watches people eat, that would be a no-no."

"Did the bartender know anything?"

"She knew Gina," Rhys said, pausing to wind spaghetti around his fork. "Didn't like her."

"Sensing a pattern," Tori said.

"She said Gina and Eddie used to be regulars, back when they were first married. Then for a while it was just Gina. Then a couple of new blokes." He paused to eat his forkful.

"Do tell," Jem said, too interested to eat.

He swallowed and said, "Bloke number one was what she called a no-hoper. Bald or balding. Apron. Harassed."

"That sounds like Jerry Berry."

"I know. I asked if she knew Jerry, or any of the shopkeepers on Silversmith Lane, and she said if they came in much, it wasn't enough to make an impression. The only reason she remembered the no-hoper is because he didn't seem like Gina's type."

"Maybe he wasn't," Tori said. "Were they, like, making out or something? If not, maybe they were just friends."

"That's what the barkeep said. Anyway." Rhys was twirling more spaghetti. "Bloke number two was halfway attractive, in her opinion. She described him as a white guy, scruffy, and dead young. Oh—and hair cut in a number two."

Jem asked, "Was he a smoker?"

"Chain-smoker. He even asked if they were planning to add a hookah room."

"T.J.," Tori said.

"T.J. the Caterpillar," Jem agreed, shaking her head in amazement. "What would Gina see in him?"

Rhys said, "I'm still wondering what she saw in Eddie."

"Maybe she liked the dangerous type."

"Dangerous? Dead idle, more like."

"Oh, well. As Emily Dickinson said, 'The heart wants what it wants.'"

"Such a librarian," Tori muttered.

Rhys was eating again. When he finished the mouthful, he said, "I know it's not much, but I'm not cut out for this super-snoop business. I couldn't think of any way to follow up, short of going door to door begging for clues. And that didn't seem advisable."

"You did great," Jem said.

"You did," Tori agreed. "Of course, it's amateur night in Chipping Norton compared to what I got."

Jem rolled her eyes. "Quit vamping and tell it," she said, digging into her spaghetti at last. It wasn't bad—nor was it good —but it was hot and filling, and she was hungry.

"All right. So. Josh and Jerry went to Exeter Police HQ. Conrad and another detective—not that constable, someone from the murder squad—took them to separate interview rooms," Tori said. "The first round of questions was separate, then a round together, then separate again. Josh said it was all very friendly, with snacks and tea and adjusting the thermostat if the room was too warm. He went in thinking all the questions would be about Eddie, since he was in custody. But after four hours he realized Conrad kept steering the conversation back to his uncle Jerry."

"How does he feel about that?" Rhys asked.

"Insulted, mostly. He can't believe anyone would suspect

Jerry Berry of murder. Just because he's always ranting and raving and threatening people and whatnot."

"So Josh didn't get the sense there was any evidence against Jerry?"

Tori shrugged. "Conrad didn't show his cards, but he acted like there was something. He said they were looking at Natalie's phone records. They'd noticed over fifty calls to The Siren just in the last couple of weeks, and almost as many outgoing, from The Siren to her. Josh had to explain they were all to and from him, either taking Natalie's lunch and dinner orders or else listening to her complain about something. Then they started asking about her laptop, and Josh remembered something he'd forgotten to tell me. When he found Natalie dead, her laptop was destroyed, too. The case was cracked and the hard drive was stolen."

Jem swallowed, washed her spaghetti down with some tea—not the ideal combination—and said, "Now that's interesting."

"Oh, I figured it was a red herring," Tori said wisely.

"What *is* a red herring?" Rhys asked. "I have no pride. I'll ask."

"Something in a mystery that's put there to send the reader in the wrong direction," Jem said.

"Why a herring?"

"Because it stinks."

"And red because red is noticeable?" Rhys shook his head as if dismissing the term as too odd to be believed. To Tori, he asked, "Do you mean Natalie's killer messed about with the laptop to send the police in the wrong direction?"

"Yeah."

"Why?"

She shrugged. "Because clever killers do stuff like that, don't they?"

"I think it might be meaningful," Jem said. "When I met Natalie, she was on the laptop the entire time. Playing solitaire, posting on message boards, and so on. I'll bet she used it to text and instant-message people. Maybe she sent a message the killer didn't like."

"Such as?" Tori asked.

"Such as, 'I know you killed Gina Marrak and I expect a payoff to keep quiet about it.' But I'm just spitballing." Jem waved it aside. "Finish your story."

"Right. Josh said finally Conrad seemed to give up, left, and came back with Jerry. Then left them alone together in an interview room for almost half an hour."

"Bet the room was under surveillance," Rhys said.

"Anyway, Josh said his uncle was red-faced. Mortified. Apparently someone, not named, told the police Jerry had a thing for Gina Marrak. That on the day she separated from Eddie, he combed what little hair he's got, put on a fresh apron, and was over at her shop like a bolt of lightning. With a bouquet!"

Jem and Rhys swapped glances.

"All right," Jem said, "I'll admit that's pretty sleuthy. You get a gold star. Did Jerry admit to being Gina's new man? He had me fooled with his line about the new one being squarely under her thumb."

"That's the thing. He insisted she wouldn't give him the time of day. That she was into someone else and wouldn't even accept his flowers."

"Once, he was a real turtle," Jem said sadly.

"Huh?"

"Sorry. Too much *Wonderland*. Then what?"

"Then he clammed up and said if the bloody police expected more from him, they'd talk to him with a lawyer present. And so he was released, and Josh, too, of course, and they were both told not to leave Penzance without asking permission first."

"Wow. That's a lot," Jem said. "I wonder if Jerry will even

open The Siren this evening. He almost cried over a late food delivery. This has probably sent him into a total meltdown."

"You would think," Tori said, smiling in a way that clearly telegraphed she had more. "But just as Josh and I were settling our bill, he rang Josh's mobile. Absolutely over the moon. So happy he seemed like a different person."

"Why? Did they already exonerate him?" Jem asked, trying not to feel disappointed. She didn't want Josh's uncle to be a double murderer, of course, but to have him cleared so soon would be a letdown. He'd barely had time to settle as her new prime suspect.

"Apparently Eddie got a solicitor, and the solicitor got him out," Tori said. "The first thing Eddie did when he was free was to check with Gina's thingummy—the person executing the estate. And sure enough, she'd never bothered to change her will. They were still legally married, and he still inherited everything, including Tatteredly's. You know what that means, don't you?" She grinned. "The deal's back on."

"Officially?" Jem asked. "Livingston's and Rich Richards are back on board?"

"I don't know about that," Tori admitted. "Jerry mentioned somebody else—she sounded like a Christmas elf, he called her something like Jingle Bells..."

"Jingle-Jangle. Keeley Jingle-Jangle, Tors, remember? We were in that vintage shop, Age of Aquarius, and the owner, Millie, mentioned her."

Tori seemed impressed. "Good memory."

Jem shrugged that off, recalling not only the brief conversation with Millie, but the scarf she'd found on offer—a whimsical orange blossoms and teacups pattern—that was identical to the scarf left behind in Tatteredly's. Was it coincidence?

Maybe I don't just have one new prime suspect. Maybe I have two.

26

A ROMANCE TO WARM THE HEART AND TURN THE STOMACH

The second night in Jem's woefully inadequate hostel went better than the first. Tori again took the sofa, Wotsit curled up on the windowsill, and Rhys took the tub. Jem didn't expect to sleep well, now that she knew how his snores echoed off the bathroom walls, but exhaustion won out. She fell asleep around midnight and didn't wake up until her mobile went off at six a.m. She even managed to brew coffee and do a fry-up without banging the skillet. The smell of bacon and coffee awakened her guests, pleasantly surprising Jem.

"Why are you up so early?" she asked Tori, who wandered into the kitchenette with her blanket draped around her like a mantle.

"When I worked for the club I was always up early. And it's time I got back to work. After brekkie I'm off to find a job."

"Oh. Right. Good on you."

"Because I'm not going back to Liverpool. And I'm absolutely not going back to live with Mum and Dad."

Nodding, Jem began portioning scrambled eggs on plates. She had a feeling she knew where this conversation was headed.

"Of course, one day I might move in with Josh, if all goes as planned," Tori continued. "But until then, I thought maybe I could stay here with you. Paying rent, of course. I can look after the flat on the weekends while you're in the islands. And there's Wotsit to consider…"

As if by prearrangement, Wotsit chose that moment to stroll in. He was a mostly silent animal, which suggested he'd spent a good deal of time on the street, but when he found Jem and Tori chatting and his bowl empty of kibble, he let out a high-pitched, heart-rending little *meow*.

"Oh! I let you run out. Be right there," Tori said, hustling to find the bag of cat food and fill the bowl like a well-trained human.

"Tori. I told you I didn't want a pet."

"Jemmie. Look at him." Tori put on a pitiful voice as she pointed at the cat, who was chowing down with happy enthusiasm. "He's doing so well. This might be his first real home."

Rhys chuckled, entering the kitchenette clad only in blue jeans, his T-shirt and socks in his hand. "Give in, Jemmie. You know you want to."

"Fine. But you and Wotsit are responsible for each other. And the two of you owe me a replacement bath rug. Jade green to match the shower curtain."

"What's up with that curtain, anyway? Someone hacked at it with scissors." As he talked, Rhys pulled his T-shirt over his head, an operation that inevitably showed off biceps, triceps, pecs, deltoids, and whatever else he had that was generally found only on superheroes. For a moment, Jem was completely captivated. Then he slipped past her, reached under the sink, pulled out an aerosol can of Febreze, went to the living room and used it to spray himself down.

"You. Are. Disgusting," Jem announced as he sprayed down his right leg and up his left.

"This is day three. I have no change of clothes. Don't you

think the least I can do is be"—he checked the side of the can—"Frosted Berries fresh?"

"Tori, I'm sorry you have to witness this."

"Are you kidding? Dave does it, too. All the lads around Finchy reek of Febreze and Lynx body spray."

"I smell like a footballer," Rhys crowed. "Achievement unlocked!"

Jem had no sleuthing chores for Rhys, so for the second day in a row, he decided to make the rounds near Gwenver Beach, looking up old friends. She suspected he might be working A.A.'s Step Four—seeking out people he'd wronged while drinking, and making amends—but she didn't quiz him on it. If he felt like sharing that part of his life, he would. She didn't want to intrude on a recovery path that was obviously working for him.

As for her, the workday wasn't bad, though her thoughts kept drifting back to Natalie Lansallos. What had compelled someone to take the risk of killing her in her home—on a quiet stretch of Weaver Road where any neighbor might have heard her scream? Just getting through Natalie's dangerously cluttered yard would have been challenging enough, and then the killer had to make his way past that security door and into a home that was surely full of booby-traps, deliberate or incidental.

But the scenario gets easier to imagine if I assume Natalie invited her killer into the house. I know Josh described her like a total shut-in, and she certainly behaved that way with me, talking to me through a window. But she said herself that not so long ago, Gina asked her to mind the shop, so she dressed up and sallied forth to serve the reading public. Or something like that. So if she'd been willing to go out when the fancy struck her, she could certainly unlock the door and let someone in. Especially if she asked for a payoff, and they were bringing the money over.

Around half-ten, Micki called to fill Jem in on Eddie's

release. He wasn't out of the woods yet, but he still hadn't been charged, and his solicitor didn't expect him to be, unless compelling evidence was found connecting him to one or both crimes.

"And now that we have a video of him leaving Tatteredly's just before the murder, his alibi's that much stronger."

"Wait, what? There's a video of Eddie on the row Saturday morning? Before the sun came up?" Jem asked, thinking she must have misheard.

"Oh, yeah. I'm sorry, love," Micki said. "Eddie wasn't totally honest when we saw him Sunday. You know he was sympathetic to the shopkeepers who wanted to sell, and he thought he could help convince Gina. Or maybe he just wanted a reason to see her and talk to her. The owners who wanted to sell the most —that bloke from The Siren, and the lady from the vintage shop, and the barber, and the electronics repair guy—heard that Gina was doing a predawn inventory and decided to ambush her in the shop. They didn't call it that, of course. They called it an intervention."

"And Eddie went along?"

"Yeah.

"And a CCTV camera caught them coming and going?"

"That's right. The owner of Hair Today, Gone Tomorrow rang the police and said they might want to see his footage from Saturday morning. It's the only shop on the row with a camera pointed toward Tatteredly's front door. The police examined it and—"

"Hang on," Jem said. She'd spent so much time on that particular stretch of Silversmith Lane, she could visualize it without even closing her eyes. "Why was it pointed that way? Why only record what's going on to the east?"

"I don't think it was meant to be oriented that way," Micki said. "But you know how birds will perch on them sometimes and make them shift. People will reach up and twist them, too, just to be antisocial. Anyway, it was pointed right at Tatteredly's front door and it filmed all the shop-keepers entering together. Then it filmed them leaving together. None of them stayed after, and Gina locked the door behind them. The camera filmed everything for the next several hours, including you and me trying to get in through the front."

"But of course we went around back," Jem said. "Just like the killer."

"Yeah." Micki sighed. "Poor Gina. But at least this film established that they all came to talk to Gina, and they all left. If the coppers want to bang Eddie up again, they'll need finger-prints, DNA, or a witness. That's what his solicitor says, anyway."

"I wonder how many people knew Gina kept a hideaway key behind the electric meter? And nothing but a dummy CCTV camera over the door?"

"Well, Eddie knew, obviously. And the other victim, Ms. Lansallos, knew. I reckon Gina's new man might have known, too."

"Did you ask Eddie those questions for me?"

"Yeah. He swears up and down that he doesn't know the new boyfriend's name. As for breakfast, he said it had to be Jones's Diner. That once upon a time when Gina and Natalie were friends, they always ate breakfast in the shop. One of them would swing by the diner and pick up two boxes to go."

Jem let out a frustrated noise. "That just can't be a coin-cidence!"

"What?"

"Never mind. It would take too long and it doesn't seem to lead anywhere. I'm glad Eddie has a good attorney. If he was really in deep, I'm not sure I could help at all."

"Well. I have new information," Micki said portentously. "Don't be cross with me for saving it. Only I think this is the first time I've really discovered something that might help with a case."

"Tell me."

"Okay, but first you'll need a visual aid. Look up Livingston's estate agency online. I'll wait."

It took slightly longer than it should have, because Jem's search for Livingston's revealed that it had recently relocated to Chapel Street, one of Jem's favorite places in all of Penzance. Crammed with quaint buildings and an eclectic variety of businesses, Chapel Street had a Victorian-era church on one end and a venerable old quay on the other. There was also Penzance's oldest pub, a Wesleyan Chapel, and the glorious Grade I listed Egyptian House, a building so bizarre Jem couldn't help but adore it.

On Livingston's web page four agents were listed, accompanied by photos and short bios. The senior agent, Rich Richards, was a hatchet-faced man with thick dark hair who'd won three awards for community improvements around town. The most junior agent was Keeley Jingle-Jangle, whose real surname turned out to be Jarmon.

Having won no awards as yet, Keeley stared rather desperately out at the viewer, as if begging someone to make a deal. Aggressively blonde, she showed not an inch of naked skin: every visible part of her face and neck was coated with make-up or darkened by self-tanner. She was reasonably attractive, if Jem was any judge, but her instincts told her the one person who mattered most—Keeley Jarmon herself—would never think so.

"Got it?" Micki asked, still audibly excited.

"Yeah. Here's Keeley. The one I think left a scarf behind—wait. Are you telling me Keeley was part of the morning intervention?"

"Yes." A pause. "Do you notice anything else? Really look at her, Jem."

She did. For what felt like a long time, nothing came to her.

Then she thought of Burberry camel check, fake bake, and cubic zirconia-studded jewelry.

"Do *not* tell me Keeley's the ex-girlfriend who cut Eddie with a steak knife."

"Yes," Micki squealed, as if they'd both won a prize. "Doesn't her nose look great? He broke it, remember? They both were charged with domestic assault and went to prison—but I left out the part where they kissed and made up just before going into the big house."

"Really?"

"For real. It'll warm your heart or turn your stomach, just as you like."

"Do you think she still has feelings for Eddie?" Jem's mind leapt ahead to the financial angle. "Do you think he supported the sale for her sake, knowing she'd get a commission when it went through?"

"Whoa, now, don't forget which side you're on," Micki said. "I said Eddie's innocent, and I believe it today as much as I ever did. He might be a slippery, smiling little git, but he's my brother, and he didn't kill anyone. He adored Gina and didn't want to be with anyone else. Now Keeley... I couldn't say. Maybe she wanted Eddie back. Maybe enough to take Gina out of the picture forever."

"Could you ask him? About how he feels about Keeley, and vice versa?"

"I already did. He said Keeley's moving up, she's trying to better herself in the real estate game, and if he can help out a little, that's fine. Nothing else, not on his side."

"What about her side?"

"He said he didn't know. Mind you, that could just be the cocky little runt's ego talking. You know he wants to believe all his exes secretly carry a torch for him."

At that point in the conversation, Mr. Atherton drifted by, pointedly examined Jem's computer monitor—currently showing the Livingston's website—shook his head and kept walking, though he paused to look over his shoulder. Jem knew this was just the first pass, and if she didn't become conspicuously occupied, he'd be hanging over her shoulder for the rest of the day.

"I'd better go. We'll talk more later. Do I have this right? The people who did the Saturday-morning intervention were Jerry Berry from The Siren, Millie from Age of Aquarius, Toby from Hair Today, Gone Tomorrow, Krish from New Day Electronics Repair, your brother Eddie, and his ex/estate agent, Keeley Jarmon. Those six, correct?"

"And the wormy little guy. I think he was a clerk in one of the shops."

"Wormy little guy? What do you mean?" Jem asked.

"Just a guy. Young. Buzz cut. Smoking on his way in and smoking on his way out."

"Okay. Got it," Jem said as Mr. Atherton veered back her way. "Thanks, Micki. We have to be getting close to a breakthrough."

"I'm sure you'll crack it any minute," Micki said as her sign-off, sounding as if she really believed it. Jem wasn't nearly so sure, but she appreciated the vote of confidence.

So what do I know? she asked herself. *I know the killer behaved as if she—or he—despised Gina and Natalie. Those deaths weren't just a means to an end to make the sale go through. Cracking Gina in the head and bludgeoning Natalie to death is personal. Emotional. Unhinged. Could Jerry Berry have done it? And when Natalie worked it out and tried to blackmail him, he killed her, too?*

Her next thought was of T.J., the person who always seemed to intersect with the circumstances around Gina's death.

He was part of the intervention. Why? He didn't work for any of the owners. Was he really Gina's rebound man? Present that morning because they were a couple? And afterward, did she throw him over? Hurt his pride so he attacked her—and then turned on Natalie even more viciously?

Despite Micki's admonition for her to remember which side she was on, Jem found herself considering Eddie Latham more seriously than at any time since Gina's death.

He has that stalkerish quality. And a conman vibe. Suppose he decided to kill her before the divorce was final so he could keep up the lifestyle he enjoyed with Gina? And when Natalie wanted to horn in, leaning on their imaginary sexual magnetism, he eliminated her, too.

But in light of her new information about Keeley Jarmon, the estate agent had jumped close to the head of the pack.

Of course Keeley was desperate for the sale to go through. That much can be assumed. If Gina died and Eddie inherited Tatteredly's, it would go on the market. And maybe more important to her—if she still cares for him—with Gina dead, Eddie himself would go on the market. Two life goals accomplished by eliminating Gina. Now that's a motive.

27

KEELEY'S STORY

Under Mr. Atherton's watchful eye, Jem found herself staying until almost four o'clock, despite coming in two hours early. Her backlog was shrinking and her work on the UNESCO project was going swimmingly, but no brilliant flashes regarding the Gina Marrak and Natalie Lansallos murders had come to her.

She had just exited the Courtney Library and started for home when her mobile *chirrup*ed. It was Rhys.

"Hiya, Frosted Berries. Sniff anything out?"

"Yeah. The crew I ran with in my drinking days aren't any happier now than they were then. It was all I could do not to give them an A.A. sales pitch."

"I thought you guys don't evangelize."

"We don't. Took everything I had not to do it anyway, that's all I'm saying. Sobriety's still new enough for me that I want to grab people and shake 'em into it so they can enjoy it, too." He laughed. "People tried to do that for me when I was drinking. It never works. Anyway, you're not going to believe this, but PayPal just *ding*ed my phone. That means I sold a painting from my online shop. It's a miracle. From broke to ballin', as they say."

"Who says that?"

"I don't know. Muppets on telly. The point is, two paths lie before me. Path number one—I ring Bart and get a ride home. Path number two—I take you out for a proper dinner. My treat. What's your fancy?"

"Dinner," Jem said without hesitation. "Wait—did you say proper? Are you casting aspersions on last night's spaghetti?"

"No. It was... edible," he said, sounding like a man who'd embraced the A.A. cornerstone of rigorous honesty. "Let's face it, we're both used to Pauley-level cooking. So let's go out and find some. I'll even let you pick the place."

"Fine. Where are you right now?"

"Near the Union Hotel."

"So you're on Chapel Street?"

"Practically."

"Why don't I meet you on Chapel near Livingston's? You'll never believe what Micki found out. When I tell you, you'll understand what I have in mind."

"I called ahead to Livingston's," Rhys said by way of greeting as he met up with Jem on Chapel Street. "Keeley was just about to pack it in for the day, but said she'd stay an extra half-hour to talk to us."

"You didn't say it was about this, did you?" Jem asked, holding up a small tissue-wrapped parcel she'd purchased along the way.

"Nope. Said it was about some property that might be due for redevelopment. Didn't have to say more. She's hot to sell something to somebody. Do you really like her for the killer?" he asked as they walked the short distance to the real estate agency. "Why not the Turtle? If he wanted Gina bad and she turned him down, that on top of ruining the sale is a pretty good motive."

"I know. He's in the running."

"There's always the Caterpillar."

"The thing that spoils T.J. for me is his behavior after the fact. I can't come up with a single good reason for him to kill Gina, dispose of the murder weapon, then recruit his best mate and Tori, practically a total stranger, to watch as he goes through the motions of trying to find it."

"Maybe it was all an elaborate way to frame Natalie."

"If so, it was too clever by half. I've either overlooked something, or missed a key detail altogether," Jem said, biting back frustration.

"Don't moan about it. Look, there's the Egyptian House. What a sight. Sheer madness."

Jem, enchanted as always, paused to fondly look it over. During that strange British architectural period known as "Egyptian Revival," Victorians had briefly gone mad for obelisks, pyramids, and sphinxes. Somehow this had led to the Egyptian House's utterly inauthentic facade, with lotus columns, stylized cornices, bright colors, and—why not?—King George III's coat of arms, including the royal motto, "God and my right," thrown in for good measure.

Rhys said, "You know, they rent rooms. It's like a boutique hotel."

"Is it? I'd like to stay there."

"Stay there with me," he said lightly, still looking up at the facade. "Not tonight. When this is over. Soon."

Slipping her hand into his, Jem gave it a good, hard squeeze. "It's a date."

With that settled, they went into Livingston's. Judging by his decorations, fixtures, and furnishings, the agency had pretentions and mostly lived up to them. Three estate agents were still at their desks, all smartly dressed and oozing fake candor. Something about Jem in her workday attire and Rhys just as himself—forever island casual—caused all three heads to come up at once. For a moment it was in doubt: which agent would get across the floor to them first? The winner was also the oldest, a gray-haired woman with a jutting jaw.

"Good afternoon! Don't you find this weather marvelous? Other places wither as autumn approaches, but Penzance is gorgeous whatever the season." As she spoke, the agent's gaze shifted from Jem to Rhys and back again. She was like a robot assassin from the future, analyzing them down to their cellular structure as her sinister operating system calculated probabilities: Siblings? Romantic partners? Seeking a home? Looking to sell?

"We adore Penzance," Jem said. "And we're actually looking for one of your colleagues. Keeley Jarmon?"

The woman sagged, her face going blank. No matter how human these robot assassins seem on first blush, they always reveal themselves at the first hiccup.

"She's in the break room," she said in a flat voice. "Through there."

Thanking her, Jem and Rhys passed through the door she indicated and into the land of tea bags, Styrofoam cups, and stale coffee. Keeley Jarmon sat alone at the Formica-topped table, frowning at her mobile. When Jem introduced herself as the person who'd discovered Gina's body and said she'd like to talk with Keeley about the deaths of Gina Marrak and Natalie Lansallos, the woman bristled.

"This is an ambush." Arising from the table, Keeley planted her feet and clenched her fists. Almost as tall as Rhys and perhaps as heavy, she fixed them with a glare that held genuine menace.

"Not really," Jem said in a determinedly reasonable tone. "Now, what you and Jerry Berry and the rest did to Gina Marrak on Saturday morning, *that* was a bit of an ambush. Or maybe an intervention, to try and get her to take pity on the other owners. I assume most of you never intended it to be violent. But it turned bloody in the end, didn't it?"

Keeley stared at her. "I wouldn't know. I wasn't part of it."

"But you were there."

"Says who?"

"Says this," Jem said, opening the small parcel from Age of Aquarius and shaking out the whimsical orange blossoms and teacups scarf inside. "The night I found Gina dead in Tattered-ly's, I saw this on a shelf and took it home," she lied, pleased at how Keeley's eyes flew wide. "Careless of me to keep it, eh? I really must show it to DS Conrad. He'd be over here like a shot to interview you, don't you think? Right now he seems stuck on nailing Eddie Latham for the crime, but this might change his mind."

Keeley let her breath out all at once. "I can't believe I risked — That you have— Oh, God, I'm so stupid! I'll never get a break," she wailed. Throwing herself back into the chair, she did the one thing Jem hadn't prepared herself for: she dissolved into tears.

"Hey, erm... don't do that," Rhys muttered, looking around for someplace to hide, or maybe a fire exit.

"Keeley, listen," Jem said, hoping to salvage something of the gambit. "This scarf isn't the only thing that places you in Tatteredly's. There's video evidence, too. Everyone knows you were dying to make that sale, and Gina stood in your way. Not everyone knows that you and Eddie had a history. Did you attack Gina? Try to scare her and go too far?"

"No! *No!* Does every single person in Penzance know that I have a record? Will my punishment ever be over?" She covered her face with her hands and cried harder.

What would Archie Goodwin do now? Jem wondered, regretting the fake evidence scheme that was direct from his playbook. *Probably take her in his arms and kiss her. Those Alloyed Age detectives lived in a different world.*

Blowing out a sigh, Jem turned to Rhys to see if he had any ideas. He shrugged, looking more than a little unnerved. Those muscles weren't good for every situation. It was up to her.

"All right. Let's start over," Jem said, taking a seat beside Keeley and motioning for Rhys, still transparently looking for the exit, to join them. "When I heard about the history between you and Eddie, and I thought about what you might stand to gain, I jumped to the conclusion that you killed Gina. Did you leave the scarf behind that morning?"

Keeley nodded, sniffling. "The meeting was supposed to be upbeat and friendly—Millie and Krish really wanted to keep things respectful—but it turned ugly right away."

"How so?"

"I think in the beginning, Gina sort of enjoyed telling us no. We'd tell her how advantageous the deal was. She'd let us talk ourselves blue, then just say no. With a smile. It started to get a little sadistic," Keeley said. "The more Jerry and Toby and Millie and Krish pleaded, the more sympathetic she seemed—but she always said no in the end. That chain-smoker who sells the sticky icky made a lot of money off Millie. She has to smoke a ton of weed to keep up her earth mother vibe."

"Right. So we know who came to the intervention. You, Eddie, Jerry, Toby, Millie, Krish, and the chain-smoker, T.J. Mallard. Who was in charge? Jerry Berry?"

Keeley frowned. "Nah. I mean, he acted like it. But really it was a mutual thing. We all wanted it so badly. Eddie for my sake, because we were still friends, and the rest because they were all underwater and needed the cash."

"Why did T.J. want it?"

"Oh, sorry, not him. He was just there."

"As Gina's rebound man?"

Keeley blinked at her. "What?"

"Gina was seen in Noughts & Crosses with two men. The description of one fits T.J. Mallard perfectly. The bartender who saw them assumed they were a couple."

Keeley laughed. "No. He was the go-between. If he went in there and chatted up Gina, it wasn't on his own behalf. He was just the messenger."

"For Jerry Berry?"

"For Toby. You know, the barber. He was madly in love with Gina. I reckon she gave him a week or two, then threw him away, just like she threw away Eddie. And just like Eddie, he didn't want to let go."

Jem and Rhys exchanged glances. The "no-hoper," as described by the bartender he'd pumped for information, had been bald, harassed-looking, and wearing an apron. Jem had imagined Jerry's food-stained white apron, but the bartender had meant Toby's black stylist's apron.

"You know this for sure? Toby told you? Or Gina?"

"Oh, Lord no, nobody told me." Keeley seemed surprised that she would ask. "It's all about observation. When you know what to look for, it's obvious."

"You said T.J. was the errand boy. The go-between," Jem said. "I don't suppose he turned up at the meeting with, well —food?"

"How'd you know?"

"Lucky guess. What kind of food?"

"Takeaway breakfast from Jones's Diner. He knew Gina liked it. I reckoned Toby was trying to make a morning out of it. Probably the way they did when they were together, if you want my best guess," Keeley said. "But she said she didn't want it, and — Oh. He left both boxes behind, in the shop. Did you find them, too, when you found my scarf?"

"Sort of," Jem said, mind whirling.

28

WWNWD: WHAT WOULD NERO WOLFE DO?

Jem and Rhys didn't have to confer about the postponing of a proper, Pauley Gwyn-level dinner; it went without saying. Jem wasn't sure what she might gain by dropping in to Hair Today, Gone Tomorrow to check in with Toby Smithfield, but she couldn't stop herself.

"I understand why you don't want to ring Conrad," Rhys said as they walked down Chapel Street toward the dusky half-circle of Silversmith Bay. "But there's always Hackman. He probably won't even scold you. It's not his jurisdiction, and you haven't done anything too crazy this time. He should give you credit for that."

"All right. Say I ring Hack. What do I tell him?"

"That you know who killed Gina, and maybe Natalie, too."

"Okay. What's my proof?"

"His motive. A man scorned—wait, is that a thing?"

"You'd better believe it is."

"Right. So, a man scorned, plus a quarter of a million pounds of desperately needed dosh. Bang."

"Motive isn't proof. What's the physical evidence?"

"Those breakfast trays from the rubbish pile."

"Not very conclusive, when you think back to how they were found in an open bin that anyone could've contributed to. Not to mention how they were dragged through the streets."

Rhys thought for a moment. "Okay, so it's a circumstantial case. I don't think Conrad would shy away from that. You said yourself that Toby's CCTV camera just happened to be pointed toward Tatteredly's front door. He arranged it that way, so he'd have a video alibi."

"Prove it," Jem said, laughing mirthlessly at the way he scowled. "I know. It's infuriating. We have some excellent leads but nothing concrete. We don't even know for sure that Toby is the rebound man. He fits a vague description—bald, harassed-looking, apron. As for whether or not he was actually seeing Gina, she seems to have kept things hush-hush. Even Keeley's declarations were actually just guesses, and she admitted as much."

"So what next? Are we going to the salon to beat the truth out of him?"

"Would you be up for it?"

"My sponsor would fire me. Solving problems with violence —not really in the program."

"To answer your question, we're going to the salon because I don't know what else to do. Now that I feel sure Toby killed Gina, maybe something he says or does will give me a clue of how to nail him. Or maybe you'll see the way, and tell me how to proceed."

"Sure. No pressure," he said, and began to walk slower. Even so, Jem found herself in front of Hair Today, Gone Tomorrow with no idea of what she would do, apart from striking up a conversation with a man who was at best a murderer, and at worst a double murderer.

Through the big picture window, Jem saw there was only

one client in the chair: a middle-aged woman, her hair dark and goopy with developing color formula. The other four styling chairs were empty.

"Maybe I should stay out here," Rhys murmured.

"Why?"

"I thought I hadn't seen Toby in years. But the minute I saw his face, I flashed back to something that happened at a waterfront club, ages ago. Short version, I was a jerk. If I talk to him, I'll have to make amends, and I'd rather not make nice with a killer just now."

"Fine. But if I turn around and gesture, come inside."

"What will you want?"

"How can I possibly know until it happens? Just keep your eyes open," Jem said, and opened the salon's door, which bonged with an electronic bell.

"Welcome," Toby said from behind the cash stand, not looking up. He was scowling at something on his computer. "I was on the verge of closing up, but if you'll tell me what you have in mind, perhaps I could— Oh! Jem." He gave her what looked like a forced smile. "Don't tell me you've decided to free yourself with a smart new cut?"

"Nope. I actually came just to talk to you," Jem said, forcing a smile right back and hoping it looked more realistic. "Could we step into the back?"

"I..." He made a dismissive gesture toward his curtained back room, which was not dissimilar from Tatteredly's. "It's a mess back there. Let's talk out here. Mrs. Lincoln won't mind, unless it's about sex, money, or murder."

"I'm fine with all those," said the color-developing Mrs. Lincoln, who sounded as if she meant it.

"Oh, well, just a few things," Jem said, eyes roaming the shop in search of inspiration. Something black on the floor caught her eye. Was it a cockroach? Jem stiffened automatically, then realized it was one of Toby's hair clips, like the one he'd dropped on Sunday while crossing the street.

"Lost another one. Here you go," she said, handing it over with some effort. She didn't want to touch, even glancingly, the hands that had killed two women. "Remember how I said I found Gina Marrak's body? Well, because of that—"

"Hang on," Toby cut in. He was smiling, but his pale eyes were sharp. "You think I'm not on to you, Scilly Sleuth? After we met up again, I looked you up online. Whatever you do, don't read the comments on *Bright Star*. People can be so cruel."

Jem shrugged. "Anyway, I'm known for sticking my nose in and right now I'm curious about a friend of my little sister. Two friends, actually. One is a very nice bloke called Josh Lansallos—"

"Good kid," Toby cut in again. "Related to Jerry Berry but doesn't take after him, thank heavens. Your sis is safe with him."

"Yes, well, it's not Josh I'm concerned about, it's T.J. Mallard. Do you know him?"

Toby shook his head slowly, as if turning an unfamiliar name over in his head. As performances go, it wasn't bad, except for his eyes, which were still razor-sharp.

"You really don't know him?"

"Sorry, Jem. This isn't St. Morwenna. I don't know every person in Penzance by name."

"Of course. Only... I heard he runs errands for you."

"Fine." Toby sighed. "Yes, I've paid him to do odd jobs for me sometimes. I'm not proud of it, given his reputation. Sorry, Mrs. Lincoln," he added, remembering his client was within earshot. "Ordinarily I don't tell falsehoods."

"Don't do it when I ask for hair advice."

"I won't, I promise." Toby, still holding onto the wayward clip Jem had picked up from the salon floor, tested the gripper mechanism on a finger. The clip fell off. "Another one done for.

Not that it matters," he said, binning it. "Today I learned Eddie Latham will inherit Tatteredly's and Rich Richards is willing to go through with his original deal. Soon I'll be opening a new place in a better location." He glanced at Mrs. Lincoln, who was examining her manicure, and added softly, "Far away."

"Anyway, getting back to T.J., I heard about the Saturday-morning intervention. And somebody else told me you gave the police your CCTV camera footage. It shows you and the other shopkeepers, plus Keeley Jarmon and T.J. Mallard, going in and out of Tatteredly's, is that right?"

Toby folded his arms across his chest. When he spoke, there was a hint of anger. "Who's been telling tales out of school? It's Jerry Berry, isn't it? He ranted to Josh, Josh told your sis, she told you, and now I'm hearing of it. Stories get distorted that way."

"You're not a fan of Jerry, are you?"

"No. If you want my opinion, he killed Gina. Probably killed Natalie, too. She was his sister-in-law, you know. Awful woman. Kind of woman who deserved whatever she got."

Jem chanced a peek at Mrs. Lincoln. The woman didn't look pleasantly scandalized, as people often do when subjected to a bit of good gossip. She looked disquieted, as if she wanted to get up and walk out but couldn't with all the goop in her hair.

She hears it. On a visceral level, she knows, just as I know.

Toby, perhaps aware that he'd gone too far, produced another smile, this one more genuine-looking than the last. "Pay no attention to me. My ship's finally come in, and it's taking me awhile to get used to feeling anything other than desperate. Can I do anything else for you, hon?"

Jem steeled herself against visibly cringing at the "hon." "No thanks," she said. "Have a good night."

~

"I wonder what's taking Bart so long," Jem said. The wind off the bay was brisk, but she wasn't cold. Rhys had his arm around her, and was blocking the worst of it with his body.

"It always takes him forever on special charters. That's why he's so cheap." Squeezing her, he added, "If you're hinting for me to stay the night, I'm game. I'll probably need a lot more Febreze tomorrow morning, but if you don't mind, I don't."

She laughed. "No, I don't want you sleeping in the tub again. You might do your back permanent damage. Do you always snore like that?"

"No. I'm semi-allergic to cats."

"Oh, poor Wotsit. You never said."

He shrugged. "Can't disrespect a cat in his own home."

She raised on her tiptoes to kiss him. It was a pleasant experience; during most of her romantic life, she'd been leaning down.

"So what's next with your investigation?" he asked, looking like he'd rather kiss her again than talk about murder, but was holding himself back.

"Ideally, I'd ask Toby to write out a confession, he'd say yes, and I'd hand it over to the police. Done and dusted. In the real world, I have no idea."

"The Scilly Sleuth can't say that."

"The Scilly Sleuth has no idea what to do next."

"Right. Then what would your book sleuth do? Archie Whosit."

"Archie Goodwin? Oh, at this point he's always stumped. Nero Wolfe takes over for the endgame. Nine out of ten times he drags all the suspects into a room together."

"And then what?"

"Then he says or does something provocative. And sometimes ridiculous. Something that makes the killer slip up and reveal themselves."

"Well, far be it from you to do anything ridiculous," Rhys said lightly. Then his smile faded. "Hang on. Tell me you aren't planning to do something provocative and ridiculous."

"I haven't dreamed anything up yet. But if I do—will you help me?"

29

BUBBLE BATH, WINE, AND BOOK

It wasn't much of an evening after Rhys boarded Bart the Ferryman's disreputable-looking converted fishing boat, *Merry Maid*, and chugged away in the direction of St. Morwenna. Jem walked home slowly, conscious of her surroundings but not appreciating them, well aware that her problem was pure ego. She'd undertaken a puzzle she'd almost solved, but she couldn't prove her theorem to satisfy even the minimum requirements of the real world. Now she was faced with the humbling prospect of taking her conjectures and not-coincidences to the likes of DS Conrad, who was certain to take the opposing view just for spite. Turning the whole case over to Hack was slightly more attractive, except the end result would be the same. It wasn't his jurisdiction, and he couldn't investigate. All he could do was pass it on to the proper authority at Exeter Police HQ; in short, DS Conrad. Jem doubted he'd enjoy that resolution any more than she would.

At home, Tori was sulking in front of the telly. It seemed that wages in Penzance were considerably lower than in Liverpool, and most of the openings hadn't been to her liking. She was probably going to have to start by taking a couple of part-time jobs and then try to parlay one of them into full-time work. Jem commiserated and asked how Josh was. Apparently the Lansallos family was busy with funeral preparations, and Tori wasn't sure how to help.

"Even Wotsit won't let me pet him," she grumbled. "He really is *such* a cat sometimes. I don't suppose I can do anything for you?"

Jem shook her head. "Eddie's out of jail, no one's arrested Toby as far as I know, and no one else has died. This might be the end of the line."

"Shut up. Really?" Tori sounded mildly crushed.

"Maybe I just need to put my mind on something else for a while," Jem said. "Bubble bath, glass of wine, book. That's the prescription. Even if it doesn't work, it should lull me to sleep, and that's something."

"Enjoy." Tori sighed, and went back her listless viewing of *MasterChef*.

After the bubble bath (which was short on bubbles because Jem had no bath potions and had to make do with a bit of Fairy Liquid) she wandered into her bedroom, moisturized her face and hands, and got into bed. That night's Alloyed Age mystery was *Three Doors to Death*. She was just settling into the first story when her mobile *chirrup*ed. It was a recorded message from Hack, who found speaking and sending easier than typing or using voice-to-text.

"Hiya, Stargazer. Do you do any actual stargazing in town, or is that strictly an Isles of Scilly thing?

"Anyhow, I don't suppose you've heard about it, being wrapped up in library stuff and your many murder cases, but I've become a bit famous. If only I could monetize it like those kayaking little buggers. You realize they get paid every time someone clicks, right? Ought to be a law.

"Just thought I'd tell you the meeting last night wasn't so

bad. The IOPC fellows were stuffed shirts, but the retired Scotland Yard guy was all right. Catered it, if you can believe that. Said we all had to eat. Must've paid a pretty penny, but I reckon a baron can afford it. He gave me a fair hearing. Said in his view my complaints on you-know-who have merit on the face of it, and he'll recommend that the investigation continue. I don't expect to be vindicated, but hey... If I am, I swear I'll legally change my name to Ignatius Hackman and make my mum the happiest woman alive.

"This whole thing is proof nice guys finish last, and playing by the rules is for suckers. I mean... not really. But the reason Conrad always wins is because if the plain truth doesn't work, he stretches it. If the evidence doesn't fit, he changes it. If the smoking gun isn't lying around, he puts a good facsimile where he'd like the evidence to be. Like I said, there ought to be a law.

"Anyway, that's all. Take care, Jem. The islands aren't the same without you."

He rang off.

Jem put the phone aside and lay back against the pillows, trying to decide how she felt. In a world where Rhys Tremayne didn't exist, she would've already done a swan dive back into the dating pool with Hack. He was cocky, sharp-witted, and sexy as hell. If she ever really got to know him, who knew how he might make her feel?

But Rhys does exist. And I already know how he makes me feel.

Three Doors to Death ended up on the nightstand next to her mobile. She switched off the light, closed her eyes, and was almost asleep when the thought came to her:

What if I put a good facsimile where I'd like the evidence to be?

30

"YOU SHOULD BE THANKING ME"

It was Friday evening—another seventy-two hours later—
before all the elements of Jem's plan came together. Looking
back on the operation, including designing the concept,
recruiting the players, coordinating between all parties, and
managing her own nervous anticipation, the hardest part was
performing her regular duties at the Courtney on Wednesday,
Thursday, and Friday. Beavering away on a Cornish mining
exhibit proposal is all very well, except when all you can think
about is murder.

As far as Tori and Josh went, Jem made the tough but necessary decision to leave them both entirely in the dark. Josh, still
grieving his aunt's death and infuriated by the cloud of suspicion around his uncle Jerry, was in a state where no one could
expect total discretion from him. In fact, if Tori had slipped up
and told him the identity of his aunt's killer, Josh might have
taken matters into his own hands. Therefore, among her friends,
Jem consulted only with Rhys and Micki, allowing Micki to
reach out to the operation's pivotal player, Eddie. Relying on
him took a rather large leap of faith on her part, and she half
expected him to bail out long before showtime, but he didn't.

Around six o'clock, her mobile received a text from him that read,

Tatteredly's at midnight, all confirmed but Krish. Keeley, Jerry, Toby, Millie, and T.J. All on pins and needles. I guess some of them think I'm a killer, and some of them think Jerry is. I hope not getting Krish isn't too big a deal.

It wasn't. After reading Eddie's text and realizing her plan was really going to happen, Jem wondered if she hadn't gone a little overboard. Still, the die was cast, and if things came right in the end, people would probably forgive her for a little foolishness along the way.

Jem took her place on stage several hours before showtime. She couldn't risk being seen entering Tatteredly's, not even escorted by Eddie Latham, who as the shop's new owner had a right to admit anyone he pleased. With Rhys and Micki scouting Silversmith Lane and communicating with Jem by phone, they advised her when it was safe to slip into the dark and silent bookshop unseen: half-seven, as it turned out, while Keeley was eating dinner, Jerry was serving pints, Toby was giving highlights, Millie was making a sale, and T.J. was inside Noughts & Crosses, probably resenting the anti-smoking ordinance.

All in all, four and a half hours proved a very long time to wait, even surrounded by more books than she could read in a year. Tatteredly's felt forlorn, and Jem found herself checking and rechecking various elements, like the ceiling-mounted security camera that Eddie had installed but Gina had never used. Now it was functioning, ready to record everything that happened during the midnight meeting. The cameras weren't rigged for audio, a gap which Jem had thought they might fill with their mobiles, but Rhys had suggested going old school. A professional-grade tape recorder, purchased for a song at New

Day Electronics, sat on the floor behind the cash stand, ready to immortalize every word—and hopefully the next best thing to a full confession.

Around 11:45 p.m., Jem concealed herself in the shop's far corner next to the *Alice* window. There she would remain unseen even when Tatteredly's front door opened and Eddie ushered everyone inside. Once the guests were in the shop, Eddie had volunteered to bolt the front door and remain in place so that no one did a runner. Little and unimposing as he was, she believed he was up to it. Unlike Josh, he wasn't at risk of taking the law into his own hands, but he very much wanted Gina's killer to pay. With him guarding the front, that would leave only the curtained back room as an exit route—and should Toby try it, a surprise waited for him inside.

That quarter-hour, from 11:45 p.m. to 12:00 a.m., was as slow and agonizing to Jem as another four full hours. Finally —*finally*—a man's voice could be heard on the other side of the shop's big picture window. It was Eddie, issuing a friendly greeting to someone. He sounded just like he had on the day Jem first met him—buoyant, good-natured, and at ease. Probably smiling that big, unfaltering smile at everyone, even Toby.

The door opened. For a few seconds Jem's view was obstructed, but then someone hit the switch and the overhead lights flickered on. Millie the boho princess entered first, rocking her pretty-granny broomstick skirt and crocheted shawl. Next came Toby, all in black as always, his faded apron still studded with plastic hair clips. Keeley and Jerry entered more or less at the same time, she glancing around nervously, he mopping his forehead with the back of his hand. Last came T.J. Mallard, whom Jem would forever think of as the Caterpillar, dressed in a dark hoodie and jeans. In his right hand smoldered a cigarette, despite the NO SMOKING notice on the door.

Closing the door, Eddie turned the bolt lock with a snap.

Calling, "Jem, love, take it away," he positioned himself in front of the door like a goalie defending his post.

"What's this?" Jerry demanded, wheeling around as Jem stepped forward.

T.J. giggled in a way that suggested he'd been sampling his own product. "Wait. Is this some kind of murder-mystery stunt?"

"I don't understand," Millie said.

"Bollocks." Toby looked around Keeley, whose towering figure was in his way, and bounced on his toes until he saw Jem step out into the open. "I don't know what this is, and I don't care. Open that door and let us leave or I'll ring the police." He started patting his apron down in search of his mobile.

"Come on, guys," Keeley announced in the inflectionless tone of a student actor recording a public service announcement. "Maybe we should hear her out. What's up, Jem?"

She fought back a smile. When Eddie had floated the notion of including Keeley as a participant, Jem had agreed only reluctantly, but the estate agent was clearly giving it her all. That earnestness made Jem like her more. Maybe if she spent time in the Isles of Scilly, she could hone her thespian skills with St. Mary's theater group.

"Sunday morning, I had a conversation with Natalie Lansallos," Jem began, pleased that her voice remained steady. A person should probably never become accustomed to being around murderers on the hoof, but maybe she was—a little, anyway. "I was one of the last people to see her alive. One of you was the last. You went to her home—inside her home, no less, which is quite a feat—and beat her to death. And you did it because of something I told her."

"What did you tell her?" T.J. asked, sounding like Eric Idle of *Monty Python's Flying Circus*.

"Quiet," Jerry snapped.

"The mallet that killed Gina was found in the rubbish bin

behind The Siren. The murderer tossed it in there. He tossed something else in, too—a couple of untouched breakfasts from Jones's Diner. He brought them along Saturday morning because he knew Gina and Natalie used to eat breakfast in the shop sometimes. He must've done it during the time he and Gina were briefly together. Then, after she ended the affair, he tried lots of little things to get back in her good—"

"You did it," Jerry growled, turning on Toby, who was at least a foot shorter. The stylist backed away. "You killed Natalie. My nephew's in a right state because of you."

"You're crazy." Those blue eyes, so sharp that Tuesday night when Jem had talked with him in the salon, were wide now and protruding slightly. When he backed away another step, colliding with Millie, she recoiled as if scalded.

Intrigued by the group dynamic, Jem continued, "On Sunday, my sis took a picture of the takeaway boxes that I thought connected Natalie to Gina's murder. Jerry's nephew, Josh, showed the pic to his aunt—"

"You thought Natalie killed Gina?" Jerry broke in, rounding on her. "Why? She hardly even left the house anymore."

"Because of T.J.," Jem replied, turning to smile at the Caterpillar. His finger still bore the marks from Wotsit's bite, which suited her fine. If she was going to have a cat, she wanted one with good instincts. "T.J. pulled me into this when he told Natalie's nephew Josh that he saw her in the alley with a bloody mallet in her hand."

"I did see her," T.J. declared, no longer sounding like Eric Idle. "He had a right to know what his aunt was up to. I even helped him look for the mallet to protect her!"

"You saw her?" Millie sounded confused. "I don't understand. If you saw her, why didn't you ring the police straightaway?"

"He didn't see Natalie," Jerry growled. "He saw Toby, isn't that right?"

"Me?" Toby cried in a high-pitched voice that did nothing to make him sound like an innocent man, falsely accused. "Why me? Eddie, get out of the way. I'm leaving. I'm the one who should ring the police. Eddie! I said move!"

"You're not going anywhere, mate," Eddie said, not budging from his position blocking the front door.

"But Teej," Millie said, appealing directly to the young man, whose eyes were darting around the sales floor as if he might be the one to go barreling toward the back room where Rhys stood just behind the curtain, waiting. "Whoever you saw in the alley, why did you try to recover the mallet yourself? Why not just tell the police?"

"My theory was blackmail," Jem said. "I reckoned if Natalie was the killer, and at the beginning it seemed like she had to be, then T.J. wanted the mallet to hold over her head." Frowning at the accidental pun, she plunged on. "But it turns out T.J. did odd jobs for Toby sometimes. And T.J. might not be the nicest guy you'll ever meet, but he's certainly not the thickest, either. He worked out the likely repercussions of Gina's death right away—the sale would happen, Toby would get a quarter mil, and as long as T.J. had possession of the mallet, Toby would be paying him to keep quiet about it."

"You are mental," Toby burst out, but while his words were directed at Jem as a sort of blanket denial, he was glaring at T.J., and everyone in the shop could guess why. Until that moment, he hadn't thought of himself as in danger from the area's small-time dealer. If he had, T.J. might have gone the way of Natalie Lansallos.

"So getting back to those breakfast trays," Jem said, speaking faster as the collective mood grew darker. "When I mentioned them to Natalie on Sunday morning, she immediately guessed that Toby was the killer. Later, when Josh showed her the pic, she must have seen it as blackmail fodder. Maybe that's why she and T.J. were friendly—their minds worked in the same way.

Anyway, by dinner time, she was dead, bludgeoned to death in her own home. I think sometime that afternoon, she contacted Toby, probably using her laptop, and told him to come round. She invited him inside to make her demands, and that's what got her killed."

"I told you, this is mental," Toby said again, striving for a more dignified tone. "You brought us here under false pretenses and you're just making things up as you go. She didn't contact me. I—"

"But she did," Millie said suddenly, eyes widening. "I rang you, remember, to ask if you thought Eddie would inherit the shop. That was Sunday afternoon around five o'clock—I used my mobile, I can check the exact time. We were talking and suddenly you said, 'Nutty Natty is emailing me.' Then you called her a very rude name and said you had to ring off." Millie shook her head in disbelief. "You really did it, didn't you? Went to her place and beat her to death."

"I ought to beat you to death," Jerry told the little man. If Jem hadn't known him to be a man of threats rather than action, she would've been alarmed by the way his fists trembled at his sides. "I cared for Gina. I would've been good for her, if she'd given me a chance. And you killed her. Just like you killed my sister-in-law, you sneaky little git."

"You should be thanking me," Toby cried, eyes roving among his fellow owners to take in Eddie and Keeley, too. "Think of the money! Think of the freedom. Saturday morning we were all in a hopeless situation. Now Eddie's set for the rest of his life and we're all getting out of here. I did that!"

"Money?" Jerry repeated, sounding stunned.

"You're sick," Millie told Toby, backing away from him into Keeley, who patted her shoulder.

"Were you really thinking of the money when you killed Gina?" Jem asked, watching his face. "It must've been humiliating, how she treated you. You were her rebound man and she was way out of your league. She didn't even want it known, did she? She was ashamed to be seen with you. That time you tried to meet her in Noughts & Crosses, she didn't like it, did she? After that you sent T.J. as your go-between."

Toby rounded on T.J., who looked more than a little impressed by Jem's deduction. T.J. said, "I don't know how she knows that, but she's got you dead to rights, man. Sorry."

"It's true that I was with Gina briefly. Ending it was a mutual decision," Toby insisted, drawing himself up to his full height with desperate dignity.

"I don't think so," Jem said. "I don't think killing her after the meeting failed to change her mind was totally spontaneous, either. You tried to make it work. You rang T.J. to pick up the breakfasts, which he did, even after his long night on the town with Josh and my sister. You and the other owners made your best arguments. But Gina didn't give a damn, did she? She wouldn't even eat the breakfast. You were so upset, you left them behind when you walked out with the others. But even then you knew the CCTV camera was filming you leaving Tatteredly's. And there was no working camera around the back to film you using the hideaway key to slip back in."

No one spoke. Even Toby was looking at Jem as if waiting to hear what came next.

"Dude. You confessed," T.J. whispered helpfully. "You opened your mouth and basically confessed."

"It's her word against mine. She confused me," Toby said. "I didn't know what I was saying."

"See that camera?" T.J. pointed. "The red light's on, mate."

"It's recording," Eddie announced, still smiling his now almost frightening smile. "I saw to that especially for you, Toby. And there's a machine behind the cash stand recording every word."

"Gina attacked me. She came at me like a madwoman. I had to defend myself," Toby said, eyes darting from face to face.

"And as for Natalie, I never touched her. I was never in her house. I don't even know how she died."

"Jerry's nephew found the body," Jem reminded him. "He was so shaken up, he didn't know what he was doing. He showed the police her laptop. The one you smashed, trying to eliminate any record of her email—which was stupid, as you have to know. He also found this near the body. He meant to give it to the police but forgot. So he gave it to me." Reaching in her pocket, she pulled out a long black clip. "Recognize this? Nearly sprung, like most of your clips. That's why it fell off your apron when you killed Natalie."

"No," Toby whispered. "No. Did I wear my apron? I couldn't have. I was in such a frenzy..." He broke off, over-whelmed, unable to pull his gaze away from the clip in her hand.

"You're a sick person, Toby," Jerry said with loathing.

The little man didn't seem to hear. His gaze shifted from the hair clip to Jem's face. "You," he cried, and launched himself at her.

"Enough! Devon & Cornwall Police. Freeze," thundered PC Stacy Kellow, who could sound quite official when she wanted to, as she emerged from Tatteredly's back room with Rhys beside her.

PC Kellow and Rhys weren't close enough to stop Toby. Jem was on too much of an adrenaline high to feel the slightest fear—she liked her chances against him in a bare-knuckle fight—but then Keeley Jarmon sprang into action. Picking Toby up like a Keebler elf, she held him a foot off the floor, short legs kicking helplessly.

"Knock it off," she bawled in his face, "or I'll break you in two."

～

As Jem knew from prior experience, wrapping up after an attack and arrest was a slow process. By the time she and Rhys were given the green light to leave Exeter Police HQ, it was seven o'clock and time for breakfast. Ordinarily she would've been asleep on her feet, but her adrenaline high wasn't quite spent. When it was, she'd belly-flop in her bed and stay there for hours, if not forever.

"I'm still flush after selling that painting," Rhys said as they stepped out in the rosy morning light. "Breakfast is my treat. Jones's Diner, I presume?"

Jem groaned. "No thanks. Anywhere else."

"All right, but we have to celebrate. Your little stunt with the hair clip worked. Toby didn't even demand to inspect it. And you went to so much trouble springing the mechanism, so it would look well used instead of brand new."

"I know. But better safe than sorry. I didn't expect the rest of the group to start chiming in," she admitted. "Millie's testimony will probably help send Toby down. Plus everything the forensics techs recover from the web. They're sure to prove that Natalie emailed some kind of blackmail threat to Toby, and he at least opened it, even if he was smart enough not to reply."

"Was it my imagination, or did Eddie and Keeley look sort of cozy in there?"

"I don't know. Eddie was all about justice for Gina. I reckon it will take him awhile to process everything," Jem said. "Plus his change in circumstances. He really is well off now. And all because he behaved like a stalker instead of going along with the divorce."

"Maybe Gina brought out the worst in him," Rhys suggested. "In which case, Keeley might do better. Now that they've already attacked each other, been to prison, been rehabilitated, and so on."

Jem smiled. "I can't tell if you're punchy from lack of sleep or giddy over how upset DS Conrad was."

"Definitely giddy. He was ready to arrest PC Kellow for solving a double murder, which was one for the record books. Remember when I excused myself to go to the men's room? I was in there laughing my arse off."

"I hope he doesn't make PC Kellow's life too hard now that she's showed him up."

"I hope he doesn't make your life too hard, next time you stick your nose in. And you will."

Jem started to contradict him, mostly from habit, but couldn't. The killer of Gina Marrak and Natalie Lansallos was behind bars, which meant one thing—Jem Jago, the Isles of Scilly's very own sleuth, had hung out her shingle on the mainland, too.

31

42M VIEWS

The next day, a better-rested Jem and Rhys sat down in front of her telly with Tori, Pauley, Micki, and Josh to watch the kayaking teens' viral Wyatt the Walrus video. Even Wotsit watched the YouTube sensation from his perch on the windowsill, though if anyone glanced his way, he shut his eyes and pretended to be napping.

There was takeaway lunch spread across the coffee table, but it grew cold as they watched the video over and over—first in amazement, then in horror, then in absolute delight. All five of the kayakers on the Scillonian bird sanctuary, Annet, had filmed Hack's encounter with Wyatt, resulting in plenty of raw phone footage shot from multiple perspectives. Someone had taken that footage, edited it with flair, and interspersed the action with testimonial-style commentary.

Everyone had their favorite part, but Jem's began with Hack sitting alone in the IoS PD's rigid inflatable. As the waves began to rock more powerfully, he just sat there, staring into the middle distance as he stewed over his upcoming meeting. On the right side of the screen, Wyatt the Walrus trundled into view. With his alternating flipper action and blowhole eruptions, no one could say he sneaked up on Hack. Yet the man never stirred or looked around, and the video cut to a testimonial from a teenager with wet hair and a gobsmacked expression.

"I mean, the poor sod was just sitting there, out to lunch, like he was pondering the fate of all mankind or something. And here's Wyatt, this great bloody beast, paddling up..." He imitated the motion. "But Mr. Policeman doesn't stir. Britain's finest, I shouldn't wonder."

The video cut back to Hack and Wyatt. Rendered in slow motion and shot from multiple angles, it showed Wyatt heaving himself aboard the RIB's aft section, carelessly flopping his vastness atop the engine. This hiccup prevented him from beaching himself on the boat, a trick he'd mastered over the summer. Hack hardly had time to shout an expletive (helpfully removed by the kids and replaced with a cuckoo's call) before he was airborne, hurled straight up like Superman.

The image froze with Hack midair. Keeping him there on the left side of the screen, the right side returned to testimonial mode, now with a different teen.

"The boys were screaming their heads off," said the girl with twin braids and a thick Scottish accent. "I turned to the other copper, the one who came ashore to tell us off. And he's just..." She mimed an open mouth. "That's it. No words, no reactions, just..." She opened her mouth and held it.

The action resumed with PC Newt gaping as Hack was flung toward the sky. Thereafter, every few moments—after Hack crashed into the sea, after Wyatt began bellowing, after *Merry Maid* chugged into view with Bart the Ferryman crooning an old love song over his boat's PA—the video occasionally flipped to PC Newt for a reaction. It was, of course, always just the same five-second loop of him gaping, thunderstruck.

"This is the funniest thing I've ever seen," Tori said.

"Greatest story ever told," Rhys agreed.

"You two shut it. You shouldn't kick a man while he's down," Jem said.

"No worries. He's up again. Yeeted, am I right?" Rhys asked Tori.

"Yep. Where'd you pick up that word, Grandad?"

"I have a thirteen-year-old in my life."

"Poor Hack. He'll never live this down," Jem said, loyally trying to drum up sympathy.

"Nope," Tori agreed. "Forty-two million views! Once *Bright Star* picked it up, he was done for."

"Yes, well, with any luck, maybe people will stop mocking Hack long enough to focus on the human interest story between Bart and Wyatt," Jem said. "I'm proud of Bart. He's finally found someone to love unselfishly."

"Even if it is a walrus," Rhys said.

A LETTER FROM EMMA

Thank you so much for reading *A Death at Silversmith Bay*. If you enjoyed it, and would like to be informed of my future releases, please sign up at the following link. I promise never to sell or reuse your email address in any way, and you can unsubscribe whenever you choose.

www.bookouture.com/emma-jameson

As readers of the first two books in the Jem Jago series may recall, Jem has decided to split her time between St. Morwenna, where she lives in Lyonesse House with her bestie Pauley Gwyn, and Penzance, home of her employer, the Courtney Library.

In this third mystery, I decided to set the action on Silversmith Bay, an imaginary version of Plymouth Harbour, and introduce some recurring Penzance characters. These include Tori Jago, Jem's spirited and happy-go-lucky little sister (half-sister, if you want to get technical), PC Stacy Kellow (who becomes her mainland ally), and the sinister DS Conrad (who will become her recurring enemy). Jem also meets a very special feline called Wotsit who's based on one of my cats, Bobby the tailless Manx mix, who looks and acts exactly the same. I don't know if Wotsit will ever take an active role in solving a future mystery, but I do know that whenever Jem is in Penzance, he'll insist on sticking a paw in.

As much as I enjoyed introducing you to some new characters, I also want to assure you that the Isles of Scilly will remain the heart of this series. Old friends like Clarence Latham and Bettie Quick will return, and although it seems like Jem has chosen to get serious with Rhys Tremayne, it's much too soon to count out Sergeant Hackman. I hope you'll return for future installments and discover what happens next!

One last thing. I often say the difference between a book that finds its way and a book that sinks like a stone is simple: reviews. Honest reviews are the lifeblood of books in today's competitive digital sphere. If you enjoyed *A Death at Silver-smith Bay* and would be willing to write a review, I would be eternally grateful. Thank you.

Until next time,

Emma Jameson

2022

www.emmajamesonbooks.com

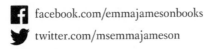

facebook.com/emmajamesonbooks

twitter.com/msemmajameson

CPSIA information can be obtained
at www.ICGtesting.com
Printed in the USA
BVHW031547150222
629077BV00011B/575